C

\
W

The
Raft

Also by Arabella Edge
and available in Picador

THE COMPANY

The
Raft

Arabella Edge

PICADOR

First published 2005 in Picador by Pan Macmillan
Australia Pty Limited as *The God of Spring*

First published in Great Britain 2006 by Picador
an imprint of Pan Macmillan Ltd
Pan Macmillan, 20 New Wharf Road, London N1 9RR
Basingstoke and Oxford
Associated companies throughout the world
www.panmacmillan.com

ISBN-13: 978-0-330-41847-8
ISBN-10: 0-330-41847-5

A CIP catalogue record for this book is available from
the British Library.

Printed and bound in Great Britain by
Mackays of Chatham plc, Chatham, Kent

To Nick, the navigator

Montmartre

———

June 1818

DRESSED, READY, THÉODORE GÉRICAULT waited in a state of dread for the arrival of his uncle. He knew that soon the shiny black landau would appear along the avenue of chestnut trees, beneath all their dark green magnificence and white candle blooms.

Always it was the same, like a scene in a play enacted for all eternity over and over again. The coachman guiding his team of six bays at a decorous pace; then his uncle stepping from the equipage, manner patrician, imperial, extending a hand to assist his lovely young wife.

Géricault stood in the doorway and greeted his patron and benefactor with a sly, sycophant's smile, unable to look his aunt in the eye, yet trembling with desire to kiss her gloved hand.

As always, supper would be interminable, tense with suppressed longing.

Géricault led the way to the dining room and they took their places at the polished oak table: Charles Caruel in the honoured position at the head, flanked on either side by his wife and his nephew. A maid lit the candelabra and closed the French doors overlooking the terrace; a chill dew had descended and the twilight sky was darkening with fast scudding clouds.

Géricault watched his uncle pour Alexandrine's wine, select the choicest morsels for her plate. How he fussed so. She submitted to her husband's attentions like the perfect child bride, remonstrating in the prettiest way that indeed she could not eat another morsel. A sight to set his teeth on edge. Seated on a straight-backed chair, Alexandrine folded her hands on her lap, modest, wifely, with an expression of demure saintliness; butter would not melt in her mouth—that pouting, waiting mouth. At times, Géricault felt himself diminished by this woman's poise and sophistication. Here was a hothouse orchid, destined for a life of elegance and ease that only the self-assured possessed. You could see it in the languor of slender wrists, the way she arranged her hair in loose lazy coils, which would cost a fortune to affect. The clothes she boldly wore. Cut in the latest fashion, those free-flowing gowns—so cruelly unbecoming to many who thronged the King's court—shimmied from his aunt's shoulders with a fascinating grace. Yet there was no attempt at artifice in Alexandrine's allure. If anything she magnified her beauty by not giving it a single thought.

Always when jealousy began to growl, Géricault found himself hating this uncle of his. He wanted to look at him and see a very monster, rouge and powder smoothing withered skin, the thin arch of his eyebrows pencilled in, leering and winking at Alexandrine, who had to avert her face from the stench of his breath. Instead there he sat, elegant, his silver hair neatly coiffed and perfumed with citrus pomade. When once again Caruel graced him with an affectionate smile, Géricault discerned in his features—the piercing cornflower blue eyes, the fine slightly hooked nose—an echo of his dead mother's beautiful face.

Géricault felt the pressure of Alexandrine's foot against his. He feigned to drop his serviette and in retrieving it managed to stroke her ankle. She lifted her gown and his fingers rasped the white silk of her stocking. It had been a month since he had touched that smooth supple flesh. He inhaled the scent of her, attar of roses, a hint of cloves perhaps, before straightening up, flushed and nervously dabbing his lips with the serviette.

They glanced at one another across the table and then away again.

The strain was wearing him out. Young, gifted gentleman artist!—how could he paint with a clear head and steady hand when he found himself pacing back and forth at night, even leaving his bedroom door ajar, hoping for he knew not what—that which could never happen—lying restlessly awake until dawn, praying to hear carriage wheels along the drive, the quick steps of a footfall. In the early hours, feverish with desire, he longed for his uncle's wife, the dark silhouette of her body outlined through her chemise. How lovely Alexandrine was, naked and in bed.

The moment this thought flared in Géricault's mind, he found his uncle staring at him with an enquiring expression.

'Do give us an account of your trip to Rome,' Caruel said, taking a delicate sip from his glass. 'You must have been inspired by the grand masters. Tell us what you are working on now.'

Géricault could not bring himself to meet his uncle's steady, trusting gaze. Instead he hunched over his plate. Lately he was beginning to notice something furtive in his own gestures, which he did not like.

What could he say to his uncle, when each morning he had woken *wanting* to work, yet the more opportunity he had the less he achieved, beginning a hundred projects which he never finished, and finally doing nothing in a mood of exhaustion. He had been naïve to think a self-imposed exile in Rome might have helped.

'For my next composition, honoured uncle,' he replied, 'I have in mind a crowd scene as witnessed at the Roman carnival, using as a central motif the riderless Barberi horses.'

He could not go on. He felt too fraudulent. Caruel the cuckold, eagerly expectant, beaming encouragement. And all the while Alexandrine's slippered caress rose higher and higher.

Géricault struggled to continue.

'Perhaps I'll begin by recording the start of the race, the athletes fighting to restrain the horses—just as I saw it in the Piazza del Popolo—which I could transform into a colonnaded forum suggestive of ancient rather than modern Rome.'

'Splendid, dear fellow,' Caruel exclaimed. 'We shall look forward to seeing the finished tableau. Won't we, my pretty one?'

Alexandrine nodded and stifled a yawn.

Géricault tried to ignore her slipper nudging his thigh.

All afternoon, he had forced himself to remain calm and organise his thoughts. He knew he should tell Alexandrine it was over. He could have written a letter. But the minute he dipped the pen in ink, he found himself anticipating a furtive encounter that would vanish in an instant, and calculating every possibility he might have of saying two or three private words to her at supper that evening.

Géricault watched Alexandrine's long slim fingers toy with the pearls of her necklace, an unconscious gesture, which made him mad for her. He longed to unclasp the gold fastening at the nape of her neck, that delicate swan-like neck, so vulnerable, yet sinuous as a dancer's.

She gave him a sharp, searching look. 'I hear the ladies in Rome are renowned for their beauty. Is that so?'

Now they were on dangerous ground, where promises and assurances might be exchanged in frivolous volleys of repartee.

Somehow he managed to address his mistress with a gallant half-bow. 'Italian women are drab as sparrows in comparison with you, Madame.'

'Well said, sir, well said indeed,' Caruel declared, giving his wife an appraising glance. Alexandrine smiled, triumphant behind her fan, all the while pressing her foot hard against Géricault's thigh.

He flinched when Caruel leaned over and gave his wife a playful kiss on the cheek. With a proprietorial gesture, he raised her hand to his lips. Submitting to his caresses, Alexandrine stared at Géricault with a disarming expression of mischievous amusement.

She's enjoying this, he thought, revelling in our deceit.

It began to rain steadily, sending chestnut leaves scattering across the lawns, splashing against the flagstone terrace like an accusation, a portent.

Signalling for his glass to be refilled, Caruel announced that tonight he had a proposition to make. He drained the wine and Géricault watched a flush of claret rise in his cheeks.

'I would like another portrait, dear nephew.'

He turned to his wife. 'Does that please you, my dearest?'

How could he not know? Or was this some test, a trap? Géricault glanced in wonder at Alexandrine, who looked lovingly into her husband's eyes, and effortlessly deceived him.

How cruel it was to know that his uncle's commissions allowed him to paint a detailed inventory of every part of Alexandrine, her arms flailing the morning air, rumpled sheets twisted beneath one fist, the curve of her throat before she uttered those sharp mewling cries which he had to suppress with his hand.

The pressure of Alexandrine's foot became unbearable. He dared not look at her. Just once and he'd be undone.

Mercifully Alexandrine excused herself and left the room.

Caruel leaned back in his chair with a self-satisfied air.

'Tell me,' he said, swirling the last dregs of wine in his glass. 'Am I not a lucky man?'

Géricault gave a mumbled assent, conscious of a guilty blush to the roots of his hair.

'Your father crams his life with business speculations when, like me, he should find himself a pretty young wife. Not that your mother wasn't a fine upright woman. Mark my words, she was.'

He could not think of a reply. He knew he was in danger of disgracing the family's reputation and denigrating the memory of his poor tubercular mother.

'And you, Théodore? No conquests in Rome?'

Appalled, Géricault stared at his plate. A terrible anguish constricted his soul.

'Oh, I know, still so shy, dear boy. In time you'll grow out of it. But surely in Italy—there must have been some dalliance, some amour?'

Now Caruel had a foxy glint to his eye, beseeching his nephew to regale him with talk of conquests and the brothel, at last. He had long voiced his concern in no uncertain terms. 'Make hay, boy, while the sun shines. Christ knows what your father will say if you don't turn out a ladies' man. And I'll be blamed for encouraging you to become an artist, even if I did persuade your father that my dear sister never wanted you apprenticed in the family tobacco firm.'

Once again Géricault found himself weaving another

web of lies. Not a natural dissembler—no one who blushed as readily as he could ever deceive with the skill that was required—he steeled himself to entertain Caruel with bawdy tales of the bordello and desire: seducing contessas in the cool sandstone shade of summer houses on the outskirts of town, skylarks bursting their song in the clear blue air; a young widow wandering the empty echoing rooms of a villa once owned by the Medicis; and how could he ever forget a watermelon seller proffering her wares on the Spanish Steps, who when he embraced her tasted of strawberries; or the febrile prowling of his landlady in his lodgings at the Via S. Isidoro, a scent of marsala and laudanum on her breath.

'Capital,' Caruel cried in delight. 'Tell me more.'

To his disgust, in recounting these fictional couplings Géricault felt himself stir. Still Alexandrine had not returned to the dining room.

Rain streamed in rivulets against the French doors. How much longer must he go on? Who else, he thought, could I have fucked in Rome?

Finally Caruel peered into his empty glass. 'I say, nephew, how about a splash of brandy to toast your new commission.'

'Trust me, sir,' Géricault replied, springing with relief to his feet. 'I'll return with the very best my cellar has to offer.'

Trust, he said *trust*. Shamefaced, he headed for the door.

'And if you see her,' his uncle called, 'shoo in my silly goose of a wife. What can she be doing in the privy that long?'

Géricault glanced back at him. As always after one of his cook's rich meals, Caruel closed his eyes and began to doze.

He hurried along the corridor. A hand caught the sleeve of his jacket. Alexandrine pushed him into the win-dowed alcove of the hall.

'I knew you'd come back,' she whispered, arms twined around his neck. 'Imagine the luxury of spending hours together every day for weeks at a time. As for the portrait, you can compose it later from memory, like the others.'

He listened to Alexandrine's voice, scheming, triumphant, telling him that she'd arrange for Louisette, the silliest of all maids, to chaperone her to his studio, where she would bribe and dizzy the girl's mind with a promised pouch of centimes and send her packing to purchase all manner of fripperies at the Montmartre fair. Nothing would make Louisette miss such an outing.

At this, Alexandrine tousled his hair and treated him to her theatrical laugh, which he was beginning to fear.

'Caruel's credulity knows no bounds,' she said, covering his cheeks and throat with her kisses. 'He actually believes the air of Montmartre brings light and colour to my eyes and skin, when it's the folly of our passion that enfevers my complexion.'

Géricault felt the heat of her breath on his. He found himself tearing at her gown, his hands riffling the crisp folds of her petticoats. To be discovered taking her against the wall like this as if she were no more than a common whore! But, he had to confess, the thought of Alexandrine straddling some bare-arsed youth in a vile alley, the exchange of coarse words, a slap perhaps, her chemise ripped from her shoulders, or stripped bare but for her boots, and a jeering crowd of men jostling, watching, waiting their turn—these images set him shuddering.

Beneath swathes of lace, his fingers twined and loosened the ribbons of her culottes.

Géricault lifted his mistress light as a child in his arms. She clung to him, her thighs about his hips.

At last he could grasp the warmth of her flesh and she bucking the empty air held him tight and tighter still. Afterwards, spent, panting like a savage, Géricault heard a sound of footsteps. He recognised the ambling tread of his cook, La Motte. Alexandrine loosened her grip on his shirt. Hurriedly they arranged their rumpled clothes.

'Return to my uncle,' he whispered. Would Caruel notice the creases in her gown, her lips flushed crimson?

On his way to the cellar he saw La Motte, standing hands on hips at the foot of the stairs and glaring at Alexandrine who scurried ahead. As he passed she gave him a baleful glance and clicked her tongue.

When his uncle and aunt took their leave, Géricault crossed the courtyard and hurried through the pelting rain towards his studio, a former grange adjacent to the house. It was a ramshackle wooden building covered in a tangle of honeysuckle, with a leaking slate roof and a rough stone floor across which draughts blew dust into spirals. Yet even on a winter's day, light streamed through the arched windows from every conceivable direction. And for that, Géricault was grateful.

Opening the heavy double doors, he stepped inside. He lit a taper and surveyed the dismal scene, with its general atmosphere of neglect—the empty easel set before the central window; his unmade cot in one corner; a model's platform stacked with wine bottles and decanters; and, at the end of the vaulted room, the divan covered with a large oriental rug upon which he had painted his aunt shamelessly, feverishly.

Everywhere sketches of Alexandrine in so many poses: standing against a dark panelled wall in a black riding habit and silk hat; dressed in a loose muslin summer dress; holding a bowl filled with peaches and pomegranates.

Géricault strode across the room and, kneeling by the divan, dragged out a great bolt of canvas, his first and only success, his *Charging Chasseur*. Unrolling it with effort, he found he still admired the composition. The chasseur turned in the saddle on a rearing stallion. Looking behind him, he signalled the charge with a raised sword. Man and horse fused in the tilted tip of one sharp hoof.

Once again Géricault took a sensual delight in his officer's uniform, the horse's magnificent apparel, the leopard-skin saddlecloth with flattened head, fangs bared. How defiant and invincible the chasseur seemed dressed à la hussarde, resplendent in his emerald-green dolman, tight breeches and plumed bearskin hat. There were so many details he had woven in: one hundred and fifty buttons of five different kinds; a satin sash embroidered with gold; the gleam in the silver sabre tache containing missives and maps hanging from the sword belt; the contrast between the leopard skin and the stallion's dappled coat. As for the setting, he had envisaged a vaporous space rather than a literal landscape, a luminous haze enveloping horse and rider as they advanced towards a flicker of fires at the horizon.

With a sigh, Géricault rose to his feet and paced back and forth before the canvas, studying it closely. He could not imagine how he had ever managed to paint in that state of nervous concentration when the walls began to glow, the roof lifted from the studio and the soul took flight.

A time before Alexandrine, he thought, before he found himself worn out with desire, leaving the wretched paints to dry completely, the palette a stained gourd, brushes rigid as drumsticks—all for a shared, but irregular, stormy love of illicit rendezvous and snatched moments. If only they could talk nonsense by the fire over a glass of anisette, but there was no time for sweet untroubled sleep or even endearments, except their whispered exchanges of where and how they would next meet.

He cast his mind back to the summer of 1812, when he had immersed himself in work like a musician practising scales. It had seemed natural, innocent, unselfconscious, like breathing itself. He had become possessed with an impulse to shine, illuminate, and to astonish the world. For months he had worked tirelessly with the conviction of a man born to show others the right way. He had even had the audacity to expect his first painting would be highly commended and he'd thrilled at what the critics might say: *a brilliant demonstration of precocious mastery*.

One day, such was the intensity of his work, in frustration he had exclaimed, 'It's too warm in here, I'm going mad!'—only to become aware of laughter and a voice behind him saying, 'Don't be ridiculous, it's been unseasonably cold all week.'

With a start, Géricault had turned round and there stood a woman framed in the doorway, curls tumbling loose from a broad-brimmed silk hat, the hem of her gown splattered with mud. Shaking drizzle from a dark green cloak, she'd fixed him with a disarming smile. Call it madness but at first all he could see were raindrops caught in the fabric—exactly what he needed, exactly right. 'Quick,' he said and, forgetting himself entirely, told her to stand quite still just where she was, the misty light slanting across her left shoulder. He grabbed his watercolours and frantically worked his brushes until, yes, finally he realised his vision, configured every dew spark on a blade of grass.

'Perhaps I should introduce myself,' the woman said, trying not to laugh each time he leaned over to scrutinise the tones and shades of her damp cape. 'Madame Caruel. Your step-aunt, I suppose.'

The confident tone of her voice shook him to his senses.

How could he have forgotten Caruel's visit?—his uncle had come to show off his new bride!

'Please forgive me, Madame,' he replied, appalled by what he'd just done. 'It was that—coming in from the wet, you glittered so.'

'I'm flattered to have been of some assistance to your art.' Standing on tiptoe, she gave him a maternal peck on the cheek. 'Please, call me Alexandrine,' she whispered.

The sun now suffused the last of the rain with a golden light. Géricault stared at his uncle's new wife in amazement. She was not the faded spinster he had imagined. Not in the slightest. She couldn't be more than thirty, only five or six years older than himself.

'My husband tells me you're a talented artist.' Alexandrine peered past him into the studio. 'And intend to submit a masterpiece for the Salon. May I see it?'

When she stepped past him, Géricault registered the chaos everywhere, his studies propped against the wall, the floor strewn with papers, pig bladders of paints, empty bottles of wine and unwashed plates stacked beneath the desk and divan.

Once again he wondered *how* he could have forgotten Caruel's visit. Then he became aware of the stains streaking his shirt, a harsh aroma of turpentine about his jacket, a three-day shadow on his chin. Attempting to smooth his tangled hair, he noticed Alexandrine was glancing at him with amusement.

'I hope we're not interrupting you, Monsieur Géricault,' she said, giving him an arch look. 'My husband and I could come back at another time, perhaps, when you might be expecting us.'

'No, not at all,' he managed to say. She stood before his canvas, which was stretched from floor to ceiling against an entire wall and surrounded by a cage of wooden scaffolding.

Before he could stop her, Alexandrine placed both hands on either side of a ladder propped against the timbers and, gathering her skirts, climbed tier after tier until she stepped onto the uneven decks with not even a rail to save her if she fell.

'I implore you, be careful, Madame,' he cried. 'Please hang on to the straps of my harness which you will find to your left and do not move until I am beside you.'

Ignoring him, Alexandrine leaned forward and gazed at the Chasseur. 'He's exceedingly handsome,' she called.

Sprinting up the ladder, Géricault managed to grasp her by the arm, at last. 'Please, Madame, you will get a much better impression of the composition from the ground. This scaffolding is rather makeshift, so I suggest we climb down at once.'

'No, really, I'm perfectly safe.' Alexandrine pulled herself free with surprising strength. She turned to the canvas. 'It's a wonder to see such a lovely tender face.'

Although flattered by the sincerity in her voice, he was taken aback by such directness. He'd modelled the Chasseur on himself, spent hours in front of the mirror at the task, and perfected a resolute yet savage expression to hold the viewer in a green-eyed gaze.

Alexandrine reached out and stroked the Chasseur's lips with the tips of her fingers.

There was a subdued recklessness about her, Géricault thought, conscious of the whiteness of her throat, the dark heavy hair coiled against the nape of her neck. They were standing close, their shoulders almost touching. A strong musky scent rose from her. She smelled of the sun and the rain, and, to his shame, Géricault found himself blushing.

They heard a sound of footsteps hurrying across the courtyard. Géricault helped Alexandrine down the ladders. She jumped lightly from the last rung.

Caruel stood silhouetted in the bright light of the doorway.

'Why, there you are, my dear,' he declared, 'making the acquaintance of my favourite nephew.'

After a tour of the gardens, Caruel had taken him aside and in the most urgent tones confessed he would like to commission a portrait of his wife. And that was how it began.

At first a mere frisson, a mild flirtation, mostly imagined on Géricault's part. He had basked in that lingering smile, the way at every visit she held out her hand just a fraction longer for him to kiss, always mocking and teasing him behind her fan, quizzing him about love and saying that for a woman of her years nothing could be more endearing than to see a young man blush.

At the Emperor's Salon, after the Chasseur received its gold medal, Alexandrine had pushed open the gilt double doors to escape the crush of the room, and Géricault followed.

She hurried along the marble corridor, her dark hair falling loose from a braided chignon. He had longed for her then and tried to take her hand. But Alexandrine darted out of reach and ran ahead, the heels of her satin slippers pattering against the polished floors. Faster and faster she went, into the Italian gallery, deserted and half in shadows. Then they'd stopped, catching their breath, aware of the delicate gold-leaf haloes, the ivory plumes of angel wings beating with portents, the beatific smiles of countless Madonnas, their ultramarine gowns the purest lapis lazuli pounded to powder. Alexandrine stood against Veronese's *Marriage Feast at Cana*. The last shard of evening light flashed on a pewter plate of figs and pomegranates. He yearned to touch the crimson and purple flesh of them, inhale the scent of frankincense and myrrh.

Yes, if Géricault dared depict this tale, he would make time stand still just there in the Italian gallery, his hands cupping her pale oval face, his lips seeking her lovely mouth. He would preserve that moment of innocence for all eternity while from every wall the Madonnas gazed down and forgave.

Now Géricault sat by the studio window and drank long into the night. How he railed against this curse, this disease called love, which wasted his young life, deadened his mind like a swamp.

From the house opposite, an ivy-covered turreted mansion that had seen better days, the sound of laughter and a jingle of tambourines drifted across the lawns. He tried not to think of his neighbour, Horace Vernet, Géricault's own tutor's son—third-generation prodigy carousing until dawn with his wild city friends.

Géricault stared across the way at the glittering panes illuminated with countless chandeliers. How he would love to show these Vernets his true mettle and find a subject that would set the world ablaze. He was beginning to despair, feared that perhaps he had lost the will to paint.

Whenever an image rose of Alexandrine—lying naked beside him, her head propped on one hand, and himself tracing the delicate curve of her spine—he saw his uncle gazing at him with the same fond expression as his mother. 'Don't worry about your father's ambitions, my lad, I've found you Carle Vernet, the best tutor money can buy.'

He thought of his father, Georges-Nicholas Géricault, a stiff upright man, the emotions forever in check behind his mercantile eye to profit and gain, a man who prided himself on an impeccable attention to etiquette. When Géricault cast his mind back to the oppressive silence of his childhood, he saw his father poring over ledgers in the study, and those meals always eaten to the endless tick of a grandfather clock.

During the tumult of the Terror, when Géricault was four years old, Georges-Nicholas had abandoned the town house in the Faubourg Saint-Honoré and taken up residence here in the rue des Martyrs, at the foot of Montmartre on the northernmost fringe of the city. They had led a private, secluded life in this house surrounded by unkempt allotments and meadows. Here they could breathe. The continual ringing of the tocsin, signalling another public execution, only drifted their way on winter winds. Géricault's mother loved this village on the heights: the calm of its country churchyard, its thatched cottages, narrow lanes, orchards and windmills.

She loved this faded, two-storey, blue-shuttered house with its ragged sweep of lawn shaded by the avenue of chestnut trees, and the communal garden—shared with the mansion opposite. She had visions of a true French garden divided into squares by wide sanded walks bordered with lavender and sorrel. But at every turn the overgrown grounds defied her attempts to landscape a rose garden in formal style and bound by clipped hedges.

She marvelled at the bold recklessness of the local women, bedecked in voluminous velvet cloaks, cheap market baubles tinkling at every step, their hair streaming loose and wild beneath sun-faded straw hats; and at the men sporting beards and moustaches, striding through the market square in baggy pants and rolled-up shirt sleeves, always a smouldering cheroot dangling from the corner of their lips. This was a raffish community of writers and artists, whom Géricault's father despised, called good-for-nothing parasites, a curse on this earth.

Even now there were times when Géricault would glance out the window and seem to see his mother in her red and yellow shawl filling a basket with wild flowers.

Géricault's parents had not had an easy marriage. In those first years of the Empire, Georges-Nicholas had chafed at his exile from the city. How he admired the hive of activity in the bustling new boulevards, the smart sophisticated shops and cafés opening on every street corner; the packed markets swarming with merchants, their cries reaching his ears like a triumphant roar in a crowd. He had relished the tidal ebb and flow of profitable trade when each morning La Bourse de Commerce flung open its polished oak doors.

But he hated the rural 'squalor' of Montmartre. This rambling house in which the rooms were all laid out for idle pleasure, the interiors pale green and blue, the walls hung with light-coloured silks figured with fruit and flowers. Everywhere his wife had imposed a frivolous arrangement of beech and walnut furnishings: a marble-topped pedestal table in one corner, a day bed with carved sabre-shaped feet by the fireplace.

Géricault rose to his feet, refilled his glass and stood in front of a portrait of his mother, which he'd painted from memory. He knew she would have admired the composition—herself seated at the harpsichord, gazing from the canvas with a remote, enigmatic smile, the eyes mournful and yearning, as if she knew that life would soon run out.

The battle between husband and wife had been fought without words. A silent combat, which raged over the head of their only child. On his birthday, Géricault's mother would buy him a brand new set of sketchbooks from Horot's in the boulevard Saint-Germain. Always the best, the covers bound in costly crimson satin. His father deplored the expense; said Géricault was neglecting his lessons, particularly in science and mathematics. But still his mother indulged him, encouraged his every artistic effort, and even posed for him herself.

In the early years of the Empire, Georges-Nicholas—one of those astute souls who thrived in political chaos and had the ability to turn the Revolution to personal profit—purchased a tobacco factory in the fashionable quarter of the Hotel de Ville. Soon he had doubled the fortune his wife had brought into their marriage, and he next invested wisely in country estates. Caruel became a chief associate in this venture, and from an early age Géricault had known that codicils and contracts were to be his destiny—he was promised as a clerk in those drear vestibules on the dull side of town. The family *firm*, he would say to himself—could there ever be a more desolate word?

If Géricault were to sketch this father of his, he would dip his brush in the darkest of indigo inks and begin with the simple forbidding cut of his black breeches and that coat worn in all seasons, the wide collar heightening the pallor of the skin; and then those shrewd eyes always ready to pick fault and criticise, which with the thin purse of the lips gave his father such a cold and haughty demeanour.

Géricault stepped back from his mother's portrait. He knew every feature of that narrow fine-boned face. He tried to remember how long it had been since he'd see her. Ten years, he said finally to himself.

That spring morning in his sixteenth year when his father stood by the bedside where his lovely young wife drifted in and out of sleep, soaking the sheets with her night fevers, desperate and defeated in those last days. Her heart was failing, the doctor had confided. Silhouetted against the window, he had given his wife a disdainful glance then turned away in disgust. He always loathed sickness, particularly in women.

It was Géricault who colluded with the doctor, held glasses of brandy to his mother's lips, soaked biscuit wafers in laudanum and placed them on her tongue.

One night, she looked at him and smiled as if at last she recognised her son. Géricault crept over and took her hand. Her face seemed tranquil, smooth, unlined as he remembered it when he was young.

He leaned over and kissed her brow. As his lips brushed the chilled pale skin, he knew it was the end. He closed her eyes and still he sat beside her for a long time.

Later he woke to a grey dawn after a night of ceaseless rain, knowing that nothing would ever be the same again.

On the day of the funeral, Géricault remembered treading softly on the damp mown grass between graves. He stood between his father and uncle, all three stiff and stern in their tailored black mourning suits, and watched the pall-bearers lower the coffin into the freshly dug earth. Georges-Nicholas was staring impassively ahead and every so often tapped his cane against the path, as if impatient to be gone. Géricault glanced at him. Never, he thought, had he felt so afraid and alone.

On that day France was celebrating Napoleon's victory at Wagram. All night, gold and crimson fireworks burst in plumes across the sky.

Through the following week, Géricault's father mostly kept to his study, writing endless missives to lawyers and attending to his wife's affairs. Then one evening in the dining room, Georges-Nicholas broke the customary silence and, over a glass of port wine, outlined his plans for the future. Now that the city was safe and business thriving, he had decided to move closer to the tobacco factory, and had leased a house in the quartier of the Hôtel de Ville.

'Convenient,' he said, 'modest, nothing grand.'

Géricault found his father contemplating him with a scornful expression.

'Your mother has left you this property and a generous legacy for life. She has done nothing but pamper and ruin you, my son.'

Géricault flinched at the undertone of malice in his father's voice.

'I should have stood my ground and sent you to boarding school. But now even Caruel has interceded on your behalf—says you have considerable talent and other such nonsense.'

At this Géricault set down his knife and fork. He waited, scarcely daring to breathe.

'So you want to be an artist. Well, prove it then.' Georges-Nicholas slammed his fist on the table. 'Let us see what you achieve—otherwise I'll drag you to the factory by the scruff of your neck. Mark my words, I will.'

Géricault bowed his head so his father would not see the look of elation shining from his face. 'Thank you,' he murmured.

All the next morning from the parlour, Géricault watched his father supervising a snaking procession of trunks and valises hoisted by a retinue of hired servants. When everything was ready, his father stood alone by the carriage and barely looked back at the house. A strong breeze sent the last of the winter leaves scurrying in sorrowful drifts across the driveway.

Géricault felt a sudden rush of filial affection for this cold unloving father of his. If only he could have reached out and touched him, laid a hand on the immaculately-stitched sleeve of his coat. Instead he almost waved watching him go.

Géricault set down the empty brandy decanter and stared out the window. It was no longer dark but not yet light. The grounds between the two properties were held in a web of stillness. The candelabras continued to blaze from Horace's house. He heard another peal of laughter, although the music had quietened.

Father, I proved you wrong, Géricault whispered to himself. I showed you with my *Charging Chasseur*—it won the gold medal! I will do it again. Yes, you'll see, I will.

The words seemed suddenly to exhaust him. He swayed slightly on his feet, then lowered himself onto the divan. There he sat with his head in his hands. Again his thoughts returned to Alexandrine.

How could he deceive Caruel so heartlessly, in cold blood, how could he transform his benefactor into a cuckold, a latrine joke of the cheapest kind?

GÉRICAULT WOKE TO A TAP on the studio window. Horace Vernet stood in the doorway, elegant, dapper, showing off muscular legs in white breeches and polished tan boots, tapping his cane in that fiery impatient way of his, as if life might run out.

Géricault sighed. Although he loved the sweep of land they shared, it also meant that Horace could visit at any time.

He glanced at the brandy decanter on the floor beside him. A whiff of spirits made the bile rise in his throat. I must undergo a cure, he thought, eat three meals a day, turn my back on the world and devote myself entirely to painting.

'You look haggard,' Horace said, picking up the decanter with a fastidious gesture and setting it on the model stand.

He contemplated Géricault's queasy countenance.

'Are you sick,' he asked, 'is that why you've returned so soon from Rome?'

Love-sick, Géricault almost replied, overwhelmed with a desperate desire to confide. Instead he hurried with his toilette.

Already Horace had grabbed Géricault's cloak and was

ushering him out the door. 'Tell me about Italy, did you faint, did you swoon before the Michelangelos?—no, tell me instead about Italian women, did they prove too much of a distraction, did they seduce you from the masters?'

Géricault winced at his mocking smile.

'Why, my dear gentle Théo, I see you still blush at the slightest emotion.'

What was there to say—endless lonely nights drinking cheap wine long and late in tawdry taverns, tormenting himself drawing endless successions of erotic fantasies: Leda pinned beneath the swan's embrace; monstrous satyrs; images of lust in all its variations. And each day surrounded and confronted at every turn by gigantic miraculous forms, unimaginable masterpieces which would never fade from him now.

'If you must know,' Géricault said at last, 'it would have undermined my spirit to stay there for long.'

'Nonsense, I don't believe you.' Horace led him briskly across the courtyard. 'You won't talk about what you've seen because you intend to keep all Rome's secrets to yourself.'

He followed Horace through the shrubberies of rhododendron past the rose garden—no longer the clipped and manicured creation Géricault's mother had planned, but tangled, rampant, the heavy blooms dropping their petals on the long damp grass as soon as they burst open. A peacock appeared on the path swishing its muddied train from side to side. Seeing them, the bird let out a mournful ululating shriek, which was taken up by another and another until the garden resounded with their piercing cries. Géricault cursed Horace's half-tamed pampered flock which he allowed to wander freely around the grounds and even into his house, where they pilfered scraps from the kitchen and flapped onto the dining room table at mealtimes, despite Géricault's entreaties that the creatures were unhygienic and primarily ornamental.

Their entire point, he often said, was to display irides-cent fans on fastidiously mown lawns. Yet Horace would be happy to have them on his bed. They glanced at each other and smiled.

In a sudden shower, they hurried towards Horace's studio in the mansion's south wing.

All around lay the usual clutter—newspapers in dusty piles, empty wine bottles, spilt paint, endless bric-à-brac. Horace was forever dragging his reluctant friend to dubious auctions in village fairs; he was an insatiable salvager of oriental vases, china dinner services, feather headdresses, pre-revolutionary wigs, a battered Indian kayak, all manner of costumes, coats of armour, carpets, military headgear, a rare collection of contemporary weapons, muskets, pistols, daggers.

Some days Géricault would arrive to find a naked male model, muscular as a gladiator, astride a white stallion, and everywhere a cacophony of drum rolls, horn calls, the clatter of fencing foils punctuated by the discordant note of an ancient piano. On other days there might be a carefully arranged composition of dead soldiers—the men complain-ing of cramp or pins and needles—lying among broken cannon wheels and bales of straw, their uniforms splashed with cochineal to resemble blood; or a young bare-breasted maid raising one fist to the heavens, the other wielding a sceptre representing liberty, equality, fraternity, victory, whichever slogan signified at the time.

On this dull, damp morning, Géricault recognised the usual crowd. A young couple sprawled asleep on a day bed by the fire, she in all her creased evening finery, he dressed for the opera, both insensible to the shouts and cries from a group of soldiers engaged in some furious debate, the morning newspapers spread out on a trestle table before them. Napoleon's demobbed troops, they seemed to have bivouacked in Horace's house for good, scrounging a drink, a cheroot. Géricault nodded their way. They would drive me mad, he thought.

A large portion of the studio was devoted to a stage hung with red velvet drapes. Seated on a gilt throne in the centre there was Joseph, a famous boxer much sought after by local artists for his dark and gleaming muscle tone. Bedecked today in silks and wearing a curious helmet decorated with ostrich plumes, he cleaned his nails with a toothpick, a frown of concentration on his noble face. At his feet a group of young cherubim in grubby gauze shifts squabbled over a game, their laurel wreaths slipping askew on braided heads, paper angel wings flapping at their shoulder blades.

'Why, you've taken your time,' one nymph said in a peeved voice.

'Don't know why we all had to be here,' muttered another.

'You usually just have one of us in a day's sitting.'

'They've been whining like this ever since you left,' the boxer announced. 'Even when I tell them they're lucky to have it so easy. For every complaint, you should dock their pay.'

His words were met with a chorus of dismay. One small child began to pummel the boxer's taut, muscled calf with her fists and, laughing, he fended her off with a wooden trident.

'Children, children,' Horace shouted, clapping his hands for silence, 'positions, please.'

Grumbling among themselves, the children shuffled into a semi-circle, their arms extended in a supplicating gesture towards the boxer. Horace's assistant, Delacroix—a youth of such luminous beauty that Géricault was often tempted to whip out his sketchbook and draw him on the spot—emerged from the shadows.

Delacroix strapped the youngest cherubim into a harness and, hauling on a pulley, sent the child flying through the air. Borne aloft, the boy managed to blow a thin tune from a trumpet held in one hand. The enthroned boxer assumed a dignified crowned-and-sceptred stance.

'Perfect, perfect,' Horace exclaimed. 'Arms less stiff, Lisette, remember you're an angel with gossamer wings.'

'Do you admire my tableau,' he said, turning to his friend. '*Restoration France, Protectress of the Arts*.' He shot him a wry smile. 'I can tell you, the King's call for the Salon has caught us all by surprise.'

Géricault glanced with irritation at the canvas. He remembered the very same composition from six years ago, Horace's homage to Napoleon's artistic patronage—then it was *Our Emperor, Protector of the Arts*. He cast a look around the framed and varnished paintings ranged against the walls, pallid martyrdoms of saints, deathbed communions of medieval kings, aristocrats returning from ignominious exile.

Horace knew history, he thought. But history as nothing more than a series of political statements imagined in paintings and tableaux vivants. Perfectly executed, of course, but lacking in depth and breadth and emotion. So accomplished, so facile, painted end to end with a maddening perfection, yet in the final analysis there was something so prescribed and formulaic about Horace's work. All at once Géricault felt ashamed of himself. He knew too well he craved his rival's success, would sell his soul to share his standing in the world, those gleaming medals from Kings and Emperors lined in triumph along the mantel.

He pressed the tips of his fingers against a throb at his temples. After the brandy of the previous night, he could feel the bright white lights of a migraine beginning to dance behind his eyes.

He became aware of Horace studying him, mischievous, expectant, waiting for him to say something complimentary about the work. 'Napoleon almost made a millionaire of you with your lavish tributes to those crazed military campaigns,' Géricault began, conscious of a querulous tone to his voice. 'And now without a qualm you receive endless commissions from the Comte d'Artois. How in good faith can you do it, my friend?'

'I know Delacroix doesn't approve either,' Horace replied with an amiable smile, nodding towards his assistant grinding powders in a pestle at the far end of the room.

In Delacroix's flushed face, Géricault recognised the same aching eagerness to please that had shadowed his own early years. Like Delacroix, he too had risen at dawn when young, to practise his drawing, and spend hours in the stables getting the tendons in a fetlock exactly right.

Now Géricault told Horace he was shameless and they laughed.

'Well, I can't afford to be anything else.' Horace gave his tableau an admiring glance. 'Father, of course, thrives on the return of the monarchy. He's gone back to painting fashionable dandies and fancy high-trotting thoroughbreds. He was never any good at Napoleon's battlefields.'

Carle Vernet . . . Géricault could never think of his apprenticeship without a pang of regret for those innocent, eager days. Vernet had taught him the *kitchen* of painting: the preparation of canvases, the use of siccatives, the correct procedures in mixing oils and in varnishing finished works. In composition, Vernet had encouraged him to experiment with the most diverse techniques—pen, graphite, charcoal, wash, watercolour and pastel. His tutor had given him every freedom to develop his own personality, and had shown him how to begin by sketching in grisaille to establish a quick and simple general effect. Never was Géricault allowed to amuse himself by painting successive parts, by making the perfect head, arm or hand, for what Vernet wanted was the life of the whole.

A small black shape appeared from behind a curtain pelmet, shimmied down a tasselled crimson cord and with a flying jump landed on the boxer's lap.

In an instant the children forgot their positions and rushed towards the creature, which sat on its haunches peering about with bright knowing eyes, one paw patting the great boxer's wrist.

Finally escaping from a multitude of clumsy caresses, the monkey leaped into Horace's arms.

'Allow me to introduce you.' Horace tickled the monkey behind silky ears and fished bonbons from a top-coat pocket. 'Monsieur Singe,' he addressed the creature now perched on his shoulder, 'I have the greatest honour in presenting my guest, Théodore Géricault, gentleman artist newly returned from Rome, who, having inherited a fortune from his mother's estates, has no need of patrons. Unlike us, he is free, free to paint any subject at will. Raise a tableau to the truth of our nation.'

The monkey examined a peppermint and gave it a cautious lick with his long black tongue.

'Pay attention, Monsieur Singe,' Horace continued, 'for you have before you a genius whose forms are full of life, and there's no other man who has ever painted a better leopard-skin rug.'

Géricault smiled but he resented the references to his wealth. Horace was right, he thought, he should relish his freedom, yet he ran through each day as if letting out rope.

Horace threw the monkey into Géricault's arms. A tawny serpentine tail wrapped around his throat, inquisitive paws twisted the buckle on his belt, then, with a chattering yelp, the creature swung to the ground and made a run at one of the peacocks, which skittered outside, but not before a feather had been snatched from its train.

How Géricault envied his carefree friend, the way he only fell fleetingly in love with his models, and how he managed to exhaust the passion within a night. Watching Horace jokingly scold the monkey for attacking one of his precious birds, he resolved to become more like him. If only he could simply flirt with some young maid, and put his name down for the King's Salon.

'Now, my dear fellow, you must forgive me,' Horace declared. 'I hear a great clamour from my cherubim and should attend to them at once.'

Indeed, in high-pitched tones the children were accusing one another of cheating at their game. Géricault wondered at the forbearance of his friend, for he would have shooed them out long ago.

Horace nodded at the soldiers hunched beneath a fug of pipe smoke. 'See that one at the end there,' he pointed out a tall man declaiming loudly and brandishing a pamphlet in his companion's face. 'His name is Colonel Louis Bros. A braver man you'll never see. Why, I'd very much like you to meet him.'

Slipping an arm through his, Horace hurried Géricault towards the raucous group.

'Hey, Bros,' he called. 'This is my dear friend, Théodore Géricault, and although I will always remain faithful to the "other"—' he saluted the Colonel—'I've warned Géricault here that for all our sakes he's not to mention "you-know-who" or Waterloo, and especially not the Russian Campaign.'

'Don't provoke me, Horace.' The soldier gave Géricault's hand a firm shake. 'I'm in no mood for it. After months of subterfuge and lies, there's news of the frigate at last. Lost the *Medusa* in good weather!—I've never heard of such a thing. It's a disgrace. The Ministry of Marine must be held to account. Of that there's not a doubt.'

Géricault felt awkward standing before these men, aware they were eyeing him now, taking in the fine cut of his clothes, the smart leather boots and polished silver spurs. Often he became self-conscious among these officers on half pay who had expected medals and glory, a hero's welcome, and had received none. He wondered whether the Colonel was among the troops who had returned defeated from Moscow, convoys of wounded streaming through Paris in thousands. Never would he forget those shattered, exhausted figures stumbling past, leading emaciated horses by the bridle.

'There should be a scandal rocking the very foundations of the nation,' the Colonel was saying. 'There should be an uproar that sees the King surrounded by hounds baying for blood, bent on revenge, the very same mob that dragged his brother kicking and squealing to the guillotine. But no, instead we're given one paragraph on the fourth page of the *Moniteur Universel*.'

Horace turned to him. 'Well, you must tell Géricault all about it. He's just returned from Rome and no doubt managed to miss this *cause célèbre*. Whereas, I—' he bowed with a theatrical flourish—'must get back to work.'

'My dear boy,' the Colonel gazed at Géricault in astonishment. 'Did you not read in Rome about the frigate?'

With great eagerness, the Colonel leaped to his feet and grabbed a chair, setting it down at the table beside him.

Reluctantly Géricault sat down. He had not had a decent night's sleep in weeks and here he was, trapped, listening to the rants of this outraged soldier and campaigner. Always it was the same. Whenever he visited Horace's studio it was impossible not to become involved in some heated debate. He noticed that the Colonel's companions had embarked on a complicated game of dice, no doubt relieved, he thought, that Bros had found himself another captive audience.

Leaning close—Géricault could smell stale liquor on his breath—the Colonel confided that, bound on a mission to reclaim the former colony in Senegal, the frigate *Medusa* had run aground on a sandbank off the African coast of Cape Blanco. Four launches they'd had!— only enough to carry the captain and the high-ranking passengers. The remaining one hundred and fifty souls had apparently been assigned to a makeshift raft, and given every assurance the boats would tow them ashore. But— due to incompetence or self-interest on the Captain's part—the ropes were cast aside, and the men abandoned, given up for dead. After ten days adrift, only fifteen sur-vivors were found.

Géricault stifled a yawn. He glanced at Horace darting back and forth before his great canvas, a cheroot dangling from his lips. Once again Géricault wondered how his friend managed to work in these conditions, the children still complaining in plaintive voices, the boxer belting out some tavern tune at the piano, the monkey leaping and swinging from the curtains. A mouse creeping behind the skirting was enough to interrupt his own concentration.

'One could say this catastrophe represents a very microcosm of France,' the Colonel declared now, warming to his favourite theme. 'The Captain as the King, his cronies the stagnant court, the *Medusa*'s officers and crew Republi-cans like myself who shed blood for Napoleon's cause and now have to watch *émigrés* taking our rightful posts.'

The Colonel riffled through one of the newspapers on the table. 'Here, read it for yourself—' He jabbed a finger at the top of the page.

With what he hoped was a polite smile, Géricault picked up the journal.

The King insists on appointing returned aristocrats who have not set sail in decades, an editorial opined. *This particular captain, who sought refuge in England, had not been to sea in twenty-five years and only then as a lieutenant. Yet the King chose this Monsieur Hugues Duroy de Chaumareys over veterans of the Nile and Trafalgar.*

'The Captain refused to listen to the advice of his second in command, his officers and experienced crew,' the Colonel continued, his voice high with rage, 'appointed one of the passengers to navigate the ship, some pilot who had spent ten years in an English gaol.'

He spat in disgust and glared at Horace, who paused at his canvas. 'It is not to be endured,' he announced.

Horace clicked his fingers and Delacroix hurried across the room bearing a bottle of Armagnac and tumblers on a tray. The Colonel bowed, filled two glasses to the brim, and slammed one down before Géricault.

'We live in shocking times. There's nothing for it but to drink, my friend.'

Géricault took a grateful restorative sip and felt a sudden flare of benevolence towards this campaigner.

'Tell me,' he asked the Colonel, 'what happened to the men who survived on the raft?'

'Most died soon after their ordeal,' the Colonel replied. 'Against all odds Henry Savigny, the frigate's surgeon, evidently returned to Paris alive.'

Despite himself, Géricault began to sift through the political implications of this tale; out of habit he compiled a list in his mind. Republicans crewing the *Medusa*; Bourbons in command—yet this surgeon, Savigny, made it back to France with an eyewitness account, the truth of the matter at last.

'So what became of the ship's doctor?' Géricault asked.

But before the Colonel could reply, the door swung

open. This time one of Horace's flamboyant actress friends, wearing a dazzling confection of satin and lace cut low at the cleavage. With a cry, she sashayed towards Horace, who kissed her outstretched hand.

When the Colonel rose to his feet, she entwined one languid arm through his. 'Tell me all your news, my dear Louis,' she cooed, leading him to a window seat at the other end of the room. 'I've not seen you in a while.' The Colonel sat there entranced, all his rage against the Ministry of Marine evaporating in the radiance of her smile.

When the carriages of Horace's wild city friends appeared at full gallop along the driveway, Géricault took his leave, slipping the journal into his pocket.

The following morning, heading along the corridor to the kitchen, Géricault passed a new maid. His cook, La Motte, imperious and exacting, must have gone through the whole district by now. Although not truly pretty, this girl displayed a certain finesse, which he admired. As he went by, she nodded and lowered flirtatious eyes.

He found La Motte sweeping the flagstone floor and grumbling beneath her breath. With its rough whitewashed walls, this kitchen had been her domain for as long as he could remember. Now, she leaned on her broom and looked up at him. Fierce, devoted La Motte, who had known him since he was a child.

'Your father, occupied with his business affairs as usual, didn't seem worried when you left for Rome,' she announced. 'But your aunt, why, she was quite beside herself, calling round most days and asking when you'd be back, as if I could provide an answer.'

How could Alexandrine be so indiscreet, Géricault

35

thought, as to come here and question his cook, when it was she who had insisted that a separation was the only way to save her marriage and their reputation?

Wearily he sat at the table. La Motte had put a letter there for him. Immediately he recognised the elegant looping hand. He snatched it open.

I shall see you at 3 o'clock, Thursday week. For my portrait, Caruel has purchased the most exquisite emerald bombazine gown plunging low from the shoulders. Be careful—it cost a fortune.

Despite himself, Géricault smiled, forgetting La Motte's reproachful gaze. There were times when he loved to undress his mistress slowly at his leisure. First the intricate brocade fastenings at the bodice, which snapped open like a sigh, next the wide sash pinned with a brooch beneath the breasts, then the gown falling with a shimmer at her feet. He liked to untie the blue ribbons of her chemise, stroke the soft flesh beneath, before his busy fingers tugged at her petticoats, the long one, which came down to her ankles, followed by the shorter shift—so many garments to unwrap, unpeel—until finally she stood naked before him.

At other times he found himself tearing at her clothes, desperate to free her from that shining carapace of taffeta and silks, unyielding hooks and eyes, stiff stitched button-holes clasping ivory and pearls.

He remembered the first time they had made love. It had been a madness between them like a dance in perfect rhythm. He had discovered exactly where his rapture could be arrived at, and realised too that until then her desire had lain dormant, never stirred.

Afterwards, Alexandrine had confided she'd been tricked into marriage by her father, who had squandered their fortune on reckless speculations. Caruel had repre-sented her father's only hope. The fortunes bestowed on her would restore the wealth he once enjoyed. She had wept and pleaded to no avail. The banns were arranged at once.

Géricault had pitied her. Tenderly he had stroked her hair and kissed away her tears. Hush, he had murmured.

La Motte slammed a pot of scalding coffee and a plate of coddled eggs before him. 'Eat, boy,' she said. 'Your mother would turn in her grave to see you so thin.'

Géricault had no appetite, wondered how long he could go on like this. Crumpling Alexandrine's letter into his pocket, he found the journal from the night before. He smoothed the pages on the table and read through the article once again.

Now, in the early morning light, he thought it beggared belief that a vessel could have run aground in good weather—barely a shipwreck at all but a bump, a shudder of the keel against a sandbank.

He tried to imagine the three hundred and fifty passengers placing their trust in the *Medusa*'s sleek bows, the farmers, soldiers and gunners bidding adieu to their homeland, even a Governor recruited by the King to reclaim African shores. The editorial reported that the Ministry of Marine had appointed scouts, schoolteachers, gardeners, bakers, agriculturists, hospital directors and their attendant families to populate the Senegalese capital of Saint-Louis, at the mouth of the Sénégal river.

Surely it was impossible, he reflected, to silence those who had survived such a disaster. Surely not even the Ministry of Marine or all the spies in the world could stopper the outrage over such falsifications and lies, all in the name of protecting the King's appointment of aristocrats who had not set sail in decades—unless of course, apart from Savigny the surgeon, no witnesses remained alive?

Idly Géricault fished a crayon from his pocket and began to sketch the masts and spars of a ship at one corner of the page. He drew the long, low lines he imagined a frigate to have. Yet he couldn't exactly picture the vessel in his mind. Was she wide and square at the stern with broad bluff bows? All he could recall were stately battleships framed in gold, by the marine artists who'd once flocked Napoleon's court. He glanced at his doodles and it struck him that surely the time had come for epic narratives to be told *anew,* gleaned from contemporary facts—as if read first thing that morning in the daily newspapers.

Perhaps even this shipwreck tale could resonate with mythic possibilities, find an echo in Noah?

At the notion something quickened in Géricault's mind, a sense of eagerness he had not felt in a long time. Beyond the open window, the morning light sent a radiant haze across the lawns. How delicious the colour of the trees, he thought, how fresh the shade when the sun shines. And he wondered if he could find some way of tracking down this ship's surgeon, witness and survivor of the wreck of the *Medusa.*

Géricault decided to walk into town. Anything to escape his studio, the empty easel gathering dust by the window, or another day idled at Horace's house.

In the cafés staked on either side of the cobbled street, Géricault hurried past the amputees, the war veterans of Napoleon's Grande Armée, who lifted glasses to their lips with shaking hands. Géricault averted his eyes from the look of blank shock on those young faces. He crossed the Place du Tertre, where each morning toothless old men gathered to play boules in the shade of the sycamores, and strolled past the few shops that had opened during the Empire, many of them still stocking the barest of essentials. He tossed a coin into the tray of the organ grinder at the street corner and ignored the cries of the paint merchant and the dealer in artist materials who each day touted their wares.

Before beginning the steep descent, Géricault marvelled at the view, the vast city shimmering below. On this bright clear morning, he could see Notre Dame, roofs and church spires, the slow sliding waters of the Seine and, to the west, the massed dark green woodlands of the Bois de Boulogne.

Always he enjoyed the sight of Paris spread out below like a promise.

Somewhere, he reflected, in one of these faubourgs, going about his business like any other man, hearing the cries of the newspaper vendors on every street corner, strode Savigny, the one who had returned to France alive.

Where to start, he thought? At the sprawl of rough taverns frequented by sailors and soldiers on the quays of the left bank? —someone there might know this man's whereabouts—or at the brothels lining the arcades of the Palais-Royal? Don't be a fool, he told himself as he marched down the hill. How could he even contemplate seeking out a stranger, and perhaps a disgraced one at that, in the massing throngs of the city? Someone, after all, who might or might not give him what he desired.

Géricault sighed. He needed something, anything to work into a tableau; he longed to be anchored to some sense of purpose at last. There lay the problem, he thought. France had run out of stories: the Restoration, that flimsy painted prop of Royalty, had brought them full circle, with nothing new to tell.

By the fountain at Pigalle, he paused to admire the models for hire, brilliantly attired in all their wild gypsy finery, hourly rates displayed on placards at their feet. Some were dressed as shepherdesses or nymphs, Neapolitans as ready to prostitute themselves as pose.

There was one resplendent in a flounced aquamarine gown. At Géricault's approach, she lowered a crimson shawl to reveal pale creamy shoulders. Smiling, she uncoiled a heavy mane of flaxen hair, which swung loose against her slender waist. He turned away; the sight of her only made him lust for Alexandrine all the more. Yet her face and costume would have worked well in the Roman carnival crowd scene at the start of the Barberi race, which he'd described to his uncle. But the moment he thought of that neglected project, it staled in his mind. Just the very notion of all those arching colonnades wearied him to distraction.

By the Palais-Royal the streets swarmed. In the meadowed district of Montmartre, he always forgot the filth, the noise of the city, pedlars pounding their fists against carriage windows, beggars pointing at their bellies and mouths or holding up an emaciated deformed child, scurrying streams of people everywhere dodging horses' hooves, the incessant rumble of wheels.

In this chaos it was hard to envisage Napoleon's plans for a Paris of long vistas, marble pillars soaring against the skyline, Corinthian monuments to military might—the Arc du Carrousel, the Place de la Concorde bombastic in ornamentation and style, where the laurel counted for more than any other plant.

In the jostle, Géricault felt suddenly tired. What was he doing, he asked himself, aimlessly wandering the streets in search of a story?

Nevertheless he pushed his way through the crowds. At the markets, he almost gagged on the stench: horses' hooves, goat heads, pigs' trotters piled in blood-stained wicker baskets; buckets of eels writhing in muddied pools; live snails heaped on platters, some prodding the air with pale translucent horns.

Making his escape, Géricault strolled the paved walk-ways of the Seine, admiring the bronze streetlights in the form of dolphins and giraffes, until he reached the Government buildings in the district of the Marais. He gazed up at those ivory-coloured stone facades, each window ornamented with wrought-iron balustrades delicate as bird-cages. This was a world apart from the frenzied markets so recently left behind. Gone were the barefooted girls on trotting mules, bunches of basil and oregano tied to the panniers. Here, groups of fast-talking men dressed in tailored black jackets and immaculate breeches marched briskly by, always in a hurry.

Géricault found himself at last outside the press offices of the *Journal des Débats*. Through an arched window he could see clerks hunched, row after row, scribbling at their desks, and a thin anxious man running between them like a frantic schoolteacher collecting sheaves of copy. He pushed open the heavy oak doors and went inside—into a cacophonous roar of voices barking orders and dictating dispatches. Liveried messengers scurried to and fro with bundles of documents clasped in their arms. In the vestibule he was immediately approached by an earnest clerk with nails bitten to the quick.

When Géricault asked if he might see the editor, the youth sprinted up the marble stairs, motioning him to follow. They walked along an endless corridor with panelled cubicles on either side, each marked with a name. Every so often a door banged open and out darted some figure, a burning cheroot clamped between his lips, an expression of intense preoccupation on his face.

Finally the youth led Géricault to an antechamber lined with books, presided over by a lean wolf of a man who eyed him hungrily, as if penned in a cage.

The clerk kept vigil by the door.

'What can I do for you, sir?' The editor drummed his fingers against the varnished surface of a globe set beside him.

Addressing him with a polite bow, Géricault enquired whether any news could be given about those fifteen souls who had survived on the raft fashioned from the stricken *Medusa*.

All at once the globe spun and rattled on its sandalwood frame. The editor stared at Géricault in silence. The brocade curtains at the open window behind him twitched in a breeze and a refined icy shudder swept across the room.

Undaunted, Géricault pressed on.

'I should explain,' he said, 'that a relative of mine was on board the doomed frigate and since that time no one has received a word. My family are most anxious to discover his fate, sir.' He slipped in the name of the illustrious tobacco factory, that respectable bastion of the bourgeois enterprise lauded as the nation's backbone.

He found the editor scrutinising him closely.

'Why have you come to these offices?' he asked. 'Surely enquiries of such a personal nature should be directed to the Ministry of Marine.'

'Every petition submitted to that institution has so far proved fruitless,' Géricault replied. He hoped he was not blushing. If anything, he was becoming a master of lies.

The editor leaned forward and clasped his hands together. 'I hope you won't mind if I give you some advice,' he murmured. 'Remember, in this case, a minister who has made a mistake doesn't like to be reminded of it. The matter is still being investigated.'

Géricault nodded. 'Indeed, sir,' he said, 'but I understand there's one survivor, Monsieur Savigny, the *Medusa*'s surgeon, who has returned to France. I'm keen to learn of his whereabouts, for perhaps from him I might know if my poor cousin is still alive.'

He was graced with the briefest of smiles. From his father he knew the expression well. Business completed, dismissed.

'Clearly, sir, you are not a regular subscriber to the *Journal des Débats*. Otherwise you would have read a summarised version of Savigny's testimony at the beginning of this month.'

Géricault flushed and explained he'd been called to Rome on urgent business at that time.

'I can tell you, however,' the editor continued, staring straight ahead with a frown, 'that from this Savigny, we were led into a web of corruption and lies. You understand, the King's advisers had hoped to divert a scandal by immediately disgracing the Minister of Marine for choosing Captain Chaumarey to command the *Medusa*. Scenting a plot against him at once, Minister Bouchage penned a deadly attack on Savigny's account and character and branded him a malicious liar. In the end, the doctor caused quite a fuss—an embarrassment all round he was.'

'What became of him?' Géricault asked.

The editor eyed him shrewdly.

'Bouchage has ruined him already, and sacked him from his post. I suspect he has gone into hiding or, if he had any sense, boarded a packet and left these shores at once.'

He shook his head. 'Suffice it to say it was a disgraceful business. I would not set much store by your relative's fate.'

Gracefully he extended one hand. 'We live in tricky times. I'd advise you to leave this well alone, young man.'

Thanking him, Géricault bowed and retreated across the room.

'By the way,' the editor called with a keen look, which for a moment animated his gaunt face, 'would you be so kind as to bestow my very best wishes to Monsieur Caruel.

Tell him he will find his business report in tomorrow's edition, page four.'

Blushing, Géricault headed for the door, which the clerk held open with a flourish. He hurried down the stairs, the clerk clattering at his side.

Damn, he thought. Would he have to return to the Barberi horses straining and rearing at the start of the race, the maddening arches of the Piazza del Popolo?

He felt a tug at his sleeve. 'Sir,' the clerk whispered, 'regarding Doctor Savigny, I believe that I might be of assistance.'

Géricault sighed. He should have known—this simpering youth had picked him out from the start. Still, there might be a story to be had.

'My name's Grassin, sir. There's a tavern close by which is quiet.'

Géricault followed the youth out onto a cobbled alleyway at the back of the building, deserted at that hour except for a ragged group of barefoot children raking sticks in the mud. Grassin led the way to a dirty wine shop without any lights. The children scampered after them, clamouring for coins.

He motioned Géricault to a trestle. A woman emerged from the gloom and set down a jug and two dusty tumblers.

'How do you think you can help?' Géricault asked, unable to hide the scorn in his voice. Now without a doubt he was wasting his time.

Grassin darted him a sly look. 'Savigny kicked up quite a scene with my boss, Ricard, in there, and threatened to get the lawyers on him at once. But Ricard had been set up, and pressed until he had no choice but to publish Bouchage's testimony. When Savigny finally left—I've never seen a man in such a rage—well, I followed.'

Grassin paused and examined his bitten fingernails.

'You see, in my profession you never know when such information will come in useful, sir . . . I reckon he's holed up somewhere in one of the alleys behind the Palais Royal.'

Not knowing whether to believe him or not, Géricault wrote out his address and placed one franc on the table.

'You can count on me, Grassin, to be your most loyal servant,' the youth said, glancing at the leather purse held in Géricault's hand. 'Speed is of the essence, wouldn't you say so, sir?'

Géricault studied his eager, expectant face and handed him another coin.

'You shall be further rewarded for your efforts,' he said, 'if you succeed in your mission.'

Leaving Grassin to finish the jug of wine, Géricault stepped outside to a harsh noon sun. Urchins were calling, taunting a rat swimming the open sewers. Géricault strode on, desperate for the familiar safety of the boulevards, the avenues of sycamore trees where he could breathe freely again.

He shuddered at the thought of Savigny—the ship's surgeon humiliated, disgraced, finding lodgings in some alley as vile as this. Let him be found, he murmured to himself.

As he retraced his steps, a couple sauntered ahead, arms entwined, without a care in the world. They were beautifully dressed. They were in love. The man stopped to buy a bunch of violets. She lifted the flowers to her face and inhaled their fragrance with an enchanted smile. He leaned forward for a kiss. You little beauty, he whispered. The sight of them drove a stake through Géricault's heart. If only he and Alexandrine could share such a moment in the open surrounded by people, sunlight dappling the leaves, how light of heart he would be. When the couple walked on again, he found himself prowling behind like Satan in Eden.

Everywhere he looked, he saw lovers whirling past as if part-nered in some waltzing dance. Even the pigeons bowing and cooing across the path seemed to mock his solitary state. He sent them scattering with an impatient swish of his cane and watched them swoop higher and higher until they soared over the trees on outstretched wings.

THAT AFTERNOON, GÉRICAULT SET his canvas on the easel. Such deceit and dissembling he would paint there, an encrypted narrative of illicit love. At Alexandrine's feet, tethered on a gold lead, would sit a monkey dressed in a waistcoat embroidered with forget-me-nots and wearing a Moroccan hat, his tail plumed against her gown. Géricault was the monkey gazing up with adoring eyes, yearning for freedom yet unable to leave his mistress's side. Where else in this picture would he pay tribute to their monstrous tryst?— long-stemmed roses arranged in a Venetian glass vase on a table; shortbread biscuits cut into the shape of a heart within reach of Alexandrine's extended hand; yes, and in the background, for his mistress, he'd paint a corner of the divan beneath the open window . . . And would he dare give just a hint, just a shadow of a white stocking draped over the back of a chair, or flung in a moment of haste across a pillow?

At dusk, Géricault forced himself to work on the studies he'd begun in Rome—*Man Led Astray by Voluptuousness and Folly*; *Man Tearing Himself from the Arms of Vice*. Guilt in all its raw and seething forms. It was only a matter of time, he thought, before Caruel found out. At midnight he stopped and examined his sketches. It had not escaped his attention that, lately, whenever he began a female nude, she turned into a predator of the most hideous kind, all teeth, haunches and matted manes of hair. Exasperated, he swept them from the table. What I have done is the work of a madman, he told himself.

Géricault smoothed a fresh page before him. Without thinking, he began to draw the wide bows and blunt wooden walls of a French frigate. He'd studied the compositions of Horace's grandfather, Joseph Vernet, the renowned marine artist, and had a better grasp now. For a moment he stared at the apparition taking shape beneath his pencil before adding the main, fore and aft masts, the booms and spars. Frowning, he attempted the complex lines and angles of the rigging, the vast sheets of canvas stretched to the wind. He worked on the curved splash of the bow waves, the frothing spume in the ship's wake. And once he had finished, he began again, until a veritable flotilla of frigates crammed the page, each one stronger and more defined than the last. On his final sketch, he inscribed the name *Medusa* at the bows.

IN A STATE OF GREAT excitement, Géricault paced the terrace and once again read Grassin's note.

The youth had done him proud—Géricault was convinced this hack would make his name as a Paris pressman. Within a week Grassin had discovered Savigny's hiding place in the Passage Saint-Guillaume, one of the endless labyrinthine alleys snaking between the galleries of the Palais-Royal and the rue de Rivoli.

Introducing himself as the valet of Théodore Géricault, gentleman artist, he had told Savigny that he would find in his master a most ardent supporter of his cause, that monsieur desired an appointment, to hear his story at first hand. And the surgeon had agreed to the proposition.

Géricault crumpled the letter in his pocket. The boy had worked hard for his pouch of coins. Grassin had even delivered a veritable dossier, including newspaper clippings, editorials, opinion pages, debates that had raged between Royalist and Republican factions, outraged letters denouncing the King and the Ministry of Marine, penny pamphlets decrying cannibalism, murder and everything most horrible, lithographs illustrating the wreck of the *Medusa*, coarse tavern ballads composed in crude couplets—and an extract of Savigny's testimony published in the *Journal des Débats*:

> *The annals of the marine record no example of a shipwreck so terrible as that of the Medusa frigate. It was in the midst of the most cruel suffering that we took the solemn resolution to make known to the civilised world all the details of our unhappy adventure, if heaven permitted we should see our country. We should believe that we failed in our duty to ourselves, and to our fellow citizens, if we left buried in oblivion facts which the public must be desirous to know. Here, we hear some voices ask, what right have we to make known to the government men who are perhaps guilty, but whom their places, and their rank, entitle to more respect? They are ready to make it a crime in us that we have dared to say that the officers of the marine had abandoned us. But what interest, we ask, in our turn, should cause a fatal indulgence to be claimed for those who have failed in their duties; while the destruction of one hundred and fifty wretches, left to their most cruel fate, scarcely excited a murmur of disapprobation?*

Géricault could not believe he had missed such a scandal in the two wretched months he had idled in Rome. He would go at once. He considered riding into town, but it was market day and he decided against it. At a fast pace, it should not take him more than half an hour to walk at the most.

For an hour Géricault had traced and retraced his steps through the alleys of ancient Paris, the dank corridors of brothels and taverns behind the Palais-Royal. Time and time again, he had plunged down a side street and then another, the heels of his boots ringing against the flagstones, but for the life of him he could not find the Passage Saint-Guillaume. He had folded and unfolded Grassin's crudely drawn map so many times that the page was becoming tattered and frayed. It had been a wretched hour of ragged child prostitutes soliciting him with solemn eyes; of hurrying past open liquor dens and drunken brawls, the seediest of brothels with snaking queues at the door; and no one, simply no one sober or willing enough to respond to his pleas for directions.

Beginning to despair, Géricault walked past a row of dilapidated shops packed one against the other.

Again he cursed Grassin. He should have insisted Grassin accompany him, instead of rewarding the youth at once, in his excitement. As for his map, it made no sense at all.

Géricault paused outside a linen-draper selling cheap phials of eau de cologne. Surely, he thought with exasperation, he had been along this way before. Of all the places he had passed, this one had looked the most approachable, except for some crone haggling over the price on a swatch of ribbons.

This time steeling himself, Géricault pushed open the door and ventured inside. When he asked again for directions, the draper crouched on a stool in the shadows threw up his hands and laughed. 'Why, monsieur,' he said, 'this *is* the Passage Saint-Guillaume.'

Géricault almost let out a sob of relief.

'There's a man I am looking for,' he said, trying to hide the eagerness in his voice. 'His name is Savigny. You wouldn't know the whereabouts of his lodgings?'

At this, the draper shook his head. 'Try the boarding house across the way.' He pointed out a makeshift timber building some three storeys high around which a perilous wooden staircase led to wretched-looking living quarters. Thanking him, Géricault hurried over the lane, where a pudding-faced concierge rocked on a chair in the doorway, swatting flies with a broken black fan.

'Where might I find Monsieur Savigny?' he asked, proffering a coin.

'Third floor, number five,' she replied, snatching the money from his hand.

Géricault climbed the creaking steps and came to a dark landing with a stained, cracked sink at each end. He fought an impulse to run down the stairs and not stop until he found himself among the laughter and light of the boulevards he knew so well.

Instead he knocked on a low door warped with damp. It swung open and there before him—it could only be Henri Savigny, leaning on a cane, his skin pitted and leathered by the sun, dressed in a ragged waistcoat and breeches several sizes too large. When Géricault introduced himself, the doctor bowed and ushered him inside.

'I'm glad you could come, monsieur,' Savigny said in a low voice. 'It is kind of you to see us.'

At first Géricault was struck by the bleakness of the room, a painted cot pushed against the wall, threadbare rugs concealing chipped terracotta tiles. Beneath the window, various packing cases strewn with charts, maps and journals served as a table.

'You find us much reduced, sir.' Savigny motioned him to sit on a frayed cane chair. 'Since our return to France, such are the vexations we have experienced that here we rot, reviled, forgotten, having exhausted all our money and resources. Even our friends have deserted us.'

It was then that Géricault noticed another man, with dark restless eyes. He was crouched by the fireplace in his stockinged feet, scraping potatoes from a bucket. All about him were kitchen utensils of the cheapest appearance. A peat fire smouldered in the grate.

Savigny extended one hand towards his companion.

'Alexandre Corréard, geographical engineer of considerable repute, cartographer of distant lands, dispatched with ten men under his command on the frigate *Medusa* to chart the unmapped coastline of West Africa.'

Corréard tried to rise to his feet but a hacking cough made him sink back. Shivering, he drew himself closer to the fire.

Géricault inclined an awkward half-bow, conscious of the smart cut of his clothes, his expensive boots polished to a chestnut sheen.

Savigny unstoppered a bottle of tincture on the table and poured out a measure, which he gave to his friend.

In his former life, Savigny would have been a tall elegant man of some thirty-four years with the watchful expression, the precise careful gestures required of his profession. In Corréard—several years older than his companion, although they both looked ravaged by their ordeal—Géricault could discern a tough sinewy strength in the broadness of his shoulders, the firm authoritative set of his jaw.

When Corréard spat into a soiled handkerchief, Géricault tried not to look at the blood-soaked cloth.

'Why, gentlemen,' he cried, 'surely there must be someone to attend to you?'

'Don't make me laugh.' Savigny gestured towards Corréard. 'When finally we reached Senegal, they took him to a hospital where he was laid out half naked on a truckle bed with one filthy sheet to cover him, reduced to meagre rations and the inattentions of a common soldier who, instead of acting as his nurse, neglected his duties by being continually drunk. He would have died were it not for the kindness shown by two Englishmen. Now, back home in France, we've been harassed, financially ruined, tricked and manoeuvred into silence. On every count denied compensation, even the chance to protest. No, my friend, we do not expect anyone to attend to us.'

By the look of fixed rage etched on Corréard's narrow face, Géricault thought he appeared more ravaged by the injustices heaped upon him than the physical cause of his suffering.

'The refusal of a decoration wounds him the most,' Savigny continued. 'When at the ministry he put forward his petition, he was shown the door by an aristocrat not more than sixteen years old who had the audacity to wear the very same ribbon of the Legion of Honour for some unknown meritorious service.'

Savigny marched across the room and pointed at a bundle of documents on the makeshift table. 'The Ministry of Marine wants us silenced. Well, it's our intention du Bouchage shall receive even more publicity. We're collaborating on a book. We've unearthed more evidence, including the narratives of several key witnesses.'

He unrolled a chart and examined it closely. 'The Arguin Bank,' he whispered. He gazed at the map, spellbound.

Géricault imagined the sound of their voices endlessly whispering, sifting over the details, examining every possibility that could have prevented the terrible outcome; their thoughts forever returning to the dazzling white sand slopes, the floating river grasses and whip frond weed that flourished in coastal shallows.

The chart slipped from Savigny's fingers and joined the piles beneath the table. Géricault knew they'd never complete the task in this wretched garret. Here they would remain suspended between two points in time, either adrift in their dreams on the raft's soaked planks or compiling pointless missives to an indifferent King who had already managed to quell the uproar and silence the scandal.

Something must be done, he thought. But not in this squalid place where rats scuttled behind the wainscot and the alleys in the streets below resounded with harlots' cries. They would need the daily ministering of a physician to restore their strength and make them feel whole again. If he walked away now and joined the flâneurs strolling the boulevards, if he abandoned these men to an ignominious fate, discredited, defeated, they would die with their tale.

Géricault became aware of Savigny studying him with an intent expression as he resisted the temptation to reach for the notepad he always carried in his pocket. He would love to catch the mobility of that mournful face, the suffering cut into the purse of his lips. Even without his tale, what a fine head this man would provide, noble and equine. He admired the graceful lines of the pose silhouetted by the window.

Had he ever caught sight of Savigny on the street, he would have stopped him in his tracks, declared he possessed the most original features he had ever seen and offered the doctor a handsome price to sit for him in his studio.

All at once he knew what had to be done.

'Gentlemen,' he cried, springing to his feet. 'Please place your trust in me as your most loyal servant. I pledge my soul to assist you in redressing the monstrous injustices you have received at the hands of our heartless countrymen.'

'I'm not sure we understand, my good fellow.' Savigny retrieved the chart from the pile on the floor and placed it back on the makeshift table. 'Explain your business with us once again.'

Giving a brief account of his background and making much more of his inherited wealth than he would have dared before the Vernets, Géricault explained how fervently he hoped against hope they would leave these vile lodgings and accept his invitation to reside at his house in Mont-martre, where they'd find ardent support for their cause.

'There are many officers on half pay in the area,' he said. 'They too were denied the rightful honours of a hero's return by the King.'

The fire had gone out. Corréard began to gather scraps of peat from a basket. He gazed at the dying embers as if the very notion of placing trust in a stranger and moving else-where had exhausted the last of his strength.

Géricault could see Savigny considering every possibility.

'You're most kind,' he said at last. 'But we're quite in-capable of reciprocating your hospitality. Not even a cup of wine or a crust of bread.'

'Why, gentlemen, I don't seek payment,' Géricault declared. 'I ask you to reside in Montmartre as my most privileged guests. I'm fortunate in having one of the best cooks in the district, who will tend to all your needs.'

Savigny glanced at his companion, then turned to Géricault again.

'Why?' he asked. 'Surely something must be required from us?'

Now Savigny viewed him with suspicion. But what did he expect when the man had no one to trust?

'I have in mind certain sketches and studies,' Géricault began, unsure how to explain, 'for a tableau which might shed the truth on your plight at last, restore your names and reputations.'

'Ah,' Savigny smiled. 'So you believe you possess greater powers than the King.'

Géricault flushed. How arrogant he must sound, boast-ing of his wealth and inherited fortune. He should not meddle with these men's lives.

'But perhaps it is possible to come to some arrangement,' Savigny continued. 'For I doubt my friend will last long here.'

Géricault assured him that in exchange for their narrative, then he would provide board and lodging. Should he require them to sit for him in the studio, they would receive a generous stipend at an hourly rate.

'In the privacy of my home,' he said, 'you will find ample opportunity to complete your book. I'm happy to hire a clerk should you require assistance.'

Again Savigny smiled as if Géricault were a mere boy.

'Indeed,' Savigny said, 'a clerk would be useful for the task we have before us.'

Slowly he crossed the room and joined his companion. 'Allow me a moment to confer with Corréard.' They drew their heads close and began to whisper between themselves.

Discomforted by the hushed urgency of their tone, Géricault stood by the window and stared at the grey slate rooftops, chimneys belching black spirals of smoke, and beyond the silver glint of the Seine. He longed to escape this place, breathe air deep into his lungs once again.

'Very well, sir,' Savigny announced at last, 'we'll gladly accept your offer.'

'I'm most honoured, sir.' Géricault shook Savigny's hand. 'And you can rest assured I will do my utmost to keep your whereabouts a secret.'

Placing three francs on the table, he promised he would send his groom the following morning to fetch them. Quite overcome by his own act of impetuosity, Géricault bowed and took his leave.

He retraced his steps through the network of alleyways leading to the rue de Rivoli and joined the promenading crowds. He knew there was something craven in his impulse to offer Savigny and Corréard refuge, which had little to do with kindness or even generosity on his part. But he longed to share that voyage to the white-rimmed shores of Senegal and bear witness to their narrative of betrayal.

He would give La Motte immediate orders for his mother's quarters—the shuttered bedroom, library and parlour—to be opened and cleaned, the furniture polished, the beds made up with fresh linen. He'd explain that Doctor Savigny, a most eminent physician, and his companion Monsieur Corréard, renowned cartographer and surveyor, were collaborating on a work of a most learned nature and on no account must they be disturbed. As for Alexandrine, she must understand that he had work in mind.

Géricault thrilled now at the prospect of offering refuge to these men. Leave the fine stallions, converging battle troops and court commissions to the Vernets and their honoured friends. Here was *his* space. Scorched implacable skies, clouds raining dust. An ocean so tumultuous and vast it would hurt your eyes to stare at it for long. Men huddled on an improbable tempest-tossed raft. Mere planks lashed by rotting cords.

Perhaps he had chanced on a subject for the King's Salon, at last.

ALL MORNING GÉRICAULT PACED the terrace waiting for his distinguished guests to arrive. They must not disappoint, he thought.

Finally the carriage swung through the gate, and the groom was the first up the steps, carrying the men's pitiful belongings. With difficulty Savigny climbed down and extended a hand to his companion.

'Shall I fetch a physician, sir?' the groom asked, setting down the trunk and running to their aid. Together they half carried, half dragged Corréard to the house. Leaning on his cane, Savigny shuffled behind.

'Good Lord,' La Motte exclaimed. 'I've banked up a fire in the drawing room. The gentlemen should be taken there at once.'

All day, fierce La Motte ministered to their needs, fearless of Corréard's ravings and fevers. Even Savigny, pinched and pale beside him, surrendered to La Motte's insistent spoonfuls of finely sieved broth and brandy. The groom returned with trusted physician, Biett, who prescribed a liberal dose of quinine and dispatched the servant at full gallop to the local apothecary. In the end Géricault retreated to the studio. There was a tap at the pane. The door swung open.

'Most peculiar,' Horace said, slumping on a chair, 'but I happened to be strolling by the terrace and could not help notice two strangers in your drawing room wearing the most threadbare clothes. One lay as if half dead on the day bed, the other dozed by his side. And seated at the table, her face illuminated in the lamp light, La Motte gazed down at them with a proud protective expression. Rather Rembrandt, I thought. Are they relatives of hers?'

Géricault stared at him with irritation. 'Yes,' he replied.

Horace always knew when he was lying.

'Well, whoever they are,' Horace said, helping himself from a decanter of brandy on the sideboard, 'they don't look very well.'

After a good night's sleep, Géricault hoped, his guests might have recovered sufficiently to receive him. He found Savigny alone in the upstairs parlour. La Motte and the groom had transformed his mother's rooms into respectable gentlemen's quarters. Charts and papers were neatly stacked and folded on a walnut escritoire by the fireplace; sad relics from their former life—a sextant, a perfume phial, a salt-stained medicine chest—were ranged along the mantel.

Wrapped in a cashmere shawl, Savigny reclined on a window seat and gazed out at the rose garden. A peacock strutted across the lawn, and, seeing a hen scrabbling among the beds, fanned his feathers in a fantastical iridescent display, all the tones and shades of lapis lazuli shimmering through his train.

'This morning I woke to an enchanted land,' Savigny said, still staring out the window. 'For a long time now, I despaired of ever clapping eyes on such a place. So hardened had my heart become that I refused to believe in the existence of Eden.'

He gestured towards a bowl of fruit on the table beside him. 'Here lie jewels almost too precious to eat.'

Picking up a peach, he held it to the light and admired the smooth ruddy skin. He closed his eyes and, pressing the fruit against his lips, inhaled its sweet sun-warmth before sinking his teeth into the fragrant flesh. Juice streamed down his chin. Géricault watched him devour the peach.

He reached for his sketchpad. Altogether there was something swift and feline about this man, a suggestion of razor-sharp claws retracted in velvet paws.

He wanted to capture the doctor's watchful, alert expression, the way he crouched on the window seat as if ready to spring. He imagined the predatory panther-plume of a tail whisking back and forth, barely concealing its contempt, its disgust with the world. How to reach behind the courteous urbane mask of Savigny's face, shaved, pomaded, presenting him now with a gracious smile, and see the rage that rankled and boiled within.

'I find your countenance most unnerving, sir.'

Startled, Géricault blushed. He did not mean to gape at his guest like that.

'This painting of yours,' Savigny asked. 'What do you have in mind?'

'It's too early to say,' Géricault replied, taken aback by the directness of the question. 'I'll need the entire story before I can begin to select a moment, a particular angle that best—'

'Depicts us as heroes,' Savigny interjected, scrutinising him with such a fierce, eager expression that he had to look away. 'That shames the court and King. Good Lord, sir, I applaud your courage. Do you dare?'

Géricault noted that although greatly reduced, this doctor was no fool, and perhaps saw him for what he was— a young gentleman of some early promise, but from the studied elegance of attire something of a fop, a dandy with too much money and time on his hands. Instead of his guests proving a disappointment, it occurred to Géricault that perhaps it might be the other way round. Did he have the talent, he asked himself, to do full justice to the tale that was about to be told?

A sudden breeze sent the cambric curtains flying wide. Savigny shivered and closed his eyes. 'I will begin,' he said.

Géricault smoothed out a page in his sketchbook and sharpened a pencil, an expensive Conté crayon of the finest graphite.

It was June 1816, less than a year after Napoleon's last gamble when he'd held all the victories of his illustrious campaigns fanned like trump cards in his hand only to sacrifice all at Waterloo. Afterwards, France's former colony in Senegal was one of the last scraps of land that remained of the Empire: not even its English captors desired it.

Having been apprenticed on Napoleon's battlefields of Ulm and Leipzig, not so much mending as sawing through shattered bones, sickened by the cries of the amputees, the criminal waste in so much butchered youth, Savigny longed to escape the carnage of France, the drunken brawls from the Austrian and Prussian garrisons bivouacked in every parkland in Paris. He craved a sea voyage, the chance to set foot on distant lands, to feel brisk trade winds cleansing the death stench from every pore of his soul.

So he thrilled at his first foreign commission, ship's surgeon on the frigate *Medusa*, in an expedition of four vessels to reclaim the former African territories.

With a sense of exhilaration he had not felt in a long time, Savigny climbed into the carriage, which would take him to Rochefort, where the squadron was anchored.

The *Medusa* lay long and low on the mud-banked estuaries off the Island of Aix. She was an ancient warship, now stripped of her battery of forty-four eighteen pounders and transformed into a passenger conveyance, store ship, barn.

Fighting his way through the crowds on the jetty, Savigny paused to admire the *Medusa*'s convoy anchored at her square stern—the *Echo*, a corvette light in the water, the *Argus*, a brig sturdy and wide at the bows, and the transport *Loire* carrying provisions.

He clambered the bulging tarry sides of the *Medusa*'s blunt wooden walls and jumped onto the wide gun deck.

Savigny would always recall the scrubbed oak planks of the *Medusa* as a stage across which dim figures carrying trunks and boxes of belongings passed or gathered in bewildered clusters. A harassed middle-aged man herded his family on board: two grown-up daughters—possibly from a former marriage—his beautiful young wife, a baby clutched to her breast, and three infants tugging on her gown.

This wooden world roared with the cries of the crew, the shrieks of livestock swinging and lowered from cranes overhead. A southwesterly that kept the ships at anchor boomed among the rigging and battered the furled canvas sails.

The Captain strode back and forth across the quarterdeck surveying the chaos about him, every so often adopting a heroic stance, hand on hip, the other twirling the points of his fine, silver moustache. Savigny watched him with interest, for word had got round that this aristocrat of ancient lineage had fled the early years of the Revolution and found refuge in England.

With a sudden tilt of the ship, the Captain almost tripped, he staggered to one side before making a grab at the helm, which rolled beneath his grasp. Equilibrium once again regained, he reached for that most authoritative prop, the glass, but a frisky breeze flipped the wide brim of his hat and sent it skimming against the rail. Springing lightly onto the deck beside him, a young officer retrieved the lost item and returned it to his superior with a low bow. The Captain rammed the hat on his head where it sat trapped at a jaunty angle.

Another more senior officer appeared, carrying the Ministry of Marine charts rolled in bundles beneath his arm. He spread one against the skylight of the Great Cabin. The younger officer, his second in command, leaned close. Both conferred in animated discussion, their fingers tracing various points on the chart. The Captain nodded and listened and every so often stifled a yawn.

Savigny stood alone in the confusion. Soldiers who formed the bulk of the passengers seemed the only ones who knew where to go. He watched them swarm past and climb into the hull. Their ragged threadbare uniforms, scuffed boots worn at the heel, the obscene oaths they uttered—there were even Spaniards, Italians and Negroes among them—made it plain they came from a low-grade battalion, mere cannon fodder pressed into service from local taverns and gaols.

Glancing around for someone in authority to sign his papers, Savigny thought that perhaps he should introduce himself to the highest authority on board, but when he glanced up at the poop deck, the Captain had disappeared, leaving the officers still poring over the charts. And he did not like to interrupt them at their task.

Everywhere Savigny looked it struck him that the *Medusa* appeared ill prepared for such a journey. Sacks of meal and flour lay piled in a muddle all around the ship's waist. Not even the barrels of salt beef and pork had been removed below, let alone properly secured, for a great many rolled and strained against the ropes. A lone roaring bull kicked and butted the flimsy poles of its pen.

The same elderly man and his family Savigny had seen earlier stood before a sailor who shrugged his shoulders at their questions and with coarse words indicated they should spend the night on rough planks. Savigny noticed people were beginning to put down blankets, squabbling to find room on the open deck. Others sat at a loss, surrounded by their luggage. Besieged by the pandemonium all around, they at first did not hear a fanfare of trumpets, the shrilling of pipes and whistles heralding the arrival of the future Governor of Senegal, his wife and daughter. These three were brought aboard with great pomp and ceremony in gilt sedan chairs carried by liveried footmen. A silence fell. Everyone stared at the spectacle. The sedans weaved through the parting crowds towards the quarterdeck, where the Captain had reappeared and stood watching and waiting. The two officers, though, remained bent over their charts, examining them closely.

The Governor gazed out the window, a bored expression on his powdered, patrician face. He wore a dolman of the finest silver brocade. The white lace of his shirt frothed at his throat and languid wrists. His wife, an elegant, faded beauty wrapped in a dark blue cloak, sat bolt upright and every so often gave a fragile dainty wave, a gesture that reminded them all of Marie-Antoinette flying past in a golden carriage. Seated in the last sedan, their daughter, hair exquisitely coiffed with blonde curls piled on her head, a hint of the Hapsburgs in the porcelain tilt of nose, barely graced the passengers with a glance, as if this voyage were no more than another turn around the Bois de Boulogne.

A small, thick-set man encased in a long black coat in the English style was the last passenger to stride up the gangplank. Looking neither to left nor right, he strutted stiffly through the silent throng and followed the swaying sedans to the quarterdeck.

To another fanfare of trumpets, the footmen set down their load. The door swung open and the Governor was the first to climb out, placing his buckled boots with care on each step. Wife and daughter lifted the hems of their gowns so as not to trip.

The Captain bowed and greeted the entourage, making a great show of kissing the rings on the outstretched hands of the Governor's wife and daughter before ushering the group below, to the illuminated depths of the Great Cabin. Chilled on the darkening deck, the passengers began to stir, bedding down among their belongings. Savigny found a sheltered corner by the bows and fashioned a blanket from his cloak. He could not help wonder at the Captain for showing such scant interest in his passengers. All night the ship swung at her anchors and contrary winds shrieked through the rigging.

THE FOLLOWING MORNING BENEATH grey dawn skies, Savigny was escorted by a snot-nosed child not more than ten years old to a long narrow hutch on the gun deck's starboard side. Entering the low wooden doorway, Savigny gagged at the stench of tar hemp and something else that reminded him of the foulest pissatières in France. In the dim light, he saw that the cabin was furnished with bunks laid like troughs along one warped, splintered wall. The floor was rutted with deep grooves carved by the vast wheels of the gun trolleys used in the days when the *Medusa* was at war. As Savigny tried to make some order of his possessions, setting out his medicine chest and hanging his clothes on two hooks above the bed closest to the door, the family he had seen earlier traipsed past, bedraggled, disconsolate, the children in tears, the mother no better, hushing the baby which whimpered at her breast. The paterfamilias marched ahead, his eldest daughter at his side.

'Our cabins are a disgrace,' he cried, 'and I demand to see the Captain.'

'Papa, we're more fortunate than most.' With the utmost tenderness, the girl slipped one arm through his.

'Any fool can see the ship's overloaded. I've tried to count and there must be three hundred of us at the very least. I will write to the Ministry of Marine at once.'

The father and daughter hurried past and were soon followed by the two officers who the previous day had been examining the charts.

'I agree with you, sir,' said one of the officers to the other. 'Already we've wasted enough time and shall arrive in a season very much advanced.'

Looking over their shoulders, they paused outside Savigny's quarters. He half closed the door so he could continue to listen unobserved.

From the authority in his tone of voice, it was the older officer who spoke: 'I found the Captain courteous but perhaps not very serious-minded, and he seemed to find it natural that I would be his obedient servant. First I made him understand that I was as true a gentleman as he and did not think I had done wrong in serving my country during the time he had chosen to go into exile.'

'I could not help notice, Mister Reynaud, sir, that at your words the Captain changed his attitude.'

'Perhaps, La Touche, perhaps,' Reynaud replied. 'But once again we must prevail on our Captain to understand that it is not the *sea* which is a danger to ships but the *shore*. We must go over the charts with him again, and thoroughly this time. We will advise a westward course until she's far out in the Atlantic, then a southerly track keeping us well clear of the islands of Madeira, Porto Santo and the treacherous Canary group.'

Hearing their footsteps recede in the direction of the quarterdeck, Savigny decided he would amuse himself by keeping an accurate log of the social course of their voyage.

By late afternoon, the tides were turning in the ship's favour and the adverse wind had fallen. At the first whistle of pipes and blast of the signal gun, the passengers crowded the breastworks to watch the endless preparations to make sail. The Captain stood with the Governor on the quarter-deck, but Savigny noticed it was the first officer, Reynaud, who gave instructions by the helm. He directed his orders towards La Touche and the other officers waiting in the ship's waist. All the while the crew scampered up the rigging and inched along the yards, the less sure-footed among them almost losing their balance, swinging perilously back and forth on the ropes as they struggled to unfasten and lower the canvas. At the bows, a group of men heaved and strained at the capstan, dragging in the ropes of the anchor cables, which came up slippery as eels and slimed with weed.

'Stand by to ease the main stay,' Reynaud roared and found his echo in La Touche who from his position in the waist looked up at the sails.

Back and forth went the commands, a hypnotic sing-song rhythm.

Deafened by the grinding yards and the creaking of ropes as the bow anchors rose dripping like leviathans from the deep, the passengers looked on, bewildered now, shrinking closer together whenever the sailors pushed their way past.

The Captain and the Governor appeared delighted with one another's animated conversation, cupping their ears against the din as if the confusion all around were no more than an orchestra playing a loud clamorous waltz. When Reynaud completed a complicated manoeuvre, roaring for all canvases to be sheeted home, and with a shudder the ship began to groan, the Captain threw back his head and let out a great peal of laugher at one of the Governor's jokes.

Glancing behind him, Reynaud registered his Captain's high spirits with a shocked expression. But before he could say a word, a cry from La Touche called him back to his duties. The wind had shifted again and now the receding flood tides threatened to bring the vessel to a standstill. Again, Reynaud gave the *Medusa*'s commander an enquiring glance. The Captain continued to banter without a care in the world.

Valiantly Reynaud worked the men hard on the sails. With all their might the crew pulled at the ropes.

Finally, with effort, the *Medusa* lumbered through thick, grey estuary waters towards a shimmer of open sea.

All eyes fixed on the blue slate spires and rooftops of Rochefort. On either side of the swollen Charente lay fields of barley and rye, bright scatterings of poppies and corn-flowers, their last glimpse of France.

When Savigny returned to his fetid sty of a hutch, he found a veritable pandemonium, a huddle of men stringing their hammocks against every available hook on the beams. His medicine chest had been knocked over and three strangers swung like bats from the deck head. In one corner, several trunks had been piled into a makeshift table furnished with packs of cards, drinking cups and all manner of cooking utensils. A tall muscular man with a wild head of flaxen hair detached himself from the mob and darted Savigny an apologetic smile.

'Alexandre Corréard,' he said, shaking Savigny's hand. 'There's been some terrible mix-up with accommodation. I've found no one in authority except a cabin boy who assured me this was all to be had.'

This was too bad, thought Savigny. They were to be crammed more densely than sheep in a pen. Surely the number of passengers on board contravened the regulations of the Ministry of Marine. He wondered if that paterfamilias had already lodged a complaint. By the way the man spoke, he had the impression he'd been to sea before.

Corréard registered his look of irritation.

'Perhaps we should have a word with the Captain,' he said. 'In this crush it's impossible even to get to the Saloon.'

So it was that Savigny made the acquaintance of his comrade in arms—Alexandre Corréard, the colony's Cartographer and Surveyor, with ten men under his command.

Despite the chaos all around, Savigny noticed the explorer displayed an authority he wished the Captain shared. The heave of the ship bearing windward, the bilious blue tilt of the horizon through the open door hatch, which made him long for a draught of laudanum, seemed to have no effect on Corréard, a natural-born leader now issuing commands for the men to stow their kits in an orderly fashion. The cartographer's disciplined manner, the gradual ship-shape trim of their quarters, everything secured and battened, gave Savigny a sense of reassurance he had not felt since he boarded the *Medusa*.

Together they went out onto the gun deck, desperate for air and respite from the cramped conditions.

Making their way towards the stern—Savigny taking care not to trip over the blocks and lines, one hand on the rail as the *Medusa* ploughed through the swell—they marvelled at the sight of the squadron's three ships, the *Echo*, *Loire* and *Argus*, bearing sail at quite some distance.

They leaned against the *Medusa*'s wooden walls, enjoying the ship's swift motion through the waves.

'She slips through the water like a racing yacht,' Corréard observed, and nodded when Savigny replied that the *Medusa*'s lines seemed as fine as her upperworks were blunt. The nausea already quelling in his throat, Savigny began to delight in the prospect of this voyage, the air so pure, the sun so bright and a flock of petrels diving and dipping in the ship's wake.

All at once the officers Reynaud and La Touche

appeared by the rail. Reynaud studied the vessels of the squadron through his glass.

'It cannot be denied the convoy proves laggard,' he said to his next in command.

'The *Loire* is made clumsy and slower by her ageing canvas,' La Touche ventured.

'We're making nine knots without topgallant or studding sails,' Reynaud observed. 'We must clew the main courses if we're not to lose the fleet astern.'

'Shall I give orders, sir?'

The officers turned back towards the quarterdeck, Savigny and Corréard strolling behind them.

The Captain had set two ornate gilt armchairs upholstered in red velvet by quarterdeck rail, for the Governor and his wife.

There they reclined enjoying the breeze while the daughter sat on a cushion prettily engaged with her sketchbook. The Captain was pouring out tumblers of wine by way of refreshment. In a chivalrous pose, he leaned close to the Governor's wife and proffered a glass, which she took with a flirtatious smile.

At the sight of this spectacle, this blatant desecration of the command deck, Reynaud stood stock-still, rigid with shock.

Seeing the two officers, the Captain waved.

'She sails roundly, we're making capital time.'

Reynaud sprang onto the deck.

'Captain, sir,' he cried. 'I must give orders to take in the staysails otherwise the convoy will be hard pressed to keep up.'

Glancing across the stern, Savigny saw the *Loire* had all but disappeared and only the corvette, the *Echo*, carrying a full suit of sails, battled to remain within sight.

'Bah, so we lose the squadron,' the Governor declared. 'Speed is of the essence for our mission. Is it not, Chaumarey?'

The Captain nodded and gave an obsequious bow.

Reynaud looked from one man to the other in astonishment.

'We've been given strict instructions by the Ministry of Marine to travel in convoy and proceed on a specific course. And those orders we must obey, sir.'

'On whose authority?' The Governor gave Reynaud a mocking smile.

'Why, the Minister, sir.'

Head held high, Reynaud stood resolute. Hands clenched behind his back were the only indication of the indignation he must have felt. La Touche gazed at his superior with an expression amounting to awe. The Captain leaned against the rail affecting an air of bored nonchalance, as if the opinions of his second in command mattered not one jot.

'The Minister—don't make me laugh!' The Governor smoothed the lace ruffles at his throat. 'Why, Monsieur du Bouchage is an old friend of mine. Indeed, we go a long way back.'

At his words the Captain beamed and made a great display of helping the Governor's wife unfurl her parasol.

'Oh my, this is too much,' La Touche whispered, casting a fearful glance at a tasselled crimson fringe twirling in the wind.

'On my last visit to His Excellency,' the Governor continued, oblivious to the look of incredulity on Reynaud's face, 'I was shown the personal files of all the officers, including you, my friend.'

He paused and scrutinised Reynaud anew.

'It appears, sir, you put up a valiant fight for Bonaparte.'

Undaunted, Reynaud continued to meet his eye.

In the long silence that ensued, the Captain flicked an invisible speck from his sleeve. 'Well, it's settled then.'

'Why, yes indeed,' the Governor drummed his manicured nails against the gilt edges of the armrests.

'The *Medusa* will arrive on the shores of Senegal
without the squadron.'

At this the Captain winced, perhaps recalling the
unmapped waters of the Arguin Bank. He glanced at
Reynaud, but that officer ignored him now, continued to
stare straight ahead.

'I believe the appearance of the *Medusa* alone would
more befit the pomp and circumstance of my rank as
Governor than a straggle of lame ships bearing bakers and
school mistresses.'

'Quite so,' the Captain rejoined. 'Allow me to refill
your glass.'

Unable to endure another moment of this charade,
Reynaud, his face quite drawn and pale, gave a curt bow and
descended the ladder to rejoin La Touche.

Savigny returned to his quarters, where he spent the
evening recalling and setting down every word of this pitiful
exchange.

GÉRICAULT STOOD BY THE window waiting for Alexandrine's carriage to appear at full gallop through the gate. The previous day Savigny had sat with him again and talked long into the night. He hoped it had not been too much of an ordeal retracing each sequence of events step by step. He must take care not to exhaust him, demand too much of this eyewitness account.

Géricault glanced at the timepiece. Alexandrine was late and would squander the best part of the day, when he wanted to enquire after his guests, to see whether Savigny had the strength to continue his tale. And suddenly it shocked him to think that at this precise moment he was in no mood for this mistress of his. If she were mine, he reflected, if she were not my uncle's wife, then I could have her at any hour.

Géricault began to sift through the sketches he'd compiled from his talks with Savigny. He held one to the light and noted with satisfaction that his frigates were coming along nicely now, this one in particular—the *Medusa* clearing the mud flats of Rochefort.

All too soon Alexandrine hurried up the path, accompanied by the sullen maid. This folly must stop, he said to himself. The strain was wearing him out. And he had something else he wanted now.

'My darling, as we drove in,' Alexandrine declared stepping inside, 'I noticed a rather disreputable-looking man strolling about the rose garden. As we passed he slunk behind the shrubberies. He must be some vagrant or thief. Do attend to him at once.'

That must be Savigny, Géricault thought with satisfaction. So he's well enough to see me today.

Drawing Alexandrine close, he explained that the man she had seen was an acquaintance of his with a companion, honoured guests who might stay several months, throughout the summer at least.

'Honoured guests, you can't be serious.' Her expression reminded him of the maid. 'Heaven knows, Montmartre is bad enough without riff-raff like that.'

Géricault noticed her cheeks were flushed from the drive, her dark eyes bright and shining. Louisette sat on a stool by the stove waiting for her bribe.

He pulled Alexandrine's cloak from her shoulders. Perhaps it was best, he reflected, to give Savigny time to linger over breakfast before re-living his ordeal.

'It's time to send away the maid,' he whispered.

Alexandrine shook herself free.

'Not with that man skulking about. There was something altogether shifty in his manner which I did not like.'

Alexandrine, he wanted to say, don't torment me like this when there's so little time.

Registering his look of irritation, she motioned the maid to wait outside the door.

'Messieurs Savigny and Corréard are learned gentlemen,' Géricault said, tugging at the buttons of her gown, 'erudite scholars who have suffered the most monstrous injustices at the hands of their King and country. Their plight would arouse compassion in the hardest of men. It was the least I could do to invite them here.'

'Really!' Alexandrine was helping him with the ribbons of her chemise—'You're no better than your neighbour across the way collecting all manner of destitutes and soldiers on half pay who scrounge around like a pack of strays. Why bother with more wastrels when already you're footing the wine bills of every artist and scoundrel in town.'

She raised her arms so he could slip her cotton shift over her head.

'When you meet these gentlemen, you'll think otherwise,' Géricault said, glancing again at the timepiece. He was becoming impatient now.

'Besides, I intend to have them pose for a series of studies I have in mind.'

Alexandrine silenced him by pressing the tips of her fingers against his lips.

'Just make sure your guests, whoever they are, never come between us,' she said.

Géricault wanted to explain that finally he might have found a way to work. But he could see she wouldn't understand.

Was Savigny sitting in the upstairs parlour waiting for him now?

'You seem distracted today.' Alexandrine stepped out of her petticoats. 'How is my portrait progressing?'

He contemplated her. Standing naked before him, she could be a Leda, a nymph carved pure and white from antique reliefs.

Slowly he traced the outline of her nipples with his forefinger and thumb. 'Your portrait is progressing very well,' he said. 'For our session today, I intend to accentuate each tone with the most delicate of brushwork.'

As he led his mistress to the divan, Géricault found himself weaken with desire. He knew it was not so much adoration or lust but a complete surrender to an infernal, dreadful love.

Alexandrine leaned against the pillows, her head resting on her arms, and gazed at him with an indolent, slightly mocking smile. She reminded him of an Oriental nude after Ingres.

'Imagine my torment,' she whispered, 'when I thought of you in Rome sketching dark-skinned models in every conceivable pose, smoking their hookahs and drinking champagne all evening long.'

Géricault stroked her thighs, the curve of her buttocks.

'Would you like me shaved like the models of the grand masters?' she murmured.

In the tussle of their embrace, Géricault pictured that delicate virgin skin, naked and exposed beneath his searching tongue, of working badger bristle—nothing but the best—in a creamy fragrant lather as if he were preparing the rarest of palettes.

Alexandrine was greedy for him and he had to hold her tight about the hips. Studies of the *Medusa* were everywhere, even one crumpled beneath her clenched fist. An image came unbidden of the Governor's wife seated on the poop deck gazing about with a haughty demeanour, her daughter sketching at her side. He imagined fucking the daughter like this and wiping the smile from her spoilt silly face.

Afterwards Géricault lay back exhausted, spent. He noticed the green tinge of a bruise on Alexandrine's thigh. He must be careful not to do that again.

He swung from the divan and rearranged his crumpled clothes. Alexandrine stirred among the sheets. Hurriedly he picked up her garments strewn about the floor.

'Quick,' he said, throwing them down on her lap. 'The maid will be back any minute now.'

Often, watching Alexandrine languidly dress, rolling white silk stockings over bare legs, Géricault would become overwhelmed with an unbearable desire to possess her again. But today he could not wait for her to be gone, so he could return to Savigny without a moment's delay.

Fastening her gown, Alexandrine darted him a reproachful glance. 'Surely you're mistaken, my darling,' she murmured. 'Look,' she pointed at the timepiece. 'We still have half an hour.'

Taking a deep breath, Géricault willed himself to remain calm. Dutifully he sat beside her. He stroked her hair and did his best not to fidget, while she chattered and tried to amuse him with her never-ending repertoire of gossip. Mostly he enjoyed Alexandrine's wit, that sharp mocking tongue. Yet now—he studied her bright, animated face—he longed for Savigny's quiet measured voice taking him far away on that sea voyage to Senegal.

Finally the maid appeared at the door. Alexandrine bid him farewell with a kiss. 'You've been so serious today,' she said, her arms around his neck. 'And not laughed once at anything I've said. I believe those guests of yours are depressing your spirits.'

Géricault stood at the threshold and Alexandrine leaned out the carriage window, her lace handkerchief fluttering in the wind until the equipage disappeared through the gate.

Then he hurried across the courtyard. But as he approached the house, Horace came striding over the lawns. 'Théo,' he called, waving his arms. He seemed agitated.

Reluctantly Géricault waited.

Horace stood before him quite out of breath.

'Those guests of yours,' he said. 'The Colonel saw them on the terrace and recognised them at once.'

Horace paused and glanced all around.

'Come on,' he gestured towards the shrubberies. 'Let's go over there where no one can see us.'

'What on earth is the matter?' Géricault said, following him through the dense canopy of rhododendron, their thick green leaves glistening in the sun.

Horace shot him an angry look.

'How can you be so naïve? Don't you know it's against the law to harbour traitors, anyone who discredits the Bourbon court? What can you be thinking of?'

Géricault stared at him in puzzlement.

'If you mean that Messieurs Corréard and Savigny—'

'Don't be a fool, these men have been disgraced, sacked from their posts and banished from the Ministry of Marine. Yet you invite them here when you know how hard I've worked to win favours from the King—who now at last no longer perceives me as Napoleon's favourite! Shame on you, Géricault.'

'I'm not sure I understand you, my friend.'

Horace stamped his foot with exasperation. 'Soon this entire district will be a hornet-nest of spies. And tomorrow, I have an appointment to discuss another commission with the Comte d'Artois. How can you betray me like this?'

Géricault flushed. It was all very well, he thought, for Horace to berate him for offering his guests private refuge. Yet *he* opened his doors to the Colonel and his retinue of soldiers, who loafed around the studio all day scrounging tobacco and wine, regaling everyone with tales of their endless military campaigns. What would the Comte d'Artois have to say about that?

He told Horace that his guests were most preoccupied with a project they were keen to begin, that he, Horace— Géricault was tempted to say *turncoat*—would rarely see them, for mostly they kept to their quarters.

'But now that the Colonel has clapped eyes on your wretched survivors,' Horace nevertheless continued in the same aggrieved tone, 'every tavern in town will soon know their whereabouts and it'll arouse the suspicions of the Ministry of Marine.'

Géricault considered his friend's selfishness, his ambitions. Talented though he might be—Horace the prodigy, who knew that history banged back and forth like a shutter in a gale—now toed a dull line by refusing to take risks.

'And of course my reputation will be tarnished by way of implication,' Horace was saying. 'Aren't you concerned about the danger you're placing us in?'

With an impatient gesture, he lit a cheroot. 'Risk your own neck by offering these men sanctuary if you wish, but, for all our sakes, don't let them out your front door. Especially if you ever see the count's carriage appear.'

Watching Horace stride back to his mansion, Géricault smiled. Horace had never imagined that he, Géricault, gentleman artist who by the end had begun to loathe the fizz and glamour of their crazed Emperor, would turn out such an anti-royalist rebel. But Géricault knew his friend. If for some reason the Comte d'Artois decided to discontinue Horace's commissions, you could count on it, he would effortlessly charm Savigny and Corréard and shamelessly steal Géricault's subject by painting them himself.

At the physician's orders Corréard remained confined to his room, cosseted by La Motte, who had made this man her charge, her personal crusade. Each day she banked the apple wood fire in his grate and darted upstairs with trays laden with delicacies.

After lunch, Savigny crossed the garden with his host. He was wearing one of Géricault's old tweed jackets, which La Motte had taken in at the sleeves and hem, and pressed black breeches with a pair of riding boots. He had his hair sleeked back, a starched white cravat pinned by a gold brooch beneath his chin, a lace handkerchief pleated in his lapel, and there was an assurance, a renewed vigour about him.

'What delight I begin to take in these grounds,' Savigny exclaimed, as they approached the studio, 'the fine aspects of the meadowlands. Such a refuge from the polluted airs of the city. Why, to think of that garret we were in!' He shuddered. 'Here I begin to breathe and sleep at last.'

When a sound of wild fiddle-playing accompanied by a clash of cymbals drifted across the lawns, Géricault found himself apologising for Horace and his wild city friends, the models and actresses who posed for his endless commissions. He assured his guest they were far too preoccupied with their confection of gossip, intrigues and scandals ever to consider visiting his dull shop across the way.

'In time,' Savigny said, 'I should like to meet your friend.'

But he agreed to Géricault's suggestion that it would be best to remain within the confines of the house and not arouse the interest of the Ministry of Marine and its network of spies. 'I can think of nowhere more pleasurable to lie low and convalesce,' he declared. 'I will seek society when I have regathered my strength.'

His words surprised Géricault. Were he in Savigny's situation, he'd have no interest in his callow countrymen—he'd be consumed only by the narrative he burned to tell.

Géricault opened the door to the studio, and Savigny stepped inside. He gazed all around.

'I'm impressed.' He gave Géricault a searching look. 'Clearly you've talent. I'm in good hands, my friend.'

WITHIN A WEEK, THE *Medusa* had cleared the Bay of Biscay and was passing Cape Finisterre on the northwest coast of Spain. Only the *Echo*, white with sail in an attempt to keep up, remained in sight. The rest of the squadron had disappeared beneath the pale, veiling mists of the horizon.

Reynaud and La Touche attended their duties in silence.

At noon, Maudet, the ensign of the watch, grimly informed them that the frigate was covering more than two hundred miles a day.

Still the Governor lay enthroned on his velvet chair by the quarterdeck rail, quaffing wine with the Captain, sometimes joined by an enigmatic stranger dressed in dark English tweed who had somehow earned the privilege of a cabin in the waist.

The passengers were beginning to enjoy the fresh southerly wind gusts, the smooth buoyant motion of the ship as she seamlessly rolled over the swell. Savigny too had become accustomed to his duties, ministering to minor cuts and bruises with ointments and plasters, suffering the occasional knock himself if he forgot to lower his head each time he entered the Saloon.

Most days the passengers milled about the gun deck sunning themselves in the shelter of the *Medusa's* high wooden walls and marvelling at the sights and sounds all around.

Today a group of porpoises skimmed across the waves in a precipitous arrowed flight, water streaming from arched grey-blue flanks. With cries of wonder, the passengers crammed the poop, breastwork and ports as the creatures circled the vessel, plunging faster and faster across the bows in a joyous leaping dance as if taunting the *Medusa* to join the race.

Mesmerised, the passengers craned over the rails, following the vertiginous display, the porpoises diving this way and that, swooping through the spume only to reappear once again before the splicing bow waves.

Dazzled by the playful creatures now veering to starboard and regrouping to recommence their game, at first the crowd did not hear a shout from Reynaud, still at watch on the quarterdeck.

'Man overboard!'

All at once a woman screamed and pointed to a boy— in his eagerness he must have fallen through one of the portholes on the larboard side. He clung to a rope, buffeted and half-drowned by the torrential spray, sinking beneath the rushing foam, only to bubble to the surface once again, his face stark with terror.

When Savigny recognised him as the urchin who had shown him to his quarters, he felt a stab of pity. Let him be saved, he prayed.

Fighting his way through the throng, La Touche swung over the topside and, stepping onto the channel, managed to grab the boy by the arm. With all his strength, he tried to heave the youth to safety on one of the lines.

But the speed of the ship loosened his grasp. In silent horror the passengers watched the boy's outstretched hands slip inch by inch from the rope—until another surge of the bows swept him astern.

Reynaud began issuing a litany of orders from the helm. The crew ran into position at the ready to halt the ship's progress by bringing her sharp into the wind. Savigny raced to the quarterdeck to be the first to assist if the cabin boy were found.

'Throw out the life raft,' Reynaud called. 'Run the flag. Fire a signal gun to alert the *Echo*.'

Only a shadow of the corvette's sails remained within sight.

Savigny watched the raft—a sturdy craft at least a metre long, fashioned from cask staves hooped together—fight to find equilibrium on swirling currents, its crimson flag fluttering in the wind. He searched the waves. Already the boy was nowhere to be seen.

Accompanied by the Governor, the Captain strode onto the quarterdeck. Frantically Reynaud screamed instructions to head the ship into the wind. The crew scurried across the waist ordering the passengers to make room, to return to their quarters.

'Tell them to bring in the sails.' The Captain stood close to Reynaud, almost nudged him from his position beside the helm. 'That will slow her down.'

'We've not the time, sir. It's too laborious a procedure. We'll lose the boy.'

When with a light tread La Touche scampered up the ladder, Reynaud rounded on him. Savigny had never seen anyone look so fierce.

'Why has the gun not been fired to second the signal?'

'None of the guns have been loaded, sir.'

'Not loaded? Why, I've never heard of such a thing.'

Reynaud glared at the Captain, who was conferring with the Governor in furious whispers.

'Launch a rescue boat at once.'

'Aye aye, sir.' And in a flash La Touche was gone.

'He calls you *sir* and ignores my commands!' The Captain bristled with indignation. 'Do you realise you could be court-martialled for less than this? Now do as you're told man and clew in the sails.'

'It can't be done, sir,' Reynaud replied, exasperated beyond measure. 'We'll lose him that way.'

'Any fool can see that fastening the sails would take the way off her,' the Captain said.

'Hear, hear,' the Governor rejoined, taking a swig from a silver hip flask.

The Captain gave Reynaud a withering glance as if he were no more than a midshipman of the lowest rank. 'Allow me to carry out the procedure that I think fit,' he cried. 'Otherwise I'll be the first to testify to a mutiny that will see you hanged by the scruff of your Republican neck.'

At this, Reynaud stared ahead, tight-lipped and pale. 'Very well, sir,' he said and stepped back from the helm.

Flustered, the Captain took his place and began calling instructions to a bewildered La Touche, who'd been intent on supervising the men lowering the rescue boat on the larboard side.

Even Savigny could see the Captain's entire manoeuvre was a fiasco from beginning to end. The sails, already drawn quarter back in preparation to tack, now slammed and battered against the yards, which soon became entangled in a cat's cradle of rigging. Ropes swung loose from the thrumming spars and whipped against the deck, terrifying the passengers, who panicked and fled. Without Reynaud's cool clear commands issued with the precision of a conductor wielding his baton, the crew flailed among a clatter of blocks and lines. All the while the mainmast groaned and shuddered fit to splitting from the strain. How Reynaud managed to stand surveying the chaos all around, every procedure of his training desecrated, defiled, the Captain incapable even of naming the correct parts of the ship, pointing at this sail and that, testified to the courage, the backbone of the man.

Even the Governor had retreated to the Great Cabin, alarmed. Only the stranger in English garb watched the Captain, with an enigmatic smile.

Finally the ship's sails were clewed, bulging and bunched in a manner than must have broken Reynaud's heart. Slowly the *Medusa* lost her speed, lurching sickeningly from side to side as she wallowed in the swell.

Miniaturised by the bright shimmering expanse of ocean that billowed towards the horizon, three men rowed the rescue boat in futile circles. Neither the boy nor the life raft was to be found, the *Echo* at too great a distance to be of assistance.

That evening the passengers retired early, their spirits made wretched by endless questions and speculations: the boy had been a strong swimmer, of that not a doubt; why were there only three men searching in a boat built for six?; perhaps he had managed to make his way to the life raft, for to be sure it was seaworthy enough; perhaps now the *Echo* had sighted the pitiful craft and rescued the lad; why had the guns not been loaded?—surely a most elemental safety procedure against pirates or an outbreak of war; and why waste crucial time bringing down the sails?

And so on until bed.

Corréard had managed to make their quarters shipshape, almost bearable. He had even rigged an office for himself, screened by coarse woollen blankets, where he invited Savigny to share a flask of brandy.

Tall and lean, Corréard perched on a chair and began to leaf through the dossier he had compiled, outlining the topography of Senegal. He pored over the papers, his sharp features accentuated by the moonlight.

He told Savigny that one account described Saint-Louis as the head of an archipelago of considerable islands. The river divided into two rapid channels carrying vast quantities of sand, which the sea flung from the coast. The left bank, called Grande Terre, was covered with verdure and fertile soil that only needed hands to cultivate it and on which grew a profusion of mangoes, palms, mimosas and magnificent baobabs.

Corréard paused and seemed to savour the syllables of the last word against his tongue.

'Let us stop a moment before this colossus,' he said, 'which by the enormous diameter it attains has acquired the title of the elephant of the vegetable kingdom. The baobab often serves the natives for a dwelling. And if you cast your eyes into the immense verdant dome which forms the summit, you will see swarms of birds adorned with the richest plumage, rollers with sky-blue wings, senegallis of a crimson colour and soui-mangas shining gold and azure, darting among flowers of dazzling whiteness.'

By the thoughtful manner with which Corréard stroked his beard, by his intent eager expression and the pensive deep-set eyes, Savigny detected in this explorer something of an aesthete, a dreamer fuelled with evangelical zeal. He could see that the details of the journey, the conflict that was beginning to flare on board, meant nothing to this man. Already he was in his stride, mapping the future maize and millet plantations, the cotton fields of Senegal.

THEY HAD BEEN EIGHT days at sea and were nearing Madeira. Savigny went about his duties unable to shake the death of the boy from his mind. A young life needlessly squandered. The loss hung heavy over them all like a portent.

Reynaud stood by the helm pale and haggard, as if he too had not slept the night. The Governor, however, reclined easily on his chair, accompanied again today by the stranger, with whom he now seemed on the most cordial terms and whom he addressed as *my dear Mr Richefort*.

'An excellent suggestion, good fellow,' the Governor was saying as Savigny took his position by the poop, feigning to be absorbed in a book.

'Why at breakfast, my wife and daughter were just remarking on the lack of fruit and vegetables to be had. A capital notion to put into Madeira for refreshments and supplies.'

A twitch of Reynaud's left shoulder was the only indication he thought otherwise.

'As I recall in my capacity as a former marine officer, the harbour of Funchal is of a considerable size, a veritable amphitheatre.' Richefort began eyeing the Captain, who leaned against the rail. 'The country houses situated on the slopes are built in extremely good taste and surrounded by fine gardens. Such is the abundance of lemon and orange groves that when the wind blows from these shores the very senses are assailed by a most agreeable perfume. The hills are covered with vineyards bordered with palms—in short, everything is combined to render Madeira a most beautiful island.'

'I will tell my wife at once that we're putting into port.' The Governor rose from his chair with a stately decorum. 'She'll be delighted. Already complains she's bored by the voyage.'

He strode past the two men and disappeared down the companionway leading to the Great Cabin.

Slowly the Captain turned to face this unexpected fount of local knowledge.

'You know the area well, sir.'

'Indeed,' Richefort replied, darting him a cunning look. 'I'm well acquainted with these seas. I vouch I could pilot this ship to the very shores of Senegal.'

The two men glanced in the direction of Reynaud, who stared straight ahead by the helm.

'Steady as she goes,' he called and found his echo in La Touche.

'Well, I dare say I could use a man—' again the Captain glanced at Reynaud— 'who could demonstrate considerable expertise in these matters.'

'You can count on my services, gratis.' Richefort bowed low. 'I'm at your immediate disposal.'

The Captain marched towards Reynaud.

'Stand aside,' he cried. 'Mr Richefort will take her into Funchal.'

Reynaud made no reply, tightened his grip on the rail.

'I said, stand aside.'

'I would counsel against such an order, sir.' Reynaud had gone pale and a pulse began to beat at his throat. 'Allowing a passenger to manage the ship contravenes the rules laid down by the Ministry of Marine.'

Savigny marvelled at his composure.

'Passenger?' Richefort exclaimed. 'I'll have you know, sir, I've been appointed Port Captain and Harbour Master of Saint-Louis.'

'Be that as it may,' Reynaud glared at the man, 'but it is my understanding you have spent the last ten years in an English gaol.'

'You go too far, sir.' Richefort purpled with indignation.

'Not another word, Reynaud.' The Captain took a step forward. 'This is the second time you've gone against my orders. Stand aside or you'll be cautioned.'

Without a flicker of emotion on his face, Reynaud retreated from the helm and watched Richefort take his place. He was about to descend the ladder and join the officers gazing up in bewilderment from the waist, when the Captain called him back.

'Remain where you are, Reynaud,' he said. 'For I'm sure our pilot,' he nodded towards Richefort, who beamed at the wheel, 'has much to instruct you on, in terms of navigation.'

All morning Reynaud had to endure the swaggering presence of this harbour master needlessly exhausting the crew by tacking back and forth across empty seas.

Savigny wondered how the Captain could place such trust in a mere stranger when even he could tell this Richefort was vain as a peacock, with ideas above his station, intent on showing off to a captain whose ancient aristocratic lineage impressed him beyond measure. As for his seamanship, the way the ship lurched from side to side and the sails slackened and flapped against their lines, the crew frantically trying to follow his confused cries—well, it beggared belief. Already they'd lost one young life, yet the Captain allowed this buffoon to work the helm as if he had been navigating for years.

Somehow, again, Reynaud managed to stand by the rail, watching this impostor prance back and forth, without saying a word.

When, at midday, Maudet and La Touche appeared to take the noon watch, they could barely look Richefort in the eye. Instead they squinted at the sun through their sextants. Reynaud continued to gaze straight ahead.

'By my calculations,' Maudet darted Reynaud an imploring glance, 'Madeira should already be in sight.'

'With this wind, her shores will appear soon enough,' Richefort retorted with a cheery wave.

La Touche held his instrument to the light and frowned.

Uncertain as to which person in command to address, he stared at his sextant instead.

'Speak up, boy,' the Captain growled.

'The position of the ship seems to indicate,' La Touche began in a faltering voice, 'that she's offset by one hundred miles to the eastern side of her course, sir.'

'Impossible,' Richefort cried, peering through the glass for a glimpse of land. 'Take your bearings again.'

La Touche and Maudet repeated the performance, lifted the brass triangles to their faces.

'What do you find, Mr Maudet?' La Touche asked, pale with dismay.

'Thirty leagues due east,' the ensign of the watch replied. 'She'll need to make a large turn to bring her bows onto the right heading. Take the best part of the afternoon, I'll be bound.'

Both contemplated this fact in silence.

Richefort glanced over his shoulder, alarmed.

'How so?'

Neither dared reply.

Shifting his weight from foot to foot, the Captain glared at Reynaud as if this error were his entire fault.

'Well, sir,' he rounded on him. 'What are your thoughts on the matter?'

Reynaud continued to gaze straight ahead.

'We're adrift, sir, on the treacherous Gibraltar current. If a north-westerly springs up, she'll be blown to Senegal before we know it.'

The Captain stood at the rail scanning the indigo curve of the horizon, as if willing the isle of Madeira to burst from the seas.

'What's to be done?' he said at last.

'Make up to wind, sir,' Reynaud replied. 'And pray she'll claw her way back on track.'

'Well, get to it, man. Get them to it.'

'Mr Maudet, La Touche,' Reynaud called. 'Prepare to tack.'

The officers scrambled to their posts.

'Come below, Mr Richefort,' the Captain entreated the pilot, who hovered uncertain, at a loss by the helm. 'Enough labour gratis for the day. Leave this tedious work to the crew. Tomorrow you shall steer the frigate through gentler waters. Meanwhile I have a fine cask of wine I'm sure I can interest you in.'

That night in the Saloon, many of the passengers were shocked by the Captain's decision to hand the vessel's command to Richefort, an upstart who somehow had managed to earn privileges over them all as well as the crew and officers they trusted. This intruder even dined in the Captain's Great Cabin, when clearly Reynaud was the most competent seaman. The elderly man with the large family introduced himself to fellow diners as Picard, an old colonial hand who had worked a plantation in Senegal when the English took over.

'I've been to sea before,' he said, 'and this Richefort fellow has no idea. Indeed, he seems to include a close approach to all the hazards that could possibly be encountered.'

Picard coloured fiercely and his daughter laid a soothing hand on his arm. At his words, a silence fell among the passengers. Soon, with a sense of unease, they retired to their quarters.

GÉRICAULT SPREAD OUT HIS studies of Richefort the dissembler and impostor on the table before him. Through the open window, a crescent moon cartwheeled above the branches of the chestnut trees.

'Imagine a toad,' Savigny said, 'sweat on his brow like slime, smiling and creeping his way about the ship.' He shuddered. 'I don't want to think of him any more.'

Staring at the sketches, Géricault resolved that this pilot would never leave his mind until he had him exactly right.

As they crossed the courtyard, the sound of laughter and a *rat-tat* of tambourines drifted across the lawns.

Once again Géricault found himself apologising for his wild carousing neighbour and promised he'd see they were never disturbed by Horace and his city friends.

'My dear boy, we would hate to put you out, on any account,' Savigny replied. A carriage tore up the drive. When it lurched to a halt outside Horace's house, the door swung open and a woman stepped out, her scarlet cloak barely concealing a low-plunging gown—the famous actress Thérèse, mistress of Racine and Corneille in five tragic acts. As Thérèse sashayed along the path, she lifted her skirts to reveal green stockings, the colour of chartreuse, and pink satin slippers with high heels and pointed toes.

Savigny stared at her with fascination. 'I'm sure we should very much like to *meet* Mister Vernet,' he said, wrenching away his gaze. 'So confined have we been in our own company that it would cheer our hearts to meet an artist of such acclaim. Why don't you ask him to join us for supper one night?'

What could Géricault say? Tell him that Horace was intent on wooing the favours of the King; that in his view Savigny and Corréard were no more than miscreants and traitors?

But he wanted to keep these survivors to himself. Hear out their tale. Begin serious work on a tableau, at last. Horace would only set out to charm them.

In the dining room, they found Corréard seated at the table, La Motte fussing over him, ladling a rich fish stew into bowls.

'I'm feeling somewhat restored,' Corréard said as he refilled his glass. 'I thought I would join you tonight.'

'Capital, dear fellow,' Savigny declared, taking a place opposite his friend. 'My word, La Motte!' He inhaled the fragrant steam from his bowl. 'This will put flesh on our bones, all right.'

Greedily he began to slurp from his spoon as if he had not eaten for weeks. Watching them devour her meal, La Motte beamed with pleasure and served more. Finally, after a third helping, Savigny mopped the last of the sauce with a hunk of bread.

At the sound of a voice singing a long trilling note, Savigny got up from the table and peered out the French doors. 'There's that woman again,' he exclaimed. 'Look at her, Corréard, now she's wearing a gold silk gown.'

His companion joined him and they stepped onto the

terrace. In their wake the room filled with a melody of fiddles. 'They're having quite some party,' Corréard said in a wistful tone. They turned back inside and once again Géricault was asked when they would meet his neighbour across the way. He assured them that Horace Vernet would make their acquaintance soon enough. Even though he hoped Horace would leave them alone.

All evening, Corréard and Savigny sat by the window drinking brandy, staring at the shadows flickering across the lawns, the illuminated rooms of Horace's house.

The following morning, Savigny arrived at the studio alone.

'Last night, I'm afraid, Corréard indulged in too much brandy and is paying for it with a return of his fever. I've warned him about taxing his liver but he so enjoys life here. A slight relapse won't do him any harm.'

When Géricault motioned him to his seat by the window, Savigny paused to inhale a scent of gardenias frothing the sill. He gazed at the peacocks strutting across the lawns. 'Such an exquisite day,' he exclaimed. 'Why don't we take a stroll across the meadows?'

When Géricault shook his head, for they had work to begin, Savigny sighed. 'Oh, very well,' he muttered.

FOR DAYS THE *MEDUSA* drifted towards the shimmering ridge of the African coast, the colours of the ocean shifting from the deepest aquamarine to pale blue. They had been at sea for two weeks but Savigny was beginning to lose track of time. Each day a white glowering sun scorched the cloudless skies.

Each day, the Governor reclined on the gilt velvet chair by the quarterdeck rail idly watching Richefort at the helm. Sometimes the *Echo* and the *Loire* appeared on the rim of the horizon, only to nudge out of sight once again. But whenever the Governor glimpsed a sail of the corvette through his glass, he urged the pilot to make speed and outrun the *Echo* at all costs.

Immaculately attired in white chiffon and lace, the Governor's wife strolled along the waist, her daughter at her side, both remarking at the pretty tints of the waves through which darting fish could be seen. A lassitude seemed to be descending on them all. There was something dreamlike about this floating world, the tireless splice of the bows through the foaming swell.

Each day at noon, Reynaud and the officers of the

watch took their sightings to fix the ship's position.

Reynaud seemed particularly over-wrought and tense at these times. 'What have you found, La Touche?' he would ask, only to spit in disgust at the officer's answer.

Every two hours, the ship sounded and each day the sounding line showed they were navigating towards shallower waters. One evening, Savigny sighted the *Echo* silhouetted in the distance. As darkness fell, the corvette began signalling. She burned several charges of powder and hung a lantern on her mizzenmast.

From the quarterdeck, a cheer followed by the Captain's voice. 'No need to signal our night course. We'll lose her soon enough.'

Savigny watched the lantern gleam for several hours before the *Echo* tacked west-southwest towards deeper channels.

Each day, unable to endure the stifling condition of his quarters, Savigny lay on a pallet beneath the quarterdeck, drifting in and out of sleep, his faculties rendered insensible by the heat, his dreams suffused with images of that shadow-flanked land drawing closer and closer.

One morning they had doubled Cape Blanco, indicating they were closing in on the Arguin Bank, when clouds the colour of whipped cream began to billow against the sky. Savigny longed for rain cool and fresh as a mountain stream. Once again he fell into a reverie and some hours later woke to Corréard crouched beside him, tugging at his sleeve. He asked if they'd arrived, for the white dune ridge seemed to loom higher, the wind scrolling the sands just as it peeled surf from the waves. Or perhaps in this heat, it was the luminous sheen of a mirage he had seen.

Corréard shook his head. He seemed in a state of considerable agitation. He informed his companion that when the Captain had asked Reynaud if Cape Blanco had yet been sighted, the good officer pointed towards some distant shape above the coast and claimed that was the cape. 'By Christ!' Corréard exclaimed and slammed his fist against the rail. 'When I looked where Reynaud pointed, all I could discern was a cape of vapour. As a geologist, at least I know how to distinguish between a rock and a cloud.'

Alarmed, Savigny sat up at the urgent tone in his voice. Perhaps it was the harsh noon sun but Corréard's face appeared stripped of all colour, and only his thin pale lips moved. Savigny watched them carefully and tried to concentrate.

Corréard told him that later he had approached La Touche and asked him to affirm that the cape had not been seen at all. The officer turned away in a distraught manner and, when pressed once again, replied that a *false* reconnaissance was the only measure they could take to persuade Richefort to stand away from the treacherous African shores. Indeed, the last accurate fix on the cape had been taken the morning of the day before.

Savigny cast his mind back in an attempt to remember but all he could recall was Richefort endlessly swaggering at the helm; the rustle of a pleated gown as the Governor's wife sashayed past on her way to the waist; Reynaud's worn haggard expression each time the soundings were read; a scene enacted day after day like some senseless shadow play.

'Where are we then?' he asked, barely able to articulate each word, such was the fear in his throat.

Corréard shrugged and stared all around, his features sharpened by the bright white light.

'Since the pretend reckoning, no one knows.'

Wearily Corréard rose to his feet and returned to their quarters. His receding steps against the bare planks reminded Savigny of the sound of nails hammered into wood.

All night, he lay on his pallet and gazed at the constellations carpeting vast windswept skies, the bear, the plough drowning in a mist of stars. Sometimes, but not often, a spark tore across fathomless horizons and vanished before he could blink an eye.

All night, the ship tilted and turned on swift-moving currents. An ebony smudge of land rose and fell on the larboard side. At times Savigny fancied he could hear galloping hooves pounding across rippled dunes, kicking great clouds in their wake, and a lone warrior's cry signalling the attack, or the crackle of desert fires, their embers scorching fine powdered sands, then the murmur of men united in some pagan prayer. All night, while the pilot snored in his bed, Reynaud paced the deck counselling his officers to steer west, double the bank—then once the danger was past they could guide the *Medusa* on a southern course bound for Senegal.

As always, by the dawn light, Reynaud and the officers of the watch were gathered on the quarterdeck to take the soundings.

'What have you found, Maudet, La Touche?' Reynaud enquired quietly, looking from one to the other. Sweat beaded his brow.

For the first time in days, Maudet smiled.

'One hundred fathoms, sir.'

A slight slackening of Reynaud's shoulders was the only indication of any relief he might have felt. He gazed up at the sails.

'The weather shows fine and the wind is not unfavourable. Steer her out to sea.'

'Very well, sir.'

Once again Savigny dozed on his pallet, soothed by the officer's words and a brisk buffeting breeze.

At nine, Richefort, the Govenor and the Captain

emerged from the Great Cabin where at their leisure they had breakfasted.

The second time the soundings were taken and five hundred fathoms recorded, Richefort rounded on the officers. Since the *Medusa* had obviously crossed the lower part of the African continental shelf, he informed them, it was now safe to resume their course and steer for Portendic.

Reynaud, who had gone deathly pale, stepped forward. 'You are nothing but an impostor,' he began.

The Captain held up one hand. 'Arrest this man,' he called to a couple of sailors, who looked up bewildered from scrubbing the deck.

When the Captain hailed the men again, they reluctantly put down their pails and climbed the ladder. Savigny noticed they could not bring themselves to lay a finger on their officer in command. Instead, with the utmost dignity, Reynaud led the way to the hold, followed by La Touche and the ensign of the watch.

Richefort surveyed their departure with a triumphant smile.

Several passengers, including Picard and his family, glanced at the pilot preening himself by the helm.

'We're safe enough,' Richefort declared, 'as Cape Blanco has been passed. I know exactly what I am doing.'

'The sighting was not accurate,' Corréard called, pushing through the throng that had gathered in the waist. 'That was no cape but a cloud.'

The Captain flushed and denied that any doubt was possible. The passengers began to murmur among themselves. Voices clamoured for a westerly course.

Richefort dismissed their cries with an airy wave.

The Governor and the Captain cheered as the ship swung round.

'We're running into danger, sir.' Picard advanced towards the quarterdeck. 'At least I know the Arguin Bank. I've been twice alongside and eight years ago ran aground because the Captain stood in too close.'

Richefort stared down at this man, this passenger who dared question his authority.

'My dear sir,' he exclaimed at last. 'We know our business. Attend to yours and be quiet.'

'Hear, hear,' the Governor murmured.

At his words, Picard made a move to rush up the ladder. 'Papa,' his daughter remonstrated and laid one hand on his arm to stay him.

'Three times I have passed this Arguin Bank,' the pilot continued, gazing at the crowd below with a supercilious smile. 'Indeed, I have sailed the Red Sea and I am not drowned.'

Perhaps it was the heat, the clammy air laden with salt that clung to every pore of their skin the moment the ship turned, but at the Captain's orders the passengers dispersed, their protests stilled. Even Picard shooed his family below. It was now half past eleven. Once again an exhausted stupor pervaded everyone. Corréard joined Savigny on the pallet. He sat cross-legged, bony wrists resting on both knees, gazing into the distance.

Ensign Maudet requested soundings be taken at shorter intervals. All morning he sat hunched over a chicken coop, which he was using as a table to calculate the ship's position.

'Eighty fathoms,' he cried.

'Capital, my good fellow,' the pilot replied, glancing at the Captain, who nodded in approval.

At noon, La Touche appeared looking careworn beyond his years. Reynaud had been banished to deeper recesses of the hold on half rations. La Touche peered at the sun through his sextant. When he whispered his findings to

Maudet, the ensign made a formal report to Richefort that the frigate was on the abrupt slope of the Arguin Bank.

'Never mind,' the pilot announced with great cheer. 'Why, we still float above fifty fathoms of ocean.'

Without Reynaud to superintend the men, the sailors had cast their lines into clear turquoise waters crying out in delight each time a plump mackerel was hauled quivering and thrashing from the hooks, blood spurting through its gills.

Again Maudet ordered the sounding.

'Thirty fathoms,' he called.

'Thank you kindly,' Richefort replied. Registering the officer's stricken expression, he added, 'No cause for alarm.'

Raising his voice so that all nearby could hear him, he repeated, 'No cause for alarm.'

The Governor's wife reclined on her chair, one arm propped against the rail.

'My,' she mused, gazing at the bronze garlands of kelp rising to the surface. 'Try and catch the colours if you can, my darling.' And head bent over her sketchbook, her daughter dabbed a brush in a box of paints.

Still Maudet insisted on taking the soundings.

'Eighteen fathoms,' he called.

La Touche, who hovered at his side, dashed off to report the findings to Reynaud cooped with the livestock in the hold.

The passengers stood riveted in the waist watching the bow wave churn through a mass of floating river grasses and long whips of weed. The waters had turned from turquoise to the palest of greens, through which rolling clouds of sand could be seen.

At the sight of the changing seas, even the sailors who had filled panniers with their catch drew up their lines and surveyed the ship's progress in silence.

'How tranquil the ocean is today,' announced the Governor's wife. 'We could not have hoped for better weather.' She glanced about with a bright smile. 'Quite perfect, is it not?'

'Indeed, Mama.' The daughter held up a sketch for her mother to admire. 'It's fortunate that tiresome wind has stopped riffling the pages of my book.'

All around them, the passengers and crew stared straight ahead, stock still as if chained to the decks.

'Twelve fathoms,' Maudet called. He leaned his hands against the coop to stop them trembling. Ashen-faced, La Touche whispered a few words to him.

Not a murmur from anyone. Only a flap of sails and creaks among the rigging could be heard.

The Governor dozed in his chair, his plumed hat shielding the sun from his face. He yawned, rose to his feet and retired to the Great Cabin. The Governor's wife continued to admire the hues of the waves. 'Oh look,' she cried. 'A shoal of fish—if we weren't in the ocean I would take them for minnows.'

No one looked up. No one answered.

Oppressed by the silence, the Captain stepped forward. He stood alongside Richefort, who beamed by the helm.

'Perhaps, my good man—' he began noticing the anxious expressions among the crew below—'we could put her a little more into the wind and slightly away from the coast.'

At his words, the sailors sprang into action and reefed in the studding sails on the shoreward side.

Maudet immediately gave orders for another sounding.

No one dared breathe as they waited.

'Six fathoms,' Maudet called, his voice tight with fear.

The Captain hesitated. He darted a glance at the officers and back to Richefort again, uncertain as to what to do next.

'Haul her in as close to the wind as she will lie,' he finally cried.

Luffing, the frigate heeled. But all at once the *Medusa* gave a shudder and scraped against the shallows. Frantically the men worked the sails. Yet she broke free only to drag on loose sands. Her canvas still billowed in the wind. No more than a bump, a nudge—then the bows ran aground. Swirling waters rushed past and lengthened into languorous lacy waves.

At first no one uttered a word. Some sank to their knees in a quiet despair. Others stood rigid with shock. The Captain steadied himself against the rail and scanned the seas as if expecting something to happen.

The officers remained still for a moment then volleyed orders in voices high and shrill. Reynaud appeared from the hold and marched towards the quarter-deck where Richefort continued to stand by the helm, unable to understand why the *Medusa* no longer moved through the swell.

'See, sir, what your obstinacy has brought us,' Reynaud cried, springing up the ladder. 'I warned you of it.'

The Governor's wife and her daughter were the only souls who seemed insensible to this disaster. Reclining on her chair, a parasol shading her from the sun, the Governor's wife peered at the chaos all around.

'Really, this is most inconvenient,' she declared at last. 'Tell me, dear man,' she addressed Reynaud with a flirtatious smile, 'how long will it take before the vessel is fixed?'

Her daughter yawned. 'It reminds me, Mama, of the time when the wheel of our coach broke loose and we were stranded for three hours in the Bois de Boulogne with no refreshments, not even a glass of water to be had.'

At this, the Governor's wife sighed. She adjusted the tilt of her parasol and snapped open her fan.

'These officers are a coarse lot. That man over there—' she nodded in the direction of Reynaud, who was screaming instructions to lower the sails and topgallant masts—'had not even the courtesy to answer my question.'

Giving the officer a haughty glance, the Governor's daughter rose daintily to her feet. 'Come, Mama,' she said, extending one gloved hand. 'We shall join Papa in the Great Cabin. Someone will inform us when the ship's mended.'

THEY HAD STRUCK AT HIGH spring tides, the worst possible time.

Although land could be seen, the slopes of the Arguin Bank rose impossibly wide drubbed by treacherous frothing currents. No one dared interfere with Reynaud now. He organised the crew into relays: some at the pumps to reduce the water leaking in through the strained seams; others in the boats to haul the anchors away from the ship and somehow drive them into the seabed; the soldiers at the capstan to haul on the ropes then, in an attempt to move the frigate.

By late afternoon, strong winds and currents buffeted the vessel. The passengers watched the men in the boats towing the great stern anchor through heavy swell. When the soldiers heaved on the capstan bars, the dripping cables came slithering towards them through soft grey mud. Again and again the boats went out. Once, with a side anchor tied at the bow, the *Medusa* veered towards open seas. A great cheer went up when the hull slipped forward—only to ground again some two hundred metres away.

Defeated, frustrated, Reynaud gave orders to jettison the fourteen twenty-four-pound guns, to lighten the ship and ease her motion in the water before sending out the boats again.

At this, the Captain demurred. 'Throw the King's cannons overboard?' he exclaimed. 'I'll do no such thing.'

Picard muttered to his daughter that the King's frigate would be sacrificed if the guns were not.

Beside himself with exasperation, Reynaud suggested the bulk of the stores be thrown over, but this was the Governor's turn to remonstrate and lift up one hand.

'Do you not know that the greatest scarcity of flour prevails in the European factories of our province?' he said, scarcely able to conceal the scorn in his voice. 'Arrive in Senegal without the wherewithal to bake bread? What would the English think?'

Hearing his words, Corréard called up from the waist and explained that they would not necessarily lose all the contents if the stores were bound together, for moisture would form a thick crust on the outside and preserve the provisions.

Grudgingly the Captain agreed to give this theory a trial. But the task of fastening the sacks and barrels together proved difficult and in the end the project was abandoned.

The Governor began a detailed inspection of the *Medusa's* four longboats, calculating how many people they could carry. At his request, Richefort scratched a list of names with a quill.

Finally Reynaud gave orders to chop down the ship's masts, yards and booms, anything to lighten the vessel. When the sawn timbers were lashed together and lowered over the side, the Governor studied them and called the Captain to his side. Both conferred closely in animated whispers then summoned the carpenter to the poop deck.

The crew went about their tasks in a sloppy half-hearted fashion. Even Reynaud seemed to flag and lose some of his zeal, undermined as he was again at every turn.

That night, darkening skies glowered with thunderous clouds. The swelling seas rammed the ship and drove her deeper into the sandbanks.

Unable to sleep, Savigny lay on his pallet anticipating each tremor of the ocean's assault. Corréard tossed and turned at his side. Strangely, Savigny had no thought yet for his own safety. The *Medusa* was not wrecked. As if in a dream, she had glided onto the soft shores of the African coast. He reasoned they could last here for months.

Whenever Savigny closed his eyes, he could see Richefort's smug smile of satisfaction as he stood by the helm, and the haunted expressions among the officers. It was no more than a *bump*, a nudge when the bows ran aground. Had the Captain not hesitated, had he turned the *Medusa* into the wind, they would have sailed to safety. All night, Savigny's thoughts drifted back and forth, raking over every detail that had them trapped on this shifting bed of silt.

By dawn, the officers gave the alert that water was gaining in the hold and the lower decks were already awash. All morning the men worked the pumps but they were unable to keep up.

At nine, the passengers were summoned to the gun deck. They crowded between the bare poles that remained from the sawn yards and masts.

The Governor hailed them with a triumphant wave.

'Fear not,' he cried. 'Should the ship be abandoned, we have come up with a plan.'

Behind him, the Captain and Richefort exchanged glances.

Leaning on the rail, the Governor explained that by his estimate there were two hundred and fifty people on board and only four boats of varied types and conditions, which could not possibly convey everyone to the African coast.

The passengers shifted uneasily like cattle in a pen.

'It is our intention to fashion a raft from these timbers,' he gestured towards the lashed masts and yards, which strained at their ropes in the surging swell.

The officers began to whisper among themselves. The Governor held up one hand for silence.

'We believe the raft will accommodate some one hundred and fifty souls, including provisions for everyone.' He looked at the Captain, who nodded in agreement. 'The boats will tow the raft towards the shore in a regular convoy. Once on land, weapons will be distributed and the entire party will march along the beach until we reach Saint-Louis, our numbers being a deterrent against attack.'

His suggestion was met with a sullen silence.

All at once Reynaud stepped forward.

'Yes, sir,' the Governor said, eyeing the officer with disdain.

'Would it not be safer, sir,' Reynaud began, 'to send the boats in relays and ferry everyone ashore, along with provisions and weapons.'

But to the last, Reynaud was ignored.

The day passed. All the fight and drive quite extinguished from him, Reynaud sat hunched on a coil of rope cradling his head in his hands while the Governor called out names from the list of his cronies—those who would join him in the boats. Many of the sailors and soldiers, who had nothing to salvage, nothing to lose, had tapped the kegs in the spirit room.

A group staggered towards Reynaud, arms folded, stamping the deck in some drunken hornpipe. The officer who had instilled such discipline and obedience in his men now barely looked their way as they careened past singing an obscene shanty. All around there were cries of confusion. Passengers dragged their trunks from below and began picking through their belongings, unable to make up their minds as to what to take, what to leave behind. Picard decided to abandon linen and a store of merchandise in favour of a manuscript on which he had been labouring for a long time. Corréard and his men had barricaded themselves in their quarters, packing their kits. The Governor's wife and daughter had not emerged from the Great Cabin since the *Medusa* struck the bank. Savigny could have sworn he heard the report of a gunshot followed by a scream and a volley of oaths. But perhaps he imagined it, such was the tumult and chaos on board. At intervals regular as a metronome, the sound of nails hammered into wood. All day in a white haze of thunderous heat, the carpenter bent to his task, melding the topmasts, yards, fishes and booms to frame the raft.

THE *MEDUSA* CARRIED FOUR BOATS. The most seaworthy was a fourteen-oared barge designated for the Governor and his family; equally capable of an ocean journey was another barge in which the Captain would embark together with twenty-seven sailors chosen for their strength and rowing prowess; a fourteen-oared pinnace with Maudet at the helm would take the Picard family and forty-two passengers; the largest but weakest vessel, a longboat commanded by Reynaud, accommodated forty-five souls.

In a parody of his embarkation in France, the Governor, first to leave the *Medusa*, was ceremoniously lowered amid a fanfare of trumpets and whistles on a red velvet armchair suspended by ropes from the bowsprit. In the same manner, wife and daughter followed, accompanied by a considerable number of trunks and valises. Richefort stepped forward and began to call out names from a list. Hearing themselves summoned, many of the passengers surged forward and scrambled down the ladders into the boats.

Savigny and Corréard had been assigned places in the longboat. But in the confusion, they and the ten men from Corréard's engineering detachment were directed to the raft. No one heeded their protests and they were caught in the crush, such was the stampede from those anxious to find refuge in the boats. With difficulty, shimmying down the ship's steep side, they pitched back and forth in the swell.

Slipping and sliding on drenched planks they clambered towards a parapet built at the centre, where at last they found equilibrium. Seeing them there and inspired by the belief that the raft would prove seaworthy after all, some twenty men climbed onto the clumsy vessel. Beneath the weight of these new arrivals, the raft sank lower and waves sluiced around their thighs. Hanging on to one another, the men fought to maintain their footing, staggering back and forth in a drunken dance. There were no adequate rails to hold.

From the frigate, the passengers watched the men on the raft and hesitated.

'For heaven's sake, get down,' the Captain shouted.

'I would rather perish on the *Medusa*,' one man cried. 'For then I shall be able to choose my own death.'

'Get down, sir,' the Captain roared. 'There's not much time.'

At his words, there was an angry tumult on deck. Only men were left there now. A crowd of them began to advance towards the Captain, waving their fists, denouncing him as a traitor, shouting that he should join the others on the raft. As for themselves, they would remain on the ship until rescue was found.

All at once, a volley of gunshot scattered wide—Richefort on the poop taking aim with a musket and a round fired from the Governor's barge. The mob retreated in silence.

'My orders will not be disobeyed,' the Captain said. 'Now get down on the raft. The lot of you.'

When he raised one hand, Richefort sent another volley into the air.

Now the people had no choice. They glanced at the raft smashing against the ship's side and back to the Captain again. There was a shout from one of the boats. Reynaud called for La Touche, who appeared at the bows in a cloud of gun smoke.

'Tell them there's no reason to panic,' Reynaud cried. 'The raft will be towed by the boats to the shore. Everyone must keep calm.'

The authoritative tone to his voice helped quell the crowd, which began to form a shuffling line. La Touche marched to the larboard side.

'Come now,' he said. 'One by one and easy does it.'

Slowly several men slithered down the ropes and scrambled onto the raft's outer edge. Spumes of surf crashed over their heads and threatened to wrench them from the bare boards. Three barrels of wine and a sack of flour carelessly tossed over the frigate's side toppled a group clustered at the stern of the raft. Corréard and his team succeeded in battening these stores so that fierce rushing currents would not carry them away.

Corréard roared for the Captain who appeared at the ship's bulwarks above.

'Are we in a condition to depart? Have we instruments and charts?'

'Indeed,' the Captain cried. 'Everything has been provided.'

'What naval officer is to come and command us?'

'It is I,' the Captain replied. When Corréard looked up, he was gone.

With a swish of oars, the Governor's barge rowed rapidly alongside and threw the first rope from its stern.

'Quick, secure it fast to the bow,' Savigny's own voice this time. 'Have faith,' he called. 'The pinnace and the yawl are lining up to take tow of the raft.'

La Touche spiralled down a rope and sprang onto the raft.

'There's Reynaud,' he shouted. 'My, his vessel's badly rigged. No room among the passengers to trim the sails and no oars to steer her by.' A ragged cheer rose when the rope from Reynaud's longboat thwacked against the deck.

Without masts and sails, how gaunt and forlorn the *Medusa* appeared, reduced to a mere hulk.

A great cry of dismay went up when the Captain was sighted scurrying down the ladder to his own barge at the bows. Richefort too was seated comfortably there at the stern.

The Captain urged his crew to run alongside the Governor's vessel. At his approach yet another rope was thrown to take the tow of the raft.

Strung out in a line, the boats began to head southeast. Crouched on the creaking planks, the men watched the waters streaming over the raft's bows. Although drenched to the skin, they managed to rally a faint cheer. Cumbersome as she was, the raft began to move away from the ship.

A sudden change of wind slammed Reynaud's vessel against the frail pinnace crammed with terrified passengers. The ensign loosened his tow. When Reynaud's boat ran clear, Maudet gave orders to turn about, pick up the rope and reform the line.

'Captain,' he called. 'Take your towrope again.'

'Yes, my friend,' the Captain replied, still surging ahead. From his precarious longboat, Reynaud called after them but without drawing a backward glance.

Dragged by the weight of the raft, the Governor's barge now drifted in senseless circles. All at once there was a shout from one of the crew, frantically trying to steady her in the bows—'Shall I let go?'

The Governor remained silent. With a splash, the rope unfurled in the vessel's wake. As if fired from a catapult, the barge shot forward. Undecided, the pinnace wallowed until finally, to Maudet's dismayed cries, their rope too was cast over.

The men on the raft drifted on fast currents beneath darkening skies. Chilled to the marrow of their bones, they refused to believe they had been callously deserted, and clung to the fragile hope that the boats had possibly seen a ship.

Standing at the stern, La Touche called to the longboat, still valiantly there, alone with the raft on churning seas. All eyes were fixed on Reynaud, who had lowered his foresail for the task of taking up the towrope.

Not the least movement was made on board the raft. Not even a cry was uttered. They seemed reduced to nothing.

When it became clear to his passengers that Reynaud intended to approach the men on the raft, angry voices erupted from his longboat. Some argued that by coming near the raft, any desperate man could leap from it to the longboat and sink their already overladen craft. Others made the point that a shoal of swimmers could strike out from the raft and haul themselves to safety over the gunwales.

Reynaud saw at last that he couldn't tow them on his own and risk *these* lives to save those on the raft. That he couldn't perform miracles.

The longboat dipped over the crest of the horizon. Darkness fell like a bolt of black velvet. No stars shone in the skies.

Starting that first night, Corréard issued rations, a spoonful of raw flour and not more than a thimble of wine.

A FLARE OF LIGHTNING AGAINST the branches of the chestnut trees heralded a summer storm. A fierce breeze sent flurries of leaves scattering across the courtyard.

Savigny sat by the window. A clap of thunder rattled the panes. 'The carpenter who built the raft was among the survivors,' he said. 'I can track him down if you like.'

Géricault lit the candles and poured two glasses of wine. He worried he might be exhausting his guest, who had triumphed over human suffering unimaginable to himself. What was he doing pampering and feeding them as if they were no more than a couple of waifs for his use? He should be ashamed. Not even Horace would pimp on their lives like this.

Roll up, roll up, come and see it. Survivors of the Medusa *frigate. No more than one shilling a head.*

When Savigny took his leave across the courtyard beneath a large umbrella, Géricault thought of the men crouched on the deck of the *Medusa*, watching the carpenter build the raft.

~

The following morning, Géricault was relieved to see Savigny seated at breakfast on the terrace, enjoying the feast set out before him. Corréard, it seemed, had not yet risen.

'Having completed the first part of my tale, I feel in need of some distraction and amusement,' he said. 'Why don't you ask Monsieur Vernet to share this wonderful repast?'

On cue, the door of the mansion opposite swung open and Horace strode down the steps with a self-conscious swagger, as if aware he was being watched. When Savigny called out and beckoned him to join them, Horace stopped dead in his tracks. He glanced over one shoulder like a conspirator and feigned not to notice.

Géricault knew he must warn Savigny about his friend's allegiance with the Bourbon court, the commissions he wooed from the Comte d'Artois. He leaned forward, about to confide, when Horace looked their way and shrugged. He hurried across the lawns, doffing his cap as if Savigny were the King of France.

When Géricault introduced them, Horace studied his guest with interest, a smile flickering at his lips.

'A dear friend of ours, Colonel Bros, alerted us to your plight,' Horace began, settling on a chair. 'Quite railed with indignation against an article published in the *Moniteur Universel*.'

Savigny frowned. 'No doubt dictated word for word by du Bouchage.'

'Why, I agree, it's a disgrace. The hypocrisy of the court knows no bounds. We're all fascinated with your story . . . Géricault in particular.' Horace graced his friend with an angelic smile. 'I must say, I've been waiting for an invitation.' This time Horace did not dare meet Géricault's eye.

Now he was going too far, Géricault thought. How, after such a long silence, dare he impose himself like this?

'But my friend can be so secretive,' Horace continued.

'He likes to keep the subjects of his tableaux to himself, like that beautiful aunt of his who vanishes into his studio the moment her carriage appears.'

'I do seem to recall seeing a young woman the second day we arrived.'

Savigny shot Géricault an amused glance. 'So this lady is your aunt?'

Shame-faced, he nodded. This was too much. Somehow he must brazen it out.

'Madame Alexandrine Caruel,' he managed to say without blushing. 'My uncle has commissioned a series of portraits of his wife.'

'Next time, we should very much like to make her acquaintance.' Again he was subjected to the sharp scrutiny of Savigny's gaze.

Horace drained his cup and leaned towards the doctor with a confidential air. Géricault braced himself for what might come next.

'Perhaps you will allow me the honour, dear sir, of giving you a tour of my studio.' Horace paused and stared at Géricault, a look of triumph. 'There's a lady, an actress, I should like you to meet. Her name is Madame Thérèse.'

'Let us go at once,' Savigny exclaimed, pushing back his chair and springing to his feet. 'Nothing would give me the greatest pleasure.'

Horace proffered an arm.

Speechless, Géricault watched them stroll along the path engaged in animated conversation. For the first time he heard Savigny laugh.

He returned to the studio consumed with a rage he had not felt in a long while, coupled with a sense of hurt and betrayal. Another peal of laughter echoed through the grounds. Seductive, theatrical Thérèse. He had not counted on her, of course.

All morning he paced up and down by the window, unable to work, waiting for Savigny to return.

At noon Horace appeared in the doorway. 'I owe you an apology, my friend,' he said. 'Savigny seems a capital fellow.'

'Where is he?' Géricault growled, exasperated by Horace's cheerful, victorious manner.

'Still with Thérèse. They delight in one another's company.'

Indeed, now he could see them seated at one of the ground floor windows.

Horace glanced at Géricault with a look of amusement. 'You seem rather wound up and I hope it's not on my account. Surely your guests are entitled to some fun? They can't be expected to remain here day after day, cooped like exotic animals in a cage.'

Before Géricault could think of a reply, Horace swaggered out the door and was gone.

IN LATE AFTERNOON, ALEXANDRINE'S carriage clattered along the driveway. Again, Géricault had quite forgotten the appointment. With a pang of guilt, he glanced at her portrait—turned to face the wall. He had not given it a single thought. Watching his mistress alight from the equipage, followed by the maid, Géricault marvelled at her grace. She was radiant in a loose flowing gown tied beneath the breasts. And yet . . . he turned away. He could not attend to her needs, a heavier more complicated responsibility than any wife, and create this shipwreck scene.

'My, what a mess,' Alexandrine exclaimed, picking her way through the piles of sketches, the paints and palette boards strewn on the floor. She paused and peered out the window. 'Your guests seem far from troubled by their ordeal,' she said in a mocking tone. 'Why, look at them playing boules on the lawn, and that fop Horace Vernet with them.'

She turned to him. 'They must be costing you a fortune.'

Géricault glanced at her and sighed. If only he could make her understand that his guests had saved him from the most wretched idleness. Savigny and Corréard had brought rescue at last from days squandered at Horace's house, watching his rival tirelessly work canvas after canvas, commission after commission from dawn to dusk.

Alexandrine was still staring out the window. 'I do declare that man—' she pointed out Savigny— 'is wearing the very embroidered linen waistcoat I gave you last summer.'

'I told La Motte to take in some of my clothes,' Géricault replied. 'As you know, they arrived here wearing little more than rags.'

He went over and put his arms around her waist. 'Why not let me tell you their extraordinary tale, then you might see why I am so keen to work their narrative into a tableau.'

'I've heard their story,' she snapped. 'No one spoke of anything else while you were in Rome. Besides,' she darted him a sharp look, 'I thought the portrait was the purpose of my visit.'

She pouted her lips for a kiss. 'Isn't it time we began?'

Géricault glanced at his oil studies stacked on the model stand, his palette congealing in a pool of sunlight, his brushes stiffening in their jars. Now he resented having to make love to order. He might as well pay a whore whom he could enjoy at a more suitable hour. Why couldn't they just *talk* on occasions, she seated prettily by the window while he worked at the easel?

From outside, there came laughter and the gentle clip of the balls as they rolled across the lawn. Alexandrine was holding him tight, twining the curls at the nape of his neck. Perhaps it was the heat, the heavy stillness of the room, but Géricault felt suffocated by her embrace.

He could hear someone cry out, 'Why, Monsieur Vernet, I do believe you're cheating,' followed by the distinct pop of a champagne cork.

'They're having quite some party,' Alexandrine murmured.

A sudden rush of fatigue swept over him. He cupped her face in his hands, conscious of the fact that not so long ago he would have been pacing the room ravenous with desire, incapable of waiting a moment longer for his mistress. Tenderly he kissed her as if they had come together for the last time. His mouth sought hers with a great yearning and sorrow for the years they had shared, the endless portraits displayed in the echoing rooms of Caruel's house.

Géricault wanted to take her quietly and calmly, with a lazy familiarity that a married couple might have. Instead, Alexandrine pressed against him with hungry caresses, and he knew that he would have to bring his mistress to her pleasure with all the art to which she had become accustomed. Dutifully, he led her to the divan.

Montmartre

———

August 1818

THEIR HEALTH VASTLY IMPROVED, Géricault's guests were growing distant and distracted. They idled away the days tickling for trout on the riverbanks; they brought the fish home to La Motte, who promised to baste the catch in pounded chervil and garlic, and bake it for supper that night. Or they strolled in the woodlands behind the house, returning with armfuls of wild flowers. Three times that week they had cancelled appointments with their host, for the most trivial reasons.

Savigny had taken to tending the rose garden, clipping and pruning the tangled blooms, digging out the briars and ripping the tufts of weeds with such devotion that the plot would soon be quite restored.

All morning from his studio, Géricault watched him pottering about the paths. Savigny wore an old paint-spattered smock, a wide-brimmed straw hat to shield his face from the sun, and a pair of leather riding gloves so that the thorns would not scratch his hands. At intervals he kneeled and poked the earth with a trowel from a basket beneath his arm. When Savigny began to clear a rangy patch of nettles, Géricault stared at him in astonishment. His very gestures, the way he stooped and raked the tall willowy intruders free, reminded Géricault of some dowager aunt, not the renowned doctor and survivor, Henri Savigny, who had pledged his soul to set the record straight, even if he must take on the King of France. Instead this gardener smiled happily and whistled some tuneless melody as he worked. White butterflies darted among the buddleia. Savigny snapped a lilac bloom and slipped it through his buttonhole. Géricault noticed Savigny was beginning to put on weight and a plump paunch had gathered around his belly, yet he'd not even been with him for a month at the most.

Glancing at the timepiece with irritation, Géricault decided to go outside and remind his guest of the hour. At his approach, Savigny gave a merry wave. 'In the words of the great Voltaire,' he called, '*il faut cultiver votre jardin*. And indeed in this, the best of all possible worlds, I have reached that age. Here contentment lies.'

He pointed at a long-stemmed crimson rose. 'Soon I shall create a paradise all of my own.'

'I've been expecting you all morning.' Géricault could not manage to conceal the indignation in his voice.

Savigny cupped a hand to one ear. 'But surely that was La Motte ringing the bell for lunch. Last week Corréard shot a hare and thought it would be very nice jugged.'

Géricault willed himself to be patient.

'Where is Corréard?' he growled.

Savigny looked vague and replied that after a careful study of the woodlands, his companion was convinced the area would yield a veritable harvest of truffles and had even hired a farmer's pig for the purpose.

At that Géricault swung on his heels and returned to the studio, slamming the door behind him. The thought of another day needlessly wasted made his heart pound. He stared out the window at his guest progressing across the lawns. Savigny gave a sudden wave. And sure enough, there was Horace hurrying towards him, arms outstretched in greeting. *He* was to blame, Géricault thought, the distraction of his actress friends, that wretched woman Thérèse.

Watching Savigny and Horace stroll through the shrubberies, Géricault slammed his fist against the window frame. Somehow he must reel his guests out of the light and cast them back into the deep, blue sea.

That afternoon the carpenter arrived. Savigny had at least done this—sent for the man himself. Thin and taciturn, with brown sorrowful eyes, this carpenter knew the value of planks and timbers. He had lashed the *Medusa*'s sawn spars and masts, and had survived on his infernal machine. One of the fifteen.

Head bowed, the carpenter stood before him, awaiting instructions and taking no interest in his surroundings. Not even in the sketches of the *Medusa* spread across the floor.

Géricault cleared his throat, unsure of how to begin.

When he explained he required an exact replica of the raft, following the dimensions of the original timbers, the angles of the bow and stern, the carpenter nodded and turned away with a sigh.

'Please take this,' Géricault handed him a heavy purse of coins. 'Buy all the materials you'll need from the dockyards.'

The carpenter gazed about the room, measuring its proportions with a shrewd eye.

'You'll have to settle for a more modest scale,' he said, 'perhaps half-size.' Ten by three metres, that would be.

Géricault agreed. That would be enough to re-enact the

exact sequence of events, under the direction of Savigny and Corréard. He glanced at the carpenter. And even this man.

'The account Savigny has so far related is of great professional interest to me,' Géricault announced with what he hoped was an urbane smile. 'Sir, I would pay a good price to hear your own version of the calamitous events that took place on the raft.'

The carpenter gave him a shocked look.

Géricault flushed and hoped he had not sounded too flippant in referring to their ordeal.

'When I was a lad,' the carpenter said, 'I'd watch the ships coming into Rochefort, white with sail, their great wooden bows splicing the waves. I listened to the shouts of the sailors rejoicing that they'd returned to France alive.'

He lowered his voice and drew close.

'Put it this way,' he confided, 'I believed the truth of this world lay somewhere else, beyond the horizon, and I longed to venture into the sea.'

He paused and weighed the purse in his hands. Géricault willed him to continue.

'My name is Lavillette, sir, and I could tell my story a hundred times over without stopping for breath, yet neither you, nor I, nor anyone for that matter, will ever understand what I have seen and done.'

These words seemed suddenly to exhaust him. He swayed slightly on his feet. Géricault wondered whether he should offer him a glass of wine. He longed to get this man drunk, get him to speak. Describe in every detail all he had witnessed; guide him deeper and deeper into the darkest depths of the shoreless sea.

'Perhaps, still, we could come to some arrangement . . .?' he ventured.

But already the carpenter had turned at the threshold. 'I will build your raft. But I hope to God you never find what you're looking for, beyond that,' he whispered. 'Stick close to the officers' account. It's as good as any. As for me, I intend to put it all behind me, make a new life for myself.'

Again an expression of great weariness passed over him.

'I'll tell you this much,' he said. 'At the hospital in Senegal, that antechamber of the morgue, many of us were dying, delirious with fever. The Governor sent his officials prowling around our stinking cot beds—'

He gave Géricault a searching glance.

'We knew him from the ship, knew his people. But we were made to sign papers, senseless things they said we had babbled during our night fevers . . . These documents were used against Savigny's testimony and were instrumental in bringing about his disgrace.'

Géricault felt a flare of admiration for Savigny. He must not press him too far with his enquiries and questions; Savigny would come to his studio when he was ready to talk.

'What was contained in the evidence used against him?' he asked.

The carpenter looked away.

'I was made to sign the memorial without even reading it,' he replied. 'One day this case will appear through the proper channels and, when it does, I shall declare my signature null and void. You mark my words, I will, sir.'

Géricault considered the implications in this unexpected revelation. He imagined the squalor of the hospital, rank with malodorous air, the spittoons by the beds, the emaciated survivors flayed with sores and ulcers, barely clinging to life, and the Governor's spies gliding among them, extracting confessions from their enfevered hallucinations.

The carpenter was bidding him farewell for the day. Géricault shook his hand, quite overcome with emotion. But I must not overreact, he told himself. No, he would remain vigilant, objective to the last. Sift through each fact with a clinical detachment.

He watched the carpenter cross the courtyard with a heavy tread, his thick leather boots ringing against the flagstones. The evening sky was beginning to darken. When the carpenter reached the driveway, he looked back. 'For all our sakes, stick to the facts as Savigny knows them,' he called. 'That's my advice, my friend.'

Géricault stood at the doorway, still watching the carpenter's tall angular form stride up the avenue of chestnut trees until he disappeared through the gate.

Unsettled by the exchange, he went inside. A sense of complete helplessness descended on him. He did not know with any certainty how to begin this tableau. He needed the entire story, the full truth. But now it occurred to him that the truth lay elsewhere, beyond his reach, in a great humming murmur of other voices shifting, halting and starting up again, finding their echo in the soft susurrations of the sea. In the stories of the dead, even, carried through the tireless tides of the deep. First he must be patient. He hoped Savigny would soon weary of Horace and his friends, including that Thérèse with her theatrical affectations and silly powdered face.

His guests having now been in Montmartre a month, Géricault was ready to begin preparations for his tableau.

Today he had an appointment with Chevreul, colourist and chemist of considerable repute, at the dyeworks in the avenue des Gobelins. He had decided that no expense would be spared, and he walked past the street-corner merchant of artist materials at the foot of the hill.

With his fastidious adherence to the primary trinity of red, yellow and blue, Chevreul had won considerable renown for manufacturing pigments of those hues: lemon yellow, crimson from the madder plant, ultramarine and, most astonishing of all, a new tint never seen before— orange vermilion, which gave a pure and delicate warm carnation, said to resemble the tints of Titian and Rubens.

Géricault craved carmine rich as Burgundy, and Tyrian purple extracted from the flower gland of the purpura mollusc, which when exposed to the light, undergoes a most miraculous alchemy from pale green to blue with finally a gleam of dark rose. He was fascinated by the latest pigments of Chevreul's inventions, by his chrome yellow, brighter and more vivid than the finest Siena ochres or Indian puri, those putrid dirty coloured balls manufactured from the urine of cows fed exclusively on mangoes.

He needed azurite pure as the clearest of cloudless skies, crimson lake with the lustre of medieval gowns, deep translucent copper resinate and honey browns. He wished there were a green as good as the chrome yellow: green earth was too weak, verdigris too cruel, ashes not sufficiently durable. Viridian, a compound of copper arsenite, would do of course, but he knew he must be careful not to lift one finger to his lips.

What bliss there was in blue, he thought, emblem of divine purity, marking the transition between dusk and night.

Eagerly Géricault knocked on the factory door, his coat pocket heavy with a fat purse. A valet ushered him inside and before he could begin to admire the thunderous clank of stone rollers and the rush of steam, the giant pestles grinding pigments against vast mortars, he was led into an office to one side of the vestibule.

At first he was struck by the number of paintings stacked against the walls. Payments, he concluded. A veritable apothecary's collection ranged along the bookshelves of rare calf-bound chemistry books, craft manuals, colour charts and sheaves of recipes tied with black velvet.

Chevreul greeted him from a mahogany desk, its surface covered with bladders of paint, display boards and a delicate set of gold scales.

A small man with dark inquisitive eyes and a self-satisfied air, Chevreul recognised the name of Géricault. Here was the heir to the tobacco firm, and Chevreul knew that today he was certain to receive gold in his palm and not some canvas which might or might not accrue value over time.

'Dear sir,' Chevreul cried, motioning Géricault to sit in a leather smoking-chair. 'What can I show you today? Perhaps this rose pink prepared from brazil wood, or this grass green from a mix of azurite and yellow ochre.'

He patted the bladders with his soft pale hands. He spread paint on a board, and it danced with the bright blues, greens and reds of his latest inventions.

'The beauty is they're harmless,' he declared, smearing a streak of carmine, which glowed like a distillation of rubies. 'I can assure you, sir, nothing here is arsenical.'

Géricault explained that darkness was the basic tone of the painting he had in mind.

'Ah,' Chevreul exclaimed, studying his samples. 'I would recommend mixing strong pure colours, a glaze of bone black with crimson lake and red ochre.'

Once again like a sorcerer, he demonstrated on the board.

Géricault admired the textures but needed subtler shadows.

'And asphaltum?' he enquired.

Chevreul frowned. 'Not something I sell often. Its use is advised against in every technique.'

He took out a clean board and squirted a tarry substance from a thick pig's bladder. Géricault watched him spread the viscous liquid sleek and translucent as a raven's wing.

'Unless applied with care,' Chevreul said, holding the board to the light, 'bitumen can shrink and wrinkle the surface layer.'

Géricault admired the ebony gleam, the seductive warmth of tone. He could just imagine the sweeping brush strokes and bold colouration, burnishing with a vitality rarely seen before.

'It does not dry properly and a thick film tends to run,' Chevreul continued. 'The durability of bitumen is largely unknown. Perhaps I can interest you in this instead.'

Picking up another bladder, he daubed a pigment brown as gravy with none of the vivid jet-black hues of bitumen.

'Bistre,' Chevreul announced, 'made from the soot of burnt beech wood or birch bark. You still need skill to make much of it in oils but I can recommend this as a far more reliable glaze which would suit your purposes well.'

But this bistre only served to strengthen Géricault's resolve. He would borrow Leonardo's technique of sfumato—where every colour was leached until a dark monochrome remained—but to reach this glazed darkness Géricault would use bitumen.

He returned to Montmartre with a dazzling display of complementaries, a combination of modern and ancient inventions: ultramarine of pounded lapis lazuli mined from northern Afghanistan; cobalt aluminate, which possessed a purer tint than azurite or indigo; extractions from the kermes insect for scarlet and red lakes; a bright green from azurite and ochre; and twenty bladders of asphaltum.

In addition to his regular-sized canvases, Géricault had ordered a vast sheet twenty metres high by eight wide. He had chosen the very best heavy-grade linen for its elasticity and fine long fibres that would not fluff like cheap cotton. This he would use for the final composition.

As for his brushes, only the finest quality would suffice: kolinsky sables from Russia for the softness of the marks they left in the body of the paint, round sables for quick, vigorous strokes, long-handled blenders of hog bristle and squirrel hair, scriptliners and stripers with chisel-sharp tips to produce broad lines.

IT TOOK THE CARPENTER a week to build the raft. First he supervised the unloading of timbers, ropes and an array of heavy ship materials from a cart lugged up the hill by a drayhorse.

From window to window, the raft's outer timbers would span ten metres long by three wide. A tight fit, Géricault had thought, watching the men heave the planks through the doorway. Enough room just for his easel and sketches, his final canvas, for scaffolding to be ranged against one wall where the ceiling was at its highest. In preparation, Géricault had removed the divan, the model stand, and he'd stripped the space bare—the world he shared with Alexandrine. Those furnishings were unceremoniously shunted into a cobwebbed alcove by the privy door. He wondered what Alexandrine would say when she saw this desecration. He tried not to think of his mistress.

Lavillette worked most days in silence. This morning dark shadows ringed his eyes. He looked as if he had not slept the previous night, and beyond his confidence of the week before, if you could call it that, he would not be drawn.

Géricault watched the carpenter join the topmasts, yards, fishes and boom from some condemned hulk with strong hessian cord. He nailed crude boards to the frame and fashioned a parapet in the centre. To make the raft more solid, he placed long pieces of wood across the planks, which projected at least one metre at either end. Along the sides, he added a low railing, just forty centimetres high.

When Géricault made the point that only a few crotches would have formed a breastwork of sufficient height, Lavillette clicked his tongue and replied that those who ordered the construction of the raft never expected to be exposed on it.

Géricault seethed with questions. Surely this carpenter, craftsman that he was, would have known that such a design would make the vessel crank. Why had he not added these crucial details of his own accord?

He watched the carpenter lash two topgallant yards against the ends of the mainmast, to form the raft's bow.

Even Géricault could see that, upheld only by the buoyancy of the topmasts and booms in the frame, the craft possessed no real form of flotation.

When asked, Lavillette muttered that the forepart, two metres in length, was continually submerged. 'Only the centre, sir, could be depended on. The officers on armed watch were stationed there. Messieurs Savigny and Corréard among them.'

Armed against what? Géricault thought. From one another? —but surely they were all in it together, a united force to overcome the infernal predicament they found themselves in.

At midday the carpenter packed away his hammer and saw, his boxes of nails. He pressed both hands in the small of his back and cast a critical eye over his work.

Géricault seized his chance and insisted Lavillette accept a glass of wine.

'Tell me,' he said, 'why were the officers armed?'

For the first time that day, the carpenter looked Géricault in the eye.

'We stood guard over the stores,' he replied, 'which were strictly rationed.'

The carpenter shook his head and drained the wine. Géricault noticed Lavillette's hands trembled when he set down the glass. Sweat filmed his brow. Obviously he would never fully recover from his ordeal. Once again the carpenter contemplated his replica of the raft.

'Did you know,' he said, 'they did not give us enough rope to properly set our mast. Instead with great haste the crew threw the main-topgallant sails over the sides and many on the raft were wounded by their heavy fall.'

Picking up his kit, he headed for the door for the last time, and took his leave without another word.

Géricault stood on the raft and swayed back and forth, trying to imagine its vertiginous motion through the swell, the roar of open sea surging towards a darkening horizon. Now he could see how it was as Savigny described—they could not sit but were forced to stand up to their waists submerged in brine. Surely their limbs would begin to ulcerate?

He crouched at the bows, imagining himself among the tangle of men, grabbing a piece of rope, a broken spar, someone's arm, desperate to keep their balance as the raft swung on senseless rhythms. Many trampled underfoot or kicked in the ribs, as if they were no more than sacks of hemp. And to think of dying in the crush, that seething pandemonium—you would have to plug your ears against the incantations of prayers, curses raged at the heavens, the stench of fear on every man's breath and always the roar of the ocean very loud.

'Theo, what on earth is the matter?' Horace stood silhouetted in the doorway. He stared at Géricault, hunched now in the bows of the raft.

'What are you doing here in the gloom when it's such a beautiful day outside?'

He strode across the room and opened the windows.

'The King will not be amused by this tale,' he said, glancing at the replica. 'Instead, take a leaf from my book. I've borrowed your pretty maid to pose for a tableau provisionally entitled *The Return of the Duchesse d'Angoulême*. Shame that Marie-Antoinette's daughter has to be so plain. It's the Hapsburg nose that lets them down.'

Try as he might, Géricault could not begin to conceive of that first night—no more than a spoonful of raw flour and a thimble of wine in their stomachs. He shuddered at the thought.

'La Motte has laid out lunch on the terrace,' Horace was saying. 'Corréard and Savigny are waiting. I must say, your guests seem most convivial of late. I would think twice about putting them through their ordeal again.'

Indeed, Géricault found them in remarkable high spirits, exclaiming over the hare with such raptures that La Motte, beaming at their compliments, took care to give them generous portions. She set down a salad of cress and celeriac, a bowl of new potatoes. A couple of Horace's city friends appeared from his house and sat cross-legged on the lawn. One played a gay gypsy tune from his panpipes. The other echoed the rhythm with a tambourine. Leaning back in their chairs, Savigny and Corréard admired the scene.

'Bravo,' Savigny called, clapping his hands. 'We would never have imagined such Arcadian delights were it not for the kindness of our friend.'

'The very reason I moved here.' Horace filled their glasses with wine. 'Although it will never be the most fashionable district in town. Have you ever tried to persuade a cab to go up the hill?'

'Let us pray it will remain unspoilt for all eternity,' Savigny declared, 'a pastoral of fields and meadows—'

'The carpenter has finished building the raft,' Géricault cut in, unable to endure another moment's waiting.

Savigny took a sip of wine and rinsed it around his mouth.

'A perfect bouquet,' he announced. 'What do you make of it, Corréard?' he turned to his companion. 'We've always been fond of a chilled Sancerre.'

'The carpenter did an excellent job,' Géricault persisted, 'although of course the raft is smaller in scale.'

He watched Savigny drain his glass. When Corréard launched into a detailed account of the Sancerre region, including climate, soil type and the particular grapes that yielded such crisp dry varietals—Géricault resisted an impulse to knock the bottle from his hand.

'Elderflower,' Savigny exclaimed, 'underlined with gooseberry, a hint of peach perhaps.'

'I expect you shall want to examine the replica,' Géricault continued, exasperated now. 'In case the carpenter might have overlooked some crucial detail.'

'Examine what, dear fellow?' Savigny gazed at him with an expression of genuine puzzlement.

'Why, the raft, of course.'

Géricault twisted his serviette into a tourniquet around his hand. He was finding it hard to remain calm.

Taking a deep breath, he explained that he had begun

a preliminary sketch dramatising the moment when the towropes were cut—sullen indifferent skies pressing down on empty seas, the line of boats receding into a darkening distance, the sense of terror and isolation of those abandoned on the raft . . .

His words were met with silence. Horace passed the potatoes and salad to Corréard, who piled his plate high.

'Why, look,' Savigny pointed towards the roof of Horace's house where, darting among the chimney tops, the monkey could be seen beating its breast and announcing its predicament in long shrilling cries. Then, from one of the attic rooms, Delacroix opened a window and swung onto the gables, enticing the creature with some sweetmeat. At the sight of his saviour, the monkey jumped into the boy's arms and nibbled the bribe, staring all around.

'That's the third time this week.' Horace flung down his serviette. 'I think somehow the little devil manages to scamper up the chimney.'

'Bravo,' Savigny called, watching Delacroix climb in through the window.

Géricault wanted to pound his fist against the table—anything now to make his guests relive their ordeal and discuss the composition he had in mind.

'Well, that was quite the most perfect lunch,' Horace exclaimed. He inclined a gracious bow towards Savigny and Corréard.

'This afternoon I'm expecting another visit from Madame Thérèse. She would love to see you once again.'

Then, to Géricault's astonishment, his guests rose from the table too, and sauntered up the path without even a backward glance or a care in the world.

When he called for the maid to bring another bottle of wine, he remembered that even she had been lured to Horace's house.

Defeated, frustrated, Géricault sat alone at the uncleared table.

A carriage appeared through the gate.

A sense of weariness overcame him. His guests being otherwise occupied, he had hoped to re-examine his studies of the moment the towropes were cut. Now Alexandrine was arriving.

'What in God's name have you done?' Alexandrine exclaimed, stepping into the studio and staring at the chaos all around, the raft taking up the middle of the room, the divan pushed into the alcove.

Instead of taking her usual place on a stool by the stove, the maid perched at the raft's bows with a smirk.

Géricault regarded her with distaste. Such a sullen, lumpen child, he thought, so distinctly sweaty after the carriage ride. He hated the impertinent way she scowled at him.

All at once his pent-up rage against his recalcitrant guests rushed towards the girl.

'How dare you! Get down!' He advanced towards Louisette. She gave him a venomous look, then slid off the raft. He wanted to shake her so hard that her teeth would fairly rattle in her head.

Alexandrine darted beside him.

'Be off with you, now,' she said, handing the maid her coins.

Flouncing across the room, Louisette slammed the door behind her with all her might. Géricault flinched at the sound. He shot Alexandrine a furious glance, which she chose to ignore.

'My,' she declared as she considered the place where the

divan had been. 'I dare say you've been occupied.' She arched one eyebrow when she saw her portrait carelessly propped by the door.

'Is this—' she pointed at the raft—'the reason why I've not received a single word for some time? It must be a week at the very least.'

Géricault sighed. He could feel a row brewing.

'This is an exact model of the deadly machine,' he began, 'on which some one hundred and forty brave souls perished. And the very man who constructed these crude planks also built the original and was counted among the few to survive.'

At his words, Alexandrine stifled a yawn.

'Ever since those strangers arrived, you've quite lost your countenance,' she announced in a petulant tone. 'I think you should send them on their way. They're beginning to drain your spirits. And surely you must have heard their tale by now.'

She brushed the fingers of one gloved hand against his lips.

'There, that's better,' she murmured. 'I'd forgotten when I last saw you smile.'

She embraced him closely, and suddenly he found himself tearing at her with a violence he'd never felt before, sending the buttons of her chemise spinning across the room. He wanted to flay that soft yielding skin. A vision burned in his mind of standing over her with a birch stick whittled for the very purpose and she cowering at his feet yet yearning for the first supple sting. The image lingered. It was unbearably erotic. It frightened him.

He took her there where they stood, pressing her down to the cold hard floor among the debris and dust, the discarded sketches and half-emptied bladders of paint.

Afterwards Alexandrine lay heavy in his arms, weighing

on him, pinning him down. He could scarcely breathe. Perhaps, he thought, it was the taint of mortality that seeped from the rank timbers of the raft. Savigny had mentioned a *cantinière*, the only serving woman on board, a sergeant's wife who had fed Napoleon's troops. Imagine that—day after day crushed among so many men. How had she alone come to be on the raft? He must discover what became of her.

Sprawled in her rumpled clothes, Alexandrine propped her head on one arm. 'Such brooding, glowering looks,' she murmured. 'A penny for your thoughts, my darling.'

Leave me alone, Alexandrine, he wanted to say. Return to your husband as an honest, obedient and dutiful wife.

When he did not reply, Alexandrine contemplated him with her wide dark eyes. How very fine and delicate is that face I know so well, he thought. He leaned over and stroked the beautiful curve of her cheekbone. If only she would allow him to work without interruption, if only she could be interested in what he was trying to achieve, or even just in the tale itself that was reeling him in fast like a hooked fish gasping for breath. Then he would not feel this anger towards her.

'You don't love me at all, do you, Théo?'

He flinched as if she had delivered him a blow. He put his mouth to hers, to silence her. He could not bear to hear what she might accuse him of next. Her face was wet with tears. He ran his hands through her heavy hair and to his shame, felt himself stir again against her thigh. Oh, Alexandrine, he thought. Together they had crossed the thresholds of their youth and he had squandered her life just like any man—a brute, selfish to the core, never comprehending she loved him as she did. And he? What answer could he give, except that all he desired now was to fuck her again without a word of endearment or a single explanation. He reached for her.

'Hush. I adore you,' he whispered.

THE FOLLOWING MORNING GÉRICAULT prepared his palette like an alchemist, beginning with lead white at the centre. On the left-hand side he set down chrome yellow and saffron, alizarin crimson and rose madder, followed by gold ochre, umber browns for deep red tinctures, and finally lamp black, pure carbon of tar, and pitch not as sleek or dark as bitumen but useful in delicate tonal gradations.

On the other side of his palette, he arranged the cold colours: ultramarine; Egyptian blue; luminous viridian greens; manganese violet, which when mixed with yellow created deep dusty lilacs and purples.

For two hours then, Géricault stood at a canvas, brushes in hand, unable to paint a line.

The towropes were cut. The boats disappeared. All night the raft rose and fell on the mountainous waves sweeping the makeshift vessel far out to sea. The forsaken hulk of the *Medusa* nowhere in sight. Under the instructions of La Touche, they managed to salvage the abandoned ropes which swirled past in racing currents. These they tied to the planks, and then they could hold on fast as the raft bucked and heaved for hours at an end.

Drenched, buffeted, they had no thought of sleep.

Several fancied that a flare of fires could be seen on some distant coastline. So they lit one of the gunpowder charges stowed with their weapons at the top of the mast at the raft's centre, and then another, which sparked and burned briefly before dying out. A soldier was instructed to fire a volley of shot from his carbine. At regular intervals throughout the night, these reports continued. But they received no answering signal.

Géricault decided to begin at dawn. Grey-green clouds threading the skies, the glint of a silver bar widening at the horizon. Strong currents had dragged the raft further out by then. Not even the blue-shadowed ridge of the African coast could be seen. Finally, with the morning tides, the swell had subsided. The waters receded and swirled around the men's calves.

Géricault painted the spars and beams projecting from the raft's sides, a ragged makeshift sail swinging from the mast. At first daylight, what a sight to behold. During the night, he knew, some thirty souls had already been swept clean away. Drowned. Imagine that. But at least there was more room on the raft.

Now Géricault concentrated on La Touche sprawled at the stern, as Savigny had described, his right leg trapped between the crude timbers. He fainted with the pain. His fair hair streamed like seaweed in the rushing currents. *My sextant, my compass!* he cried, searching his pockets, before losing consciousness again. Savigny the surgeon crouched beside him and freed his leg with the sharp blade of a scalpel. All morning he bent to the task, dressing the mangled wound with the sleeve of his shirt.

Corréard managed to rouse himself and organise small rations of wine from the cask lashed to the parapet. He appointed two soldiers to stand guard over the meagre stores. After the first night, everyone swayed and leaned against their comrades, drifting in and out of dreams and fitful sleep.

Savigny had imagined he was strolling through an avenue of cypress trees. Thrushes shrilled from hedgerows of lavender and dogrose. He inhaled the fragrant air deep into his lungs. Against green-tinged hills, the pale stone spire of a cathedral appeared. He passed orchards laden with fruit and paused to pluck a peach from a low-lying branch. All at once someone beside him stirred. He opened his eyes—and once again found himself adrift on the monstrous raft, the makeshift bows heaving through empty seas. An injured boy struggled to disengage himself from the mass of men. Seeing Savigny awake, the youth shook him by the hand. 'Don't worry,' he declared. 'I'm off to fetch help. I'll be back soon.' And without another word, he strode off the raft and disappeared beneath the waves.

'Good idea,' a soldier announced. 'I'm going for a nap below.' And he too stepped over the side.

Savigny called for help but no one heeded his cries.

All day the raft drifted on swollen seas. All day a beating sun scorched brine-blistered skin. Not a cloud in the pale sky or a single bird on the wing. Only this timber hulk lumbering towards the horizon. A silence among the men. Although the swells had subsided, waves still slapped against their legs. Even Corréard and Savigny at the raft's centre could not escape the sluicing foam cascading across the bows. And always the roar of the ocean, the incessant beat of the wind.

Géricault wondered where to place the *cantinière*, the only woman on board the raft. There in comparative safety near the stores? Under the protection of her husband, a sergeant armed with a musket.

My, she was a brave, gap-toothed crone with ruddy apple cheeks and a ready smile. He imagined her generous and kind-hearted as La Motte. He could just see her wheeling a trolley across blackened battlefields, delivering soup.

IT WAS A SCANDAL THAT the *cantinière* should be among these men. She leaned against her husband and stared at the vast echoing ocean, her eyes dull and vacant. At noon when an implacable sun pinpricked the vaulted skies, there was a shout. One of the men gave a frantic wave from the stumbling mass gathered at the stern.

'A ship,' he cried, peering into the distance. 'I see it plain, the outlines of the boom, rig and topgallant masts coming towards us out of the mist. We must light the gunpowder and discharge a signal at once.'

Everyone gazed in the direction towards which he was pointing. Hoping against hope that one of the boats had alerted a rescue ship, or having landed their passengers had returned to find them. Help, salvation at last. But nothing appeared across the tirelessly tossing seas. Still they continued to keep watch for a long time. Later La Touche, fighting to retain some sense of reason, managed to enquire if anyone among the sailors possessed a compass. A shout went up. The carpenter Lavillette cried out that indeed he had a pocket compass, had sewn it into his coat and quite forgotten until now. A tremor ran through the drenched men swaying together on the wet boards. Fervently an instrument the size of a large coin was passed like a talisman from hand to hand towards La Touche, until it reached a cabin boy who allowed the compass to slip from numb fingers and fall through a gap in the planks. Inconsolable at this loss, once again the men fell into a silent vigil.

By late afternoon, the seas whitened with a great number of cuttlefish shells. The raft nudged through the floating mass. On close inspection every one of them was covered with kelp fleas and flies blown by cruel gales from distant shores. At the raft's approach, they swarmed in a thick brown cloud and descended on the men and the soaked timbers.

But perhaps their appearance was yet another mirage— a trick of the light, nothing more than a phantasmagoria, the imaginings of some deluded dream. Or perhaps they were running close to the African coast once again.

This last possibility so possessed their thoughts that at regular intervals someone gave an excited cry.

'Land,' La Touche called. 'The port of Saint-Louis. There's the harbour master's house at the mouth of the river.'

At this all craned forward, crazed with renewed hope, yearning to be the first to catch sight of safe haven where they could strip bare, wash in fresh, clear water, and temper the horrors of their misfortune at a tavern followed by a visit to the local brothel—for it was said the Senegalese women were slim-hipped and doe-eyed.

At the twilight hour, the skies broiled with thunderous clouds. A yellow moon spilt like a cracked yolk across the horizon. Streaks of orange vapours pelted the raft with sharp scatterings of sand. A howling wind scorched fever hot by the Sahara panted over the seas. In answer the waves rose higher and higher. Clinging onto the parapet, La Touche urged his fellow survivors to divide into rows, link arms and hurtle back and forth to counterbalance the perpendicular force of the swell.

But the men faltered and floundered each time a mountainous wave crashed over their heads. One racing crest clawed several men over the side. In the chaos all around, morale finally broke down.

All afternoon, Géricault worked without pause, rendering the figures on the raft with broad even strokes, a blanket of shadows against the dark pitch of his charcoal.

Exhausted, he stepped back from the canvas.

But no, he had not got it at all. He turned away in anger and frustration. It was impossible to convey an accurate sense of the scene, of the raft when it was half submerged in tumultuous waters, and how the desperate men flailing up to their waists were unable even to crouch to seek respite from the beating foam all around.

Géricault examined his studies of when the towropes were cut and the raft abandoned to its fate. Perhaps this episode best fitted his tableau. Most certainly it was the event that Horace would have chosen.

He'd sketched the Captain's thin-lipped smile at the sight of Richefort, who wielded an axe, the sharp blade shining in the moonlight; Maudet calling for the boats to resume their positions and take up the ropes; the Governor's barge, where busy fingers fumbled with a knot, and the shout, 'We abandon them'; the raft plunging into a void of darkness and the boats mere specks against the horizon.

And then the hero Reynaud, valiantly attempting to return to the stricken raft in an overladen vessel, although it was clear he could not haul them to safety alone. No choice in the matter. There it was done—the cord cast over the side. La Touche in the bows of the raft watching his brave officer go. Adieu.

Géricault poured himself a glass of wine and considered the Captain, the moustachioed villain seated at the boat's bow, and Richefort, his cloaked henchman severing the tow. Studying his sketch more closely, Géricault wondered if perhaps this first act of treachery was too much of a set piece, too politically charged.

He knew his guests would be disappointed, for both believed that in terms of dramatic tension, this episode best summed up their ordeal, and that the composition would point an accusing finger at the King and the Minister of Marine. But it seemed to him that the scene was weighted with a theatricality and melodrama more fitting to a lithograph bought for a couple of sous in any café in town. No, for his sake and theirs, he would find another way of telling this tale. Besides, he reasoned, they were still at the beginning.

He took a sip from his glass and enjoyed the fragrance of the fine Beaujolais against his tongue. He thought.

Hour upon hour on restless seas they had endured, clinging to every crack and crevice of their vessel. In their situation Géricault wondered what he might have done. Follow the lead of several soldiers, who, believing they would not survive the night, had tapped into a cask of wine? Swiftly tin cups had been passed around. Soon the exhausted senses of those men had reeled, with just a spoonful of raw flour in their stomachs and two nights without sleep, awash with brine.

Standing at the canvas, Géricault tried to visualise Savigny's account.

One soldier, an Asiatic, had drained his cup in one.

'Get rid of the officers,' he'd shouted, swinging an axe

above his head. 'Destroy the raft so we may all meet our deaths.'

Géricault imagined this man possessed of a colossal stature and strength. 'Make way,' this soldier called and he cut a great swathe through the air with his axe.

Terrified, the men fell back as the soldier strode towards the officers huddled by the mast. Adrift on the delirium of feverish dreams, swaying among the crowd on the parapet, La Touche was insensible now to the mayhem around him.

A boy no older than sixteen stepped in the Asiatic's way. 'Proceed no further,' he cried. 'Return to your post.'

With a roar of rage, the soldier swung his axe and in one brutal strike lopped off the boy's head. A jet of blood spurted across the raft's deck and splattered the clothes of the men standing close by. 'Destroy the raft so we may all meet our deaths!'

The soldier's followers began to slash the hessian cords binding the planks. Snatching their muskets, the officers, Corréard and Savigny among them, fired into the darkness towards the crazed mob.

Outside, a full moon rose between the chestnut trees. Géricault opened the window and inhaled the fragrance of the garden as it cooled after the day's heat. From Horace's house came the tinkling of a piano and the thump of a tambourine. Someone accompanied the melody with a haunting whistled refrain, panpipes perhaps.

To his surprise, Savigny and Corréard appeared at Horace's doorway. The music quickened as, ceremoniously, they advanced hand in hand down the steps and along the path. The moon lengthened their shadows, transformed the darkening silhouettes into caricatures, grotesque puppets from some grand Guignol. Turning to one another, they began an old-fashioned quadrille, arms outstretched, palm against palm. Horace and his friends crowded outside and watched the spectacle. Savigny and Corréard moved with a stately decorum, as if part of a pageant, a procession lifting and stamping their feet in unison, their boots ringing against the night air. A youth playing the panpipes followed, skipping from side to side.

Faster and faster they went, to an insistent rhythm, the tambourine's tap and a jingle of bells. 'Bravo,' Thérèse called. When the pipes reached a shrilling pagan crescendo, the two men then clicked their heels in a wild, quick-footed gypsy dance, sashaying across the lawn to clamorous applause, their shadows jumping and darting in their wake.

Géricault closed the window and drew the shutters tight to muffle the sound of that infernal merriment, the endless parties his guests attended night after night.

He snuffed out the candles and only the embers of the stove pricked the darkness. He stripped off his clothes until he stood pale and naked in the half-light. He crouched on the parapet at the raft's centre and took out his knife.

It had not been so much a battle, he sensed, not so much the organised revolt of Savigny's tale, but a hideous scrimmage, a merciless mass of men kicking, biting, shrieking. And all the while the storm had hissed and hurled the tilting vessel towards ravaged skies.

By dawn the raft drifted on a listless swell. Again the waters had miraculously subsided. When Corréard woke, he found himself among a pile of cadavers, even the *cantinière* sprawled senseless beside him. No one stirred in the silence. The waves sluiced the planks—was the raft riding higher out of the water? At first Corréard believed only he had survived. He called for Savigny, for his company of men. But still no one moved among the prostrate figures all around.

Corréard staggered to his feet. Cautiously, not daring to breathe, he picked his way through the tangle of corpses. The sheer monstrous scale of it, hacked torsos, severed limbs. A boy swung from the mast, arms outstretched, his wrists slashed to the bone.

Still no one moved. Only the creak of the ropes against timbers and the rushing ocean could be heard. As if in a dream Corréard stumbled through the carnage. He would end it if he were the only one alive. There was a sudden splash from the stern. Startled by the sound, he wheeled round.

A young man bumped against the currents, his leg trapped between two loose planks and knotted rope. Pale pink filigrees streaming from a wound to his chest spread a lacy halo around his head. Leaning forward, Corréard tried to catch hold of the boy's belt.

A swift dark shadow shimmied in the raft's wake, followed by another and yet another. All at once a flash of blue-grey fins surrounded the boy in a thrashing welter of blood and spray, until only a crimson pool bubbled on the surface. He stared at the frothing, incarnadine stain. By all accounts a quick death, he had read.

Corréard the cartographer, well versed in the writhing tentacles, the tail glints, the barnacled maws of the deep, steeled himself to jump.

A hand warm as sunlight, firm and steady on his shoulder, held him back. Savigny, his companion and friend, a purple sword-cut across one cheek. And others began to stir from numb exhausted sleep. The *cantinière* opened her eyes and gazed all around. A child who could have been her son rolled lifeless at her feet.

La Touche called to Savigny for a tot of wine. 'I fear I'm losing my mind,' he whispered as the surgeon lifted the cup to his lips. 'Please tell me that last night no one tried to gouge out my eyes.'

Savigny remained silent and tended to the deep gash across the officer's brow. Unwrapping the bandages around La Touche's leg, the surgeon observed that the wound grew gangrenous. He hoped his blade had not rusted, would saw through the bone when it was time.

Even the mutineers, the perpetrators of the crimes still clutching their carbines and sabres, stared all around with looks of shocked disbelief. Some tried to kneel in tearful attitudes of repentance, and begged forgiveness for their sins. Said they'd panicked. Knew not what they had done. Savigny passed from one to another like a saint, agreeing that all had succumbed to some mysterious night fever. One by one, the good doctor prayed for the dead aboard, before tipping them over the side.

Only sixty souls alive. At least the raft had lightened. Waves no longer sluiced around the men's waists. Those at the parapet found they could stretch out and snatch a moment's respite. Others still sat propped in the water swilling across the planks.

All morning those who had survived surveyed the ocean in a listless trance, seared by the heat of a blanched desert sun. All morning they drifted in and out of sleep. Someone asked whether anyone had heard strange cries of despair during the night, the clash of swords and sabres, but perhaps it had just been the wind peeling spume from the waves? An illusion, a dream? All morning the *cantinière* stared at the sky with the same vacant eyes, a red bandanna tied around her head to protect her from the sun.

In the noon light, Corréard stumbled towards her. 'Last night, didn't I hear you implore the Lady of Laux?' he cried.

'There's a place of that name in the Upper Alps. Do you come from there?'

'Indeed, sir,' she eventually replied. 'But I left twenty-four years ago . . . the Italian campaign and . . . others.'

The *cantinière* produced a box of snuff. She offered it to him.

She talked then: 'Often I've risked death in the battle-field to help those brave men. You see, it's a useful woman you've saved.'

Corréard snatched the box from her outstretched hand and snapped open the lid, inhaling the soaked tobacco fragrance pounded to the finest of powders.

'I always let them have my goods, whether they had money or not,' the *cantinière* murmured. 'Sometimes my debtors never returned, poor fellows. But after a victory— why, then others would pay me more than they owed. So I too had a share in Napoleon's glory.'

With a sigh, she slumped against her sergeant and closed her eyes.

Corréard foraged beneath the woman's apron and searched her pockets: a hatpin, an empty perfume phial, several coins. Nothing he could eat.

As to the stores, the water barrels, the precious sacks of flour—all gone, thrown in the mayhem over the side. Three kegs of wine remained.

Overwhelmed by the deepest despondency, filled with revulsion by the carnage of the night, the men on the raft kept a silent vigil, seawatchers all, praying for a ship to appear on shifting horizons.

Savigny returned to the fragrant meadows and cypress-lined avenues of Tuscany, a shining white church outlined against an azure sky. He was crossing an emerald green plain. With each step, his walking stick pierced the moist rutted earth, so dark and fertile that he stooped to crumble it between his fingers and inhale the rich fecund scent. In the distance he glimpsed the broad glint of a river and through a glade of oaks, the slate turrets of a magnificent estate—

Someone nudged him in the ribs. Corréard crouched beside him, sweating and enfevered. 'I remember we've been deserted by the boats,' he whispered. Savigny noticed saliva flecking the corners of Corréard's lips. Skin peeled from his face in great ragged scrolls. When he smiled, his teeth began to chatter.

'But fear nothing,' Corréard said. 'I've just written to the Governor and in a few hours we shall be saved.'

Savigny closed his eyes. A golden barge emblazoned with fleur-de-lys floated down the river, burnished in the sunlight, crimson pennants streaming from her stern.

When he opened them again, Corréard leaned close, eager and expectant.

'That's good,' Savigny murmured. 'Have you a pigeon to carry your orders with as much celerity?'

All day the raft sank and rose with each rolling wave.

GÉRICAULT WOKE TO A fierce morning sun beating against the window. He must re-enact the scene. Cadavers glimpsed at dawn, Corréard stumbling through the devastation and wreckage of that second night.

Later, he found his guests seated at lunch in the dining room, La Motte fussing with laden trays, setting a carafe of cooled white wine, a plate of cheeses, a dish of quail eggs, and bread rolls on the table before them.

'Such bounty,' Savigny exclaimed, rubbing his hands with satisfaction.

Corréard unfolded his serviette and lifted the lid from a silver *bain-marie*.

'Braised calf's livers,' he said, inhaling a cloud of steam. 'Your cook spoils me, for she knows it's my favourite.'

Géricault took his place in silence and watched Corréard pile his plate. Savigny peeled an egg. 'Such a pretty speckled shell.'

'Quail, bantams,' Corréard rejoined. He speared a piece of meat with his fork. 'Did we ever imagine we should clap eyes on such fare?'

Before Savigny could reply, Géricault told them he

needed their opinion regarding a series of studies in which he had attempted to dramatise the mutiny scene, for he was not sure if he had it quite right.

'How so, dear boy?' Savigny was buttering his roll. 'Corréard, can you pass me that exquisite piece of chevre.'

Géricault waited for the exchange to be completed. His guests, the hapless survivors he had saved from starvation in a garret, now glowed with radiant health. But they seemed indifferent to the technical problems he faced in composing their narrative.

'As a central motif,' he explained, 'this battle against the officers carries dramatic biblical resonances—the Last Judgement, for example, and in this case, the fall of the mutineers into damnation.'

Savigny reached for another egg. 'So, you believe God presided on our behalf?'

'My dear fellow,' Corréard mopped his plate clean with a hunk of bread. 'It was not Christian virtue but strength that triumphed.'

The door burst open and in marched Horace followed by Delacroix, who eyed the food with a hungry look. The maid appeared with more plates and graced Horace with a bold lascivious smile. Horace had bedded her, Géricault could tell.

'The main problem is that too much is going on,' Géricault continued, motioning Horace and Delacroix to sit down. 'There's the forward surging movement of the mutineers advancing towards the officers on the parapet, who begin their defence firing volley after volley into the night skies. There's the hideous hand-to-hand combat, sabres lifted to the heavens, people drowning beneath tempest-tossed seas.'

Horace filled his glass. Gaping at the feast before him, Delacroix stuffed an entire roll in his mouth. His cheeks bulged with the attempt to chew and swallow.

'And if the timbers are half submerged in water,' Géricault said, 'you can't paint the raft.'

'Of course, the following morning, it would be considerably lighter,' Savigny offered as he scooped a spoonful from the *bain-marie*. He turned to Horace. 'What are your views on the matter?'

Géricault flushed with anger. He must intervene. Look at Horace now, leaning back in his chair and adopting the same wise expression as his father.

'In terms of narrative, I believe you're taking a considerable risk with this episode.' Horace at last fixed Géricault with an insolent stare that made his blood boil. 'If you're hoping for a conflict between the damned and the innocent, the good officers and the crazed mutineers, aren't you implying that this mass of humanity abandoned on the raft were not victims at all, but responsible for their end? They died not from the raw elements of nature but by their own hand.'

Savigny set down his knife and fork.

'I think your friend has a point,' he said, glancing at Corréard.

'Although we can't deny we're attracted to the dramatic tension in our *heroic defence* against *murderous villains*,' Savigny smiled at his companion, who nodded agreement. 'Perhaps the political implications of the tableau you have in mind will be made too explicit by hinting at a darker aspect of humanity.'

'Tainting us all,' Corréard offered, taking a delicate sip from his glass.

'Quite so, my friend,' Savigny replied.

'Shame,' Corréard murmured, 'to have abandoned the scene when the towropes were cut.'

'Good God!' Géricault cried, flinging down his serviette. 'It's not the themes I'm finding a problem but the compositional effect.'

He marched out of the room, slamming the door behind him.

To his shame, he then kneeled and crouched at the keyhole.

'My word, gentlemen,' Horace exclaimed. 'This story of yours is making quite a prima donna out of him. Any fool can see that the cutting of the towropes is the moment he should have chosen.'

'Exactly,' Savigny rejoined. 'Of course, we can't prevail on you, Monsieur Vernet.'

'I'm most flattered,' Horace said with a satisfied air. 'But I can hardly keep up with my commissions.'

He glanced over his shoulder as if he knew Géricault was eavesdropping behind the door.

'Besides,' he whispered, 'it would be unfair to betray my friend. I'm too much of a professional to steal his ideas.'

This had nothing to do with friendship, Géricault wanted to cry out for all Montmartre to hear. Horace wouldn't dare risk his reputation. Not when he hoped the Bourbon court would make a millionaire of him. More so than Napoleon, his erstwhile hero, who showered him with awards and gold medals.

Whichever way Horace sides, he thought, he never settles a single account at my house. Still views me as a dilettante with time and wealth on my hands.

'How about a glass of champagne?' Horace summoned the maid. 'Our friend the gentleman artist finds himself perplexed by the logistics of your tale. But he's come far. Surely that's a reason to celebrate.'

And they laughed.

Géricault hurried away along the corridor, and the maid passed him on the way, skipping behind the groom as he descended the steep steps to Géricault's cellar.

Once again Géricault returned to his studio alone.

Setting out the sketches again, he realised with a jolt of disappointment that somehow he had failed to capture the *brute force*, a central governing movement in those tumbling cascades of bodies setting on one another like a pack of wild dogs. The composition was ruined by confusion. The officers firing their carbines appeared more menacing than the mutineers armed only with sabres and knives. And on whose behalf, he asked himself, was the group in the foreground imploring the heavens?

He must try again.

This time, he saw the raft at a fair distance driven by the wind billowing its sail. Sprawled on the raised prow, the wounded, the dying. A man attempting to lift a corpse from the water. Beneath the mast, an exhausted officer holding a broken sword. Behind, the battle still raging, hatchets and sabres flailed the air. A crazed mutineer flinging himself into the waves. Clusters of men tumbling from the raft's stern.

Géricault studied his canvas. Now it occurred to him that part of the problem lay in the fact there were too many of them. Perhaps he should wait for more to die.

He would commission Horace's model, Joseph the boxer, to pose as the Asiatic mutineer. Corréard and Savigny as themselves. Delacroix and Horace as soldiers. And the corpses—how, he wondered, would he manage that?

An image came to him of his mother laid out on a white winding sheet, dressed in a lace gown embroidered with lily of the valley at the sleeves and hem. But just memory, he told himself, would not do for the raft. He needed to record every hue and tone in lifeless flesh and set down the moment when the soul took flight.

He rejected the heroic postures of Horace's battlefields, the soldiers sacrificed, sanctified, prettified, *pro patria mori*. No, in order to capture the raw nerve of the experience, he first needed to understand it. And when the time came to compose his final tableau, he would have to paint as if he too were a witness, a shipwreck survivor. All at once it dawned on him—the Beaujon Hospital. Why had he not thought of it before? The wards of the sick and the dying would be his true school of art.

Striding out the door, Géricault gave orders for the groom to prepare the carriage. His guests were playing cards with Horace on the terrace.

'How can you bear to go into town on such a hot day?' Savigny called as Géricault hurried towards the stables. Indeed the sun was beating down, parching the lawns. La Motte appeared carrying a jug of lemonade. But his resolve did not weaken. He urged his horse into a trot along the driveway. Damp patches of sweat stained the back of his shirt. Despite the heat, he would furnish the raft.

Through Pigalle the models for hire languished by the fountain, fanning themselves like a flock of exotic birds. When Géricault reached Saint-Germain, he noticed how deserted the district seemed, many families having left the city for their country estates during these listless dog days.

He rode along the river and then along the boulevard du Général Leclerc, until he came to an imposing granite edifice—Beaujon, the hospice.

Here Géricault explained his business to a bored young man seated at a vast mahogany desk and doodling in the corners of a ledger. When Géricault declared himself an artist who wished to study the ravages of disease, the youth looked up at him with a mixture of interest and suspicion.

'Is there a physician who can take me round?' Géricault asked, glancing at the scurrying figures darting back and forth.

The boy stared at a timepiece ticking above the door. 'My shift's over,' he said. 'I'd be happy to act as your guide.'

When Géricault handed him a coin—it seemed the

right thing—the boy introduced himself as Coudin, apprentice apothecary. Géricault followed him up a broad flight of oak stairs and along a wide corridor. Finally Coudin led him into a ward with cots ranged in rows.

'What manner of death are you seeking?' he asked. 'Tumours, syphilis, dropsy, king's evil, pox, kidney worm, croup, diphtheria, typhoid, colic—here we have every mortality imaginable except of course the plague.' He laughed.

Géricault said he needed only to study someone for whom death loomed close.

'Young, old, male or female?'

Géricault shrugged and shook his head.

Coudin escorted him to a narrow bed beneath an open window. 'Less chance of contagion,' he confided. 'Scarlatina, this one. I'd hold a handkerchief to your mouth.'

A woman tossed and turned on drenched sheets. Géricault could not tell her age, so emaciated had she become, every bone sculpted against skin, her hands clutching the cot rails like claws, dim restless eyes in dark sockets, brittle hair plastered against a damp pillow. He could feel the heat of her fever.

Bringing over a stool, Coudin motioned his charge to sit at the woman's side.

'It won't be long now,' he whispered. 'I'll be over there,' he pointed to a bench by the door.

Géricault took out his sketchbook, a nub of charcoal, his pens. It felt unseemly that he should be here. Would she know? He wondered why there were no relatives or loved ones to farewell this woman.

He began with the sharp angles of her cheekbones, the sunken shadows at her temples and brow, the nose so aquiline and fragile it reminded him of a statue unearthed from the sands of antique lands that might be smashed with one clumsy jolt of a spade. The woman moaned, every breath rattled in her throat. Her grip tightened on the rails. When Géricault looked up, he found her eyes on him. Unsettling, he had to admit. He tried to concentrate on their colour, pale as blue-flecked glass. He glanced over at Coudin, looking bored, just as he had first seen him.

Géricault stared at the woman once again and waited for the next rasping gasp. It wouldn't come. Perhaps he should call someone? That nurse carrying a spittoon and walking with a brisk click-clackety step towards the door.

Ah, there it was at last, fainter this time, a soft susurration beneath the sheets. At the sound, Géricault felt a surge of relief.

She continued to inhale the fetid air. Blood pounded through her veins, the heart still beating. Her eyes remained fixed on his. Géricault leaned forward and smiled. No reaction. What did he expect?

He felt he should know more about this woman, her name, her life. Where she was born. Whether she had lovers, children, someone to hold close from time to time. How sad, he thought, to die on this cot alone. Again he waited, and was rewarded with the rustle of a sigh like the twirling fall of a leaf.

The woman loosened her hold on the rail. Géricault pressed the woman's hand between his palms. He noticed no one had bothered to clip her nails, curved stained talons scrabbling the sheets. She would not have liked that, he was convinced. She would have said, I intend to die with dignity and grace.

Gone. Her form flattened, shrunken, no more.

Géricault examined the expressionless mask now, her face. Then, turning round, he called Coudin.

Coudin led him to a boy not more than ten years old, convulsively tossing on the narrow bed, rolling his head from side to side, his features clenched in an agonised grimace.

'Diphtheria,' Coudin whispered. 'Steadily the infection spreads.'

Géricault gazed down. The child's breath came out in great shuddering spasms accompanied by a growling rattle at the back of his throat. Every effort of the flailing limbs strained towards each intake of air into his lungs. Géricault set down his stool and took his place beside the boy's bed. Now the child had flung off his sheet, and with a gasp of shock Géricault steeled himself to sketch that stiffened body, wasted to the bone, the wizened face stained with sweat and tears.

He glanced about him and became aware of the chorus of broken cries and groans gusting through the ward like some savage lament or prayer.

Géricault rested his pencil against the blank page. Still the boy thrashed from side to side, buffeted by the roaring tides of his fever. Something must be done to end this torture, he thought. Surely one of the physicians here could quell the violence of these convulsions. Beginning to panic, he noticed that Coudin was no longer at his side. Two nurses hurried past towards a long high-pitched shrilling from the far end of the room. He turned again to the boy, who now suddenly lay limp, utterly exhausted, tensing his arms and legs.

I can do nothing, Géricault said to himself, except follow all phases of suffering, from the first seizure to the final agony, and study the traces they imprint on the human body.

Gently he leaned over and stroked the small, puckered face. Did he imagine it or had the boy quietened?

He drew back his hand and picked up the pencil once again.

For hours Géricault set down every hectic motion of this child splayed on his infernal rack. There was no remorse or relief. At times, he became overwhelmed with disgust to see the boy fighting with all his puny strength, left to die alone with not even a gathering of mourners at his bed.

And then, when Géricault thought he could bear no more, the child lay without moving on the soiled drenched sheets.

Slowly he gathered his sketchbook, his pencils and pens, and rose to his feet. He stumbled through the ward, past the scurrying nurses, those midwives of death. He had seen suffering enough to last a lifetime. For the dozing Coudin, a coin. Then Géricault walked through the door.

Géricault returned gritty with dust to Montmartre and found his guests playing boules in the afternoon shadows. Seeing the carriage appear, Savigny waved.

'Do come and join us,' he said. 'We need an umpire. Horace keeps changing the rules.'

All around them lay glasses and empty champagne bottles.

Géricault could still smell the death stench of the morgue, the sour odour of sweat and stale urine in the blankets and sodden sheets. He could not shake the image of the boy from his mind.

He wanted to round on his guests and call them to account. In the name of the suffering he'd just witnessed, who did they think they were taking advantage of his hospitality like this, yet deliberately withholding the information he still needed to create his tableau? He would offer them a choice, either they would continue to describe in every detail the events that took place on the raft, or he would throw them out of the house, simple as that.

A metal ball rolled across the lawn and bumped against Géricault's boot.

'Don't stand there dreaming,' Horace cried. 'You're right in our way.'

Consumed with fury, Géricault drew back his foot to give the ball a vicious kick—but Savigny scooped it up in the palm of his hand.

Savigny graced everyone with a bright smile. 'I believe it's my turn,' he called, 'if our host would be so good as to step aside.'

Géricault did not trust himself to speak. He gave a brief nod and left them to their games.

Very well, he thought to himself, returning to the studio and pouring a glass of wine. He would do it alone.

He toiled into the night, not even distracted now by the music and sounds of laughter drifting through the windows from Horace's house. He was becoming meticulous in ranging the bladders of paint in the correct order on the trestle. His palette carefully cleaned in spirits. The brushes neatly stacked in their jars. Evidence that finally he had found a way to work.

At midnight, Géricault surveyed his canvas. Beautiful, quite perfect. He had succeeded in recreating the exact pose of the first murdered men. He would need Corréard and Savigny to correct him on this matter, but say the Asiatic swung his sabre to the left, the boy would have fallen to the right, lying just so, supine, his palms pressed against the deck, his torso arched with the last convulsions. So too his companion sprawled on the other side gave Géricault a forward movement, an open path towards the parapet, where tomorrow Corréard and Savigny must stand firing their muskets in defence.

He sat for a long time admiring the choreography of the figures on the raft. He was tempted to pick up his pencil and begin another sketch, but decided to wait. From the gardens, a soaring note of panpipes followed by a voice echoing the refrain. 'La, ley, la, ley, la ley.'

Géricault woke at dawn eager to see his canvas in the first light. He dressed and saw beyond the window the sun rising in a pink sky, tinged green behind the woodlands.

In the studio he thrilled again at his composition. It was *good* what he had done.

With care he prepared a fresh palette and arranged his brushes. As he concentrated on the study, using his sketches from the Beaujon Hospital for the boy, he cursed the years he had squandered, and those idle weeks in Rome lusting after Alexandrine, when he could have been engaged in a subject which consumed him with a passion like this. If only, Géricault reflected, he had chanced earlier on such a tale—then never would he have allowed himself to become seduced by his uncle's wife.

For hours he surrendered himself to the men on the raft, the rictal grimace on the face of the dead boy, the Asiatic advancing towards the officers grouped on the parapet. Géricault's wrists ached with the frantic speed of his brushwork.

At noon he stepped back and marvelled at the way in which the anguished pallor of the officers now balanced with and heightened the bloodless corpses in the foreground. Nothing in life could be finer, he mused, than this burst of inspiration from the moistened point of his sable.

The door swung open. A shadow slanted across his easel, eclipsing the source of light. In exasperation, Géricault wheeled round—and there stood Alexandrine, the sour pasty-faced maid at her side.

'My darling,' Alexandrine cried. 'You can't have received my letters, for you've not sent a word.'

With a pang of guilt, Géricault glanced at the pile of missives half hidden among his paints on the table. Quite simply, he had not had the time. Each morning, La Motte had handed him the notes with a stern look of disapproval and each day he had meant to open them and reply.

'Caruel is most concerned at the progress of my portrait,' Alexandrine murmured, proffering her cheek for a kiss. 'He complains it seems to be taking longer than usual.'

Again she twined her arms around his neck and again he suffocated in her tight caress.

It was warm in the room. A hot sun now beat against the panes. Géricault looked at his canvas.

'Please,' he implored Alexandrine, motioning her towards a chair by the trestle and taking up his palette, 'it should not take more than an hour at the most. You have no idea how long I've toiled at this work.'

Alexandrine stared at him in amazement. Even Louisette was gazing his way, open-mouthed.

'Wait? Like some court lackey—for an hour?' Alexandrine exclaimed. 'Who do you think I am?'

The maid suppressed a giggle and Alexandrine rounded on her. 'Get out,' she cried, 'before I give you a good sound slap.'

Géricault stood at his canvas, intent on darkening the plunging waves with deft rapid strokes of bitumen. He could not stop now, surely she would understand.

But Alexandrine advanced across the room and began to berate him in a loud shrilling voice, declaring it beggared belief that he should neglect his mistress for those vile vagrants, those *guests* of his, and how dare he humiliate her in such a fashion—that she should be dismissed with an airy wave of his hand in front of Louisette!—why, no one would countenance such behaviour.

Géricault remained silent and continued to work at his easel. This heat was impossible, the brushes unwieldy in his hand. Alexandrine's tears and reproaches he had seen before, but never her rage.

'Caruel has paid good money for this commission, yet deliberately you insult him,' she was saying. 'When I tell him you prefer to paint these grisly scenes in favour of a portrait of his wife,' she gave his canvas a contemptuous glance, 'he will not be pleased.'

This reference to his uncle was too much. What right had she to ambush him like that?

'Please lower your voice,' Géricault said in what he hoped was a calm, even tone. 'It would not do for my guests and the servants to hear you.'

'Don't speak to me of your guests, those pitiful beggars you scraped from the streets. Why, they must take you for a fool—guzzling your best wines and champagne, lording it over you in the house, while you slave over their story which is nothing more than a pack of lies.'

She stamped her foot. 'Shame on you, Théo.'

And with that Alexandrine stormed from the room.

Géricault set down his brushes with a sigh. Through the window, he watched her stride towards the carriage, calling out to the maid, who scurried fearfully to her side. Her hair had fallen loose from its chignon and, as she as she hurried up the path, she lifted her gown, revealing those slender ankles and an elegant pair of emerald-green satin slippers.

For a moment, Géricault felt himself weaken. He was tempted to run after her, to complete the portrait, as he had promised, by leading her to the divan where he would follow the line from her breasts to her belly with his tongue.

How he could tease her. And the declarations he would make at the moment of her climax, 'I can't resist, I love you,' and other such nonsense which he would believe at the time.

Instead he turned away. Even diluted, the bitumen was sticking to his brush like burnt treacle. He would write a long loving letter and make it up to her with a bouquet of expensive flowers. But not now, he murmured, contemplating his canvas. No, he did not want to think of Alexandrine now.

THAT EVENING SAVIGNY surprised him with an unexpected visit. He even apologised for being perhaps remiss of late, but the air of Montmartre had definitely revived their spirits and they did so enjoy the company of Horace Vernet. Such a charming young man, he declared.

Carefully steering Savigny away from the subject of Horace and his friends, Thérèse in particular, Géricault guided him to the raft.

'What do you think?' he asked, realising with surprise that this was the first time Savigny had seen the replica.

Savigny shuddered at the sight of those bare planks. 'Exactly right,' he murmured, retreating to a seat by the window.

Savigny talked long into the night. Moths flickered among the candelabras and Géricault brushed them away, making sure that at regular intervals he refilled Savigny's glass with the finest Burgundy his cellar had.

The fourth night began with swelling tides lifting the raft

over the rippled flanks of each wave before the precipitous plunge seawards again. A yellow shard of lightning flared in the sky and illuminated the deep raging troughs into which they were about to descend.

And then borne upwards again in a tumultuous dizzying flight to where, racing on a roaring sheet of foam, the raft seemed to find her equilibrium, in a pause, no longer than an intake of breath, before the mountainous crest curved and toppled, sucking the vessel through a thunderous tunnel of black rushing waters. And then spat it out again like something rank and rotten that not even the ocean could stomach.

For the men sobbing and spewing brine on the raft, it was a torment, terror without end.

Each man—how they pushed and screamed and shoved—braced himself for the next spiralling dive. No mercy there should you lose your grip and tumble from the planks of the raft.

And the salt spume, it corroded every man's lips so that blood was all they could taste, caked and sour in parched throats, bitter on swollen tongues.

Each man to his own without a care for friends or companions or anyone who might loosen their hold on the rough ropes, which ripped their palms to shreds. No one heeded the cries of the men clutching the outer reaches of the raft, their fingers wedged between swollen creaking poles until, unable to withstand the battering swell, they were swept from the heaving vessel.

Another victim gone, lightening the load.

Imperceptibly the huddle on the raft shifted each time and seemed to expand, filling the space left behind.

Hour after hour, the men pledged bargains with God, forged pacts with the stars, those infernal pinpricks of light bright and mocking in the heavens. Entire families were bartered in exchange for one single life.

'Take them all so I can return to Rochefort alive. Don't let me die. Not like that man—' flayed and bleeding, his mangled leg trapped between the planks, the seas tearing him apart. 'Not even Jesus expired like that.'

So spoke the damned.

And grouped on the parapet at the centre of the raft, the officers held their weapons close and kept a constant vigil over the men. Savigny burned with a fever. Still, steadying himself against a sudden lift of a wave, he surveyed the clinging mass pummelled at the bows and stern. He crooked his finger beneath the trigger of his carbine and longed to silence their screams. They must pull themselves together. Show some backbone. Above all, he declared to no one in particular, we must enforce order among these raw recruits from the taverns and gaols. When he turned to Corréard for his advice on the matter, chandeliers swung in a glittering burst from the skies. Several of the soldiers had taken up their instruments and, bowing, launched into a waltz. A liveried butler bearing a silver tray appeared at Savigny's side. All too well, the surgeon recognised the dreams of delirium and struggled against them, although these crazed visions of the night seemed to possess all on board.

At first an angry murmur of voices from the crush, a scuffle at the stern, then a sudden rush of men brandishing cutlasses and knives, and the cry— 'To arms! Advance on the officers—'

It was not yet midnight. But now that fourth night unravelled its hours like a great bolt of silk, surging towards dawn with the same momentous rhythms as the waves, heavier and slower now, effortlessly lifting the raft across their wide foam-flecked backs.

This was a night of hand-to-hand combat fought in slow motion, each movement weighed with exhaustion, blunted blades *sawing* through flesh and the effort of it all just to swing that heavy sword or run a dagger through sinew and bone to its bloodied hilt. And later, before the moon had fled over the horizon, those without the strength to wield their weapons lunged at one another without reason or restraint. Savigny found himself pinned by a sailor, who with a crazed savagery sank his teeth into his thigh, tore at his hair and clothes, and tried to gouge out his eyes with his bare hands. In desperation and rage, Savigny too clawed at the man, had him around the throat and, kneeling on his chest, pierced him four times over with the point of his bayonet and another through the heart just to make sure. When the boy lay dead in Savigny's arms, he remembered a sweet docile lad carving whalebone in the shadow of a sail, the billowing canvas of a French frigate once called the *Medusa*.

In the madness, two barrels of wine were breached and thrown over the side. Only one cask remained and forty souls alive.

ON THE FIFTH DAY, the survivors drifted on their makeshift vessel pursued by fitful dreams. Corréard imagined he presided at the head of a glorious banquet where dish after dish appeared on golden platters: lark wings; a roasted suckling pig served whole with an apple in its mouth; an entire carp dressed in aspic; capons basted with their own juices and garlic; a cassoulet prepared in the manner of the Languedoc region, thick with legumes, seared pork fat and duck; fantastical pyramids of fruits from all seasons; and such cheeses!—a brie fit to bursting, creamy white rolls of chevre sprinkled with pepper and tarragon, a slab of Emmental the colour of buttercups. As for the wines, Corréard's cup overflowed, and each time he took a sip they seemed to match the dish he had chosen: with the fish a fine Sancerre, the pork a Bourgogne. He ate and drank, licked the plates clean and sucked gravy and grease from each finger.

A soldier was the first to succumb, knew what had to be done if he were to survive.

All morning he watched a Portuguese gunner, badly injured in the brawl, sink in and out of his fevers, a gash to the bone across one arm leaching all his strength. All morning he listened to the shallow breath become fainter and fainter. Every so often he gazed at La Touche and inhaled the stench from his leg. Hour after hour the soldier waited, saliva curdling his tongue, asking the question: *Who will be the first?* Images of food besieged this man's mind. For a long time he had been tormented by the savoury scent of roast chicken, one slaughtered and plucked that very morning at his mother's farm. He could see the steam rising from crisp-cooked skin basted with thick lardons of bacon. His hands trembled at the thought of carving that moist white flesh, a leg and now perhaps a wing, of reaching for a jug filled with wine-fragrant gravy. He almost wept at the vision of braised chestnuts cramming the cavity of that plump, juice-glazed breast. All morning he waited for the gunner to die, and leaped forward when he did. 'I will just help myself to a wing of chicken over there,' the soldier cried, and pushed his way through the dazed men.

Before anyone could stop him, he sliced a portion of flesh from the thigh of the corpse, which he began to devour with the same alacrity as in his dreams. No one moved. They watched him before returning once again to their reveries, the crazed cauchemars of the night. All day they continued to doze in a stupor, a trance. No one followed the soldier's example but the idea weighed like stone ballast in their minds.

An early morning light streamed through the shutters and cast shifting patterns on the replica of the raft. A breeze billowed the curtains like sails. Géricault inspected his latest sketches.

Although he admired the composition, he was not sure about the mutiny. Perhaps he had laboured too long at the task. The chaos, the darkness and the waters rushing over the raft—all had the same problems as the earlier scenes of carnage.

Géricault pictured his guests in the breakfast room, La Motte appearing with a baked leg of ham, which Savigny would carve with deft, meticulous strokes. Corréard piling his plate high.

He could not begin to understand it. But then, once the stores were lost over the side, how had they survived? Unless of course they had indeed resorted to the unthinkable, those rumours sensationalised in the papers and retold in every tavern in town. Could Savigny the surgeon have brought himself to feast on his dead companions? Géricault had tried to imagine it—but always an image rose of the good doctor dabbing his lips with a starched serviette. And Corréard the cartographer with ten men under his command, what of him by that fifth day on the raft?

He riffled through the dossier which Grassin had given him, mere opinions all—pressmen sensationalising and milking this ghoulish episode for all it was worth.

We feel our pen drop from our hand; a deathlike chill pervades all our limbs; our hair stands erect on our heads! Reader, we beseech you, do not feel indignation towards men who are already too unfortunate, but have compassion for them, and shed some tears of pity on their unhappy fate.

Those whom death had spared, fell upon the dead bodies with which the raft was covered, and cut off pieces, which some instantly devoured.

Géricault stuffed the papers back into the file. No, he needed to hear the truth from their mouths and not from some hack with a glass of rough ale at his side.

Crossing the courtyard on his way to the house, Géri-cault wondered how to examine his guests on this matter. He found them still seated at the table.

'Gentlemen,' he declared, taking his place beside them, 'after much deliberation, I've decided to abandon the mutiny as the central subject for my tableau.'

Corréard set down his fork. Savigny paused in the act of buttering his bread.

Géricault forced himself to look them straight in the eye. 'Instead I must ask you to describe in every detail how you managed to survive without food and water, sustenance of any kind, except the last keg of wine, which was severely rationed.'

There, he had said it. This time he would not allow them to dodge the issue. He would persist until they yielded every part of their tale.

'Really, dear fellow,' Savigny pushed away his plate. 'Much as we are grateful for your interest in our cause, this is neither the time nor place,' he glanced at the servant girl wheeling in pastries and coffee on a trolley, 'to discuss such matters.'

With an offended air, Corréard carefully folded his serviette.

'No indeed, I agree,' he replied in a grieved tone. 'Particularly as I seem to remember we spent that day chewing the leather of our hats, cartridge pouches and belts.'

Savigny stared at his host coldly. 'We fished. We made lures from identity tags carried by the soldiers, but soon the lines became entangled and useless . . .'

'We bent a bayonet into a curve to fashion a shark hook,' Corréard put in. 'And my, did one of those monsters make a dash for it, racing through the swell. Opening its great gap-toothed maw, the creature swallowed the bait but could not be caught, and almost dragged four men overboard.'

'And what did you use for bait?' Géricault asked.

Savigny dipped a spoon into a jar of black cherry jam.

'Any kind of food-gathering required great mental and physical effort.'

He bit into a pastry and chewed pensively for a moment.

'As for killing a shark,' he shot Corréard a knowing glance, 'no, we were not up to the job.'

'Which is why you—'

'I must insist, sir!' Corréard exclaimed. 'You go too far in this matter.'

'I will not create a tableau in which you munch on your buckles and belts,' Géricault cried. He had expected a certain resistance, yet surely they must know that sooner or later he would question them on this. Besides, he reasoned, if they had eaten dead flesh it was because there was no choice in the matter. And had he been in their situation . . . who could tell?

'No, instead you deliberately falsify our narrative in order to sensationalise your art.' Corréard glared at him, his face suddenly pale with rage.

Géricault took a deep breath. He must remain calm. It would not do to provoke his guests into storming out of the house.

'Well, gentlemen,' he said, 'let us return to the story. Although buffeted by winds, you've said, the sixth night passed peacefully enough. Consumed with shame, many of the mutineers had thrown their weapons over the side. You huddled together, beaten and wretched . . . ?'

'The following morning,' Savigny began, 'we woke to a shoal of flying fish, the size of herring, a few of which became trapped among the projecting side timbers. Eagerly we scooped them up and devoured them raw. The remaining we stored in a barrel.'

'And with this,' Géricault asked, determined to steer them back to the point, 'did you not mix a portion of—'

Savigny slammed his fist on the table. 'No, sir, I will not allow you to fabricate this fiction!'

Géricault was beginning to despair. These men were too sharp for him by half, he thought, always one step ahead with their sanitised account.

'Why must you persist in this matter?' Savigny cried. 'Perhaps you would have more luck if you focused on a single detail—Corréard, for example, saving the *cantinière* from the waves. Or myself, fighting hand-to-hand combat through the mutiny.'

'Portray you as heroes?'

'Well, why not?' Corréard interjected. 'Isn't that the whole point? Isn't that the reason we're here?'

Géricault stared at his guests, furious.

'You don't understand,' he said at last. 'To do so would be nothing short of the cheapest propaganda illustrating some polemic, a political manifesto. Not even our Emperor would have gone so far. No, I need the entire story, the facts as you know them, before I can even begin to select the precise moment that best encapsulates your tale.'

'Very well,' Savigny said in a weary tone. 'I shall explain in every detail how we survived.'

At last! Géricault leaned forward. He felt proud of himself. He had stood up to his guests and shown them he was no fool to be trifled with.

Now Savigny told him that he and his companions were racked more with thirst than hunger, there being as he knew only one barrel of wine, which was severely rationed. So much so that many did not drink their share straight off, but slowly sucked the liquid. Of course, they resorted to moistening their parched lips with urine, which they stored in tin cups.

He observed that some men's urine was said to taste more agreeable than others, in whom it had become thick and acrid. He noticed that drinking it made them all want to urinate again. 'Perhaps one day,' he mused, 'I will write a scientific treatise on the phenomenon, entitled: *Observations sur les effets de la soif éprouvée après le naufrage de le frégate la Méduse.*'

Corréard, who had been listening to every word, described how among their belongings they discovered a phial containing spirits of cloves and cinnamon, for cleaning teeth. At intervals, the tincture was solemnly passed among the officers like a pipe of peace, a talisman. The smallest drop produced a delightful sensation on the tongue and for a moment provided release from the thirst that consumed them.

Savigny then recalled that the most prized possession became an empty perfume bottle belonging to the *cantinière*. This too they passed with reverence around and, when it was sniffed, attar of roses could still be inhaled, flooding and empowering the senses with the deepest joy.

Géricault could envisage this scene, the huddle of ravaged men each reaching for these tricks against thirst, a stale rose scent rising in the fetid air, a sharp taste of cloves against the tongue.

The problem was he did not believe them.

Supposing that, unable to withstand the sight of the mob, Savigny had taken out his scalpel and with expert hands flensed the meat from one of the dead? Perhaps with the last of the gunpowder, Corréard had lit a small fire on top of a barrel and they roasted the flesh. Afterwards their spirits would have immediately revived, and they'd have felt almost content when they sipped their ration of wine, better equipped to face the ordeal ahead.

Géricault glanced at his guests. With an aggrieved air, Savigny was drumming his fingers on the table. Corréard had gone over to the window, where he stood with his hands clasped behind his back.

He tried to imagine it. You find yourself lost at sea, or marooned on a desert isle or in some inhospitable terrain inhabited by hostile tribes. One by one your companions die—snake-bite, starvation, fever. As each day passes, the links loosen to the person you once were—erudite, clever, charming, a man of letters, of the world. Your personality, the very core of your being—decent, caring, compassionate, Christian perhaps—becomes as ragged and shredded as your clothes, that brand-new uniform you once wore with such pride, adorned with gold braided epaulettes. All you know is a burning corrosive desire to survive. To witness another dawn, a moonrise. Nothing to do with humanity, but a primitive and pagan craving. When, against all odds, you return as a hero to your homeland, to the speeches and banquets, the pretty women hanging on your every word—in another time and place this could have been Savigny and Corréard, were it not for the political blunders of the King—you simply make a joke of it, tell the beauty seated on your right that you boiled your boots, cooked quite a stew from them. My, how she will clap her hands and laugh—

Suddenly it occurred to Géricault that perhaps he stood to make his name with this—a subject seldom touched on in European art. If only he could discover the truth about these men on the raft.

'What have we here?' Horace strode into the room, carrying a brace of pheasant—'Didn't even need the dog to snuffle these out.' He slapped the pheasant on the table. Blood seeped from the shot in their breasts and stained the white linen tablecloth. 'Perfect for supper tonight.'

Taking his place opposite Savigny, Horace leaned over and whispered: 'Madame Thérèse is so taken with you she has booked a box at the theatre tonight. *Andromache*—she's fabulous, all quivering bosom and plunging knives.'

Savigny gave him a weak smile.

Horace helped himself to a plate of poached eggs, which no one had touched.

'Corréard,' he said, noticing him by the window, 'will you not join us?'

'I've already eaten,' he replied in a low voice. Pushing back his chair, Savigny joined his companion.

'I think we'll take a walk,' Savigny murmured. 'Please excuse us, gentlemen.' They bowed and hurried out the room.

'Off so soon?' Horace called. 'See you at the theatre tonight.'

Fork poised, Horace glanced at Géricault. 'What have you said to them?' he asked. 'They seem most put out.'

Géricault left him to finish his meal without a reply.

Returning to his studio, Géricault thought of the book his guests had intended to write, those fat dossiers gathering dust in his mother's parlour. Cooped in that wretched garret, how they had burned to tell their tale and railed against the injustices heaped upon them. Now Géricault knew he'd been a fool to invite Savigny and Corréard to his house. That rank room would have fed the furnace of their discontent, no apothecary to attend to them, none of La Motte's rich meals to quicken their zest for life.

He needed them desperate, weakened, pouring out their story in a torrent of rage.

Instead, he now realised, it was he who was trapped in the absurd position of playing host to an endless banquet at which even Horace's assistant, that boy Delacroix, considered himself invited.

Géricault stared out the window. No sign of his guests or Horace, who were no doubt wandering the meadows. He cursed them. He had reached an impasse with no means of moving on. It was a form of torture, he thought.

All day he toiled at the task.

Crouched like beasts over the bodies in the foreground, the men on the raft gnawed hanks of meat, sucked soft glutinous marrow from the bones. Out of decency, Géricault had left the *cantinière* out of this study. He concentrated instead on the men, muscular and naked, burrowing like maggots through soft cadaver flesh.

But in the end, in the final analysis, he had to admit this composition did not work either. Again he studied the sketches. Why? Where had he gone wrong?

He must tackle this problem. There are men dying in the water. Others, their arms lifted, weep to the heavens. In the centre, a group. No more men than apes, they hunched back-to-back, grinding and chewing through gristle and sinew. And always the bilious tilt of the raft against the horizon.

It was a matter of tone, Géricault decided, once again scrutinising those crouching figures, gobblers of dead companions. Shakespeare understood, he thought, recognised how swiftly the comic tides seeped into the darkest tragedy. He exploited it even, that scene in *Titus Andronicus*, for example, when the hero sought revenge by serving the Queen's sons, those murderous thugs, as meat pies. How she and the Emperor devoured them. How the audience laughed at every mincing sycophantic gesture. Andronicus the cook, deferential waiter, even a starched serviette folded on one arm. Anthropophagy presented as farce.

No.

Géricault decided to pardon his guests' crimes.

A PALLID DAWN REVEALED thirty deaths in the night. Delirious and burning from some fever, the *cantinière* sprawled among the corpses. Resigning himself, Savigny counted. Only twenty-seven souls alive. He gave orders for the bodies to be rolled over the side, except for three cadavers to be kept as supplies.

Again not a ship or a ridge of land in sight. All morning they wallowed on grey marbled seas. After six days submerged in cruel waters, their legs throbbed ulcerous and raw, their ragged clothes caked to blistered skin. La Touche shivered and sweated on the parapet. Crouched by his side and mopping the officer's brow, Savigny had decided against amputating the diseased limb. Why blunt his blade when La Touche could not last?

By noon the currents acquired a curious iridescent sheen. The bow planks drove through a glutinous jellied mass of transparent creatures, which glinted and shone beneath a merciless sun. Pulsing pink and blue, they slanted in formation, propelled by a thin veined membrane billowing open to the wind. One of the soldiers leaned forward and scooped several onto the deck in order to inspect their translucence more closely. All at once he screamed. Long pink tentacles wrapped around his arm and scored his flesh with crimson welts. Then a sudden swell washed over the raft, flaying the survivors with stings sharper than a nettle rash. Savigny fainted with the pain. Many attempted to crawl towards the higher reaches of the parapet to avoid the poisonous jellyfish strokes, which Corréard identified as a specimen known as Portuguese men-of-war, an endless flotation spreading for miles around catching an offshore breeze to escape land. So perhaps now the raft was drifting closer towards the African coast?

By late afternoon the raft slapped against clear seas. A pack of sharks, which had been following the vessel at a sinister blue-finned distance, now began to nudge the beams of the outer sections. Their grey blunt snouts bumped against the stern.

Maddened by the heat, and the itching fever of his skin, Corréard rose to his feet and announced that he usually bathed at this hour. No one looked up when he swung over the side. Ah, to be lifted by the cool glass-green curve of each wave. He allowed himself to float arms outstretched in the pose of Christ or a saint. A shark brushed by and nuzzled his ribs with wide slackened jaws. Another gave him an indifferent push before shimmying away. Staring up at pale skies streaked with faint swathes of clouds, Corréard laughed out loud. 'I disgust even these beasts,' he cried. No one heeded his words. The men slipped in and out of their world of dreams.

At dusk, easing their aching bodies on the parapet, Corréard and Savigny prayed for sleep. Once again Savigny pursued those Italianate spires always beyond the next valley, the next village, on the other side of a riverbank and never a bridge in sight. Corréard found himself crossing the Alps, gazing down at a lush verdant valley tinkling with cowbells.

Upwards and onwards he climbed, stones rattling beneath the heels of his stout leather boots.

The *cantinière* returned to the joys of her youth. Her fair braided hair garlanded with wild flowers, she danced round and around a maypole, gracing her suitors with an enigmatic virgin's smile. All the while her husband moaned and tossed at her side. The sergeant imagined he was slaughtering a pig fattened on acorns and swill throughout the year. He slit its throat with the sharpened blade of his knife and listened to the whistle of blood spilling into a bucket. His mouth watered at the sight of his wife's plump fingers kneading breadcrumbs for boudin, rillettes and all manner of sausages to be stored in the pantry for winter solstice feast days.

La Touche lay awake and counted the last vanishing stars among the heavens. All night he waited for a final anointment in the sluice of a wave. Silence on the raft. Dreams crept over the sleeping figures like dragonish clouds.

All night Géricault crumpled study after study of the raft into the fire. Flares from the burning papers cast strange flickering shadows against the walls. In one he had recorded their dreams, the raft lying low on the water, lacy swirls of spume frothing across wormed planks. He had even imagined the dreams of the dead.

When morning came, Géricault found his guests in the rose garden.

'By the eighth day,' he asked, 'how many were mortally sick?'

Savigny leaned on his rake and stared at him in silence. Corréard cut his finger on a thorn and cursed.

'Thirteen souls,' Savigny finally replied, 'delirious, dying, including La Touche, the *cantinière* and her husband.'

Géricault thought back to the hospital—that woman's eyes fixed on his, her hand slipping from the cot rail. Surely the strong fierce *cantinière* survived. Her stout form could not be reduced to bones stitched with ragged sinews of flesh. And brave La Touche, his hero's second in command, he could not die!

'Our numbers had been reduced to twenty-six,' Savigny said, 'and clearly the last of the rations would not sustain all. We had barely a quarter barrel of wine, which would not last more than four days.'

'Particularly after we discovered two soldiers siphoning precious supplies from a reed placed through a hole they had bored into the wood,' Corréard volunteered to Géricault's surprise.

'The villains were lying down side by side feigning sleep but we soon uncovered their ruse and, according to the laws we had drawn up, they were summarily—'

'By my calculations,' Savigny interjected, glaring at his friend, 'even if the sick were placed on quarter rations, we could not have endured.'

'And the soldiers you discovered pilfering the wine, what became of them?'

'Executed,' Corréard replied, 'and thrown over the side.'

In the silence that followed, Savigny rounded on Géricault.

'Since you rejected the most dramatic and crucial episode when the Captain cut the towropes and abandoned brave loyal men to a dreadful fate—well, now what do you have for your great composition? Twenty-six starving souls ravaged by thirst and the burning sun, half of whom were dying anyway and might not last the night. And you think this scene would make the better painting? Well, I can tell you, my friend, you're wrong.'

Savigny looked at him then with such a sorrowful

expression that Géricault found himself flinching from that gaze.

'I had to make a decision that would have broken many a man,' Savigny continued in a low, tremulous voice. 'To put the sick on such an allowance would have diminished them by degrees, a lingering, intolerable end. Perhaps you've forgotten, we were not on the raft by design. The deception of our fellow countrymen had placed us in this situation.'

His eyes brimmed with tears. 'Leave us for now,' he whispered. 'I have no wish to go on.'

Shamed, Géricault turned and walked slowly up the path. What right had he to interrogate them in this fashion? He had shared no part in their suffering. He was not forced to decide who should live and who should die, separate the healthy from the sick, the innocent from the damned. How could he do justice to their ordeal when he'd led such a pampered and sheltered life? His every whim indulged, deluding himself that he understood the true nature of betrayal. Yet if truth were known, he could not even begin to apprehend the true nature of their experience. And the irony did not escape him that unlike Savigny and Corréard, he would not have survived.

Filled with remorse, Géricault closed the studio door behind him.

Géricault was staring at the canvas. Perhaps Horace was right, he thought. Perhaps he should abandon this dark tale of theirs.

The *cantinière*, who once wheeled her trolley through the rutted battlefields of Europe bringing solace, nourishment and twenty years of service to Napoleon's troops, now writhed, moaning and sweating in agony. Her husband, the brave sergeant, raved, delirious from a seeping sabre cut to his brow. La Touche, who with his officer could have navigated the *Medusa* to Senegal, drifted in and out of consciousness, his suppurating limb so gangrenous that not even the good doctor could bring himself to tend the wound.

That the sliding seas should be their tombs—

There was a clatter of hooves along the drive. From the window, Géricault was surprised to see Alexandrine's carriage, great clouds of dust rolling in its wake. He had received no word and not found the time to write or send flowers. Now the horses had been driven hard and froths of sweat stained their flanks.

Géricault opened the door and Alexandrine stood before him. He noticed dark hollows beneath her eyes. Her face was gaunt and strained.

She stared at Géricault in silence, before giving the maid her bribe and stepping inside.

He was shocked by her pallor. Yes, he'd neglected her, to be sure. He took her hands in his. 'Alexandrine,' he whispered, 'are you unwell?'

She looked at him with a sad, defeated air. He prayed she had not arrived to make another scene.

'I've come to tell you that I intend to visit my cousin in Versailles. I'll be away for a month at the very least. As you know I find the heat in Paris trying at this time of the year.'

She gave him a wry smile. 'So now you can devote yourself to this great composition without any interruption.'

To his shame, Géricault felt a flooding sense of relief. He was free to paint at last. And when she returned, surely she'd understand they could not go on as they were.

Despite himself, he appraised her beauty. Longed to hold her, light as a child, and savour her just one last time.

Alexandrine glanced around the studio and when her

eyes rested on the unfinished portrait, she blinked for a moment.

'Farewell, Théo,' she murmured.

He was not prepared for such haughty indifference, for the way she stood there so aloof and imperial. How dare she treat him like this? He studied her. Unless—the sudden realisation brought bile to his throat. So their secret was out!

He had known all along this moment would come. He imagined his father sitting at a desk, sifting through his papers, and Caruel striding in with the news, enraged, betrayed, demanding an answer. Scandal. Already he could hear the whispered gossip, the sudden silence whenever he walked into a crowded room.

'Favourite nephew too, poor man, what can he be going through?'

'Always thought Madame Caruel something of a hussy.'

'Refused to go into the family business, fancied himself as an artist but never said no to his uncle's money.'

With effort Géricault tried to quell the clamour in his mind.

'Tell me,' he cried, 'how did Caruel find out?'

Alexandrine shook her head. Tears began to course her cheeks.

She allowed him to lead her to a seat by the window where she sank down and buried her face in her hands, her entire body convulsed with sobs. 'Oh, Théo,' she whispered. 'I've no idea where to begin.'

He kneeled at Alexandrine's feet and tried to make her look at him.

When at last she spoke, her voice was low, almost inaudible.

'Yesterday, in despair, I went to the market herb seller and requested a certain potion. But, feeling my belly, the old woman shook her head, saying I'd left it too late for such a remedy.'

She pressed the tips of her fingers against her temples as if warding off pain. 'And Caruel, poor old man, the impotent cuckold we've made him, who only managed to consummate our marriage once, on our wedding night—it's not his child I carry.'

The word sliced through Géricault like a knife. He stared at his mistress, shocked to the core. She carried their child. He'd been careless and could not remember when he had last taken her in a sheath of catgut, for the unwieldy prophylactic had always seemed cheap and shabby as if she were a young model he had bought for a couple of sous. So this was how it ended, a scandal beyond his wildest imagining.

He began to pace the room, his mind racing. What to do? Alexandrine continued to tell him in breathless whispers that she must leave for Versailles, that Caruel was growing more suspicious by the day, and as for his housekeeper, the way she looked at her, she was certain the woman knew. Why, the other morning she had found her skulking by the door when she came out of the privy. And she didn't trust Louisette, although no one would pay attention to a maid's slanderous lies.

Géricault wanted to stopper his ears against this profane confessional. Surely, they'd announce their love and elope. They had committed no crime. They were children of the Revolution. No rules bound them now.

Instead he remained silent, aware of a cowardly shrinking in his soul.

He found Alexandrine studying him as if trying to read his mind.

'I should explain,' she said. 'There's a convent in Versailles where the nuns are renowned for receiving unfortunates like myself.'

'No,' Géricault exclaimed. 'We'll leave for Rome tonight. Then you will be free at last.'

There, he had said it. Yet the thought of abandoning his canvases filled him with a dread of the future so profound that it took away his breath. He could not imagine such an existence, the two of them exiled, disgraced, and one day hearing that Horace had reached the very height of his powers.

Alexandrine had wiped away her tears and her cheeks were flushed and swollen.

'What makes you think that you can set me free?' she said. She sat still and very straight, her hands clasped in her lap.

At the sight of that expressionless face, Géricault felt he would burst out with a nameless fury, commit some terrible violence towards her, but he mastered himself, swallowing and breathing deeply.

Alexandrine looked up at him, her huge dark eyes holding him steady in her gaze.

'When in a month my confinement becomes visible to all,' she declared in a cold hard voice he did not recognise, 'I have decided to retire behind the convent walls.'

Géricault felt a swirling in his head, a dryness in his mouth like an onset of fever.

'No, I'll not allow it.' He was aware of a strange sense of detachment as if he were reciting lines from some play, a monstrous theatrical with no idea of how it would end.

'Not allow it?' Alexandrine laughed out loud. The sound terrified him.

'What presumption, Théo. What self-deception. What makes you think I would choose a life with you in Rome, and suffer your pity and indifference?'

'You don't know what you're saying.'

Géricault found himself holding her tightly by the wrists as if she might strike him.

'Oh yes, I do,' Alexandrine replied, snatching away her hands. 'I've made my choice and found *freedom* at last.' She rose to her feet, white faced and trembling.

Who is this woman, he thought, who stood stern and unforgiving like a judgement before him? Where was his mistress with her pouting charm and pretty ways, the Alexandrine who once loved him?

She was staring at him pityingly.

'Caruel is a proud man and fearful of gossip that might damage his reputation. He'll silence all rumours with money and lies. I doubt there will be much of a scandal.'

Géricault flushed in anger and shame. Alexandrine, he wanted to say, don't punish me like this. And it struck him how little he had considered Alexandrine and Caruel as husband and wife, the years they had spent together. He tried to imagine their lives, the conversations they might have had, the walks they'd enjoyed, the countless evenings—she seated prettily at a harpsichord, he listening with rapt attention by the fire—and found it impossible to conjure one single image of them at all. His aunt had always been his mistress, his uncle the benefactor he had deceived. Alexandrine equalled lust, his uncle guilt and betrayal. That was how it had always been.

A great sense of helplessness overwhelmed him. Now Alexandrine had turned on her heel and was striding towards the door.

She paused on the threshold and looked back at him.

'Yesterday,' she announced, 'a gypsy woman came to the house and I asked her to divine the sex of my child with an emerald pendant, the one you gave me. When she swung the jewel back and forth above my belly, she pronounced a boy. I shall call him Hippolyte.'

And without another word, she hurried up the drive, the maid at her side.

Géricault could not bear watching her go.

A son, she carried their son. She had even given him a name—he imagined a boy, bowling his hoop across the lawn, the joyous sound of his laughter ringing through the grounds, and Alexandrine in the shade of the chestnut trees gazing lovingly his way, perhaps another baby held tight in her arms. And he—Géricault glanced at his canvases.

He rushed to the open window. 'Alexandrine!' he called. But already the carriage was retreating fast.

An image came to him of Alexandrine, a sombre figure dressed in black like a woman in mourning, walking along a wide gravelled path flanked with high hedges of yew and privet towards the convent, where on the granite steps a nun stood waiting, her habit and veil blowing out like dark plumes of smoke.

How savage he'd made the swell, how dark the parting waves and that murderous granite sky pressing down, pressing down. Alexandrine would have survived on the raft.

HE COULD NOT QUITE believe that Alexandrine had gone from him forever, that the passion of their affair in which he had floundered for so many years was finally spent. He felt himself stir for her then. He went over to the side table and poured himself a glass of brandy.

A rush of desolation swept over him, a keening force he had never felt before. He'd hoped for something he had not found in Alexandrine and might never know. Would he ever discover it, or would he end his days like his uncle, an old man clinging to beauty out of sheer vanity and loneliness?

Géricault drained his glass and shuddered at the thought. He was suffocating here, and he craved air and light. Studies of cadavers everywhere he looked, strewn on the model stand and across the floor—men gnawing hanks of rotten flesh, the torn and amputated limbs of the dead.

He needed to ride his horse at a wild gallop without any purpose or destination, only to keep moving, moving, and not think any more.

Hurriedly he threw some clothes in a travelling bag and crossed the courtyard, calling for the groom to saddle his horse.

~

From the rose garden, Savigny and Corréard glanced up in surprise as he cantered past.

Ah, the sheer beauty of the open fields and meadows, the corn and barley stooks ranged in burnished rows. A hawk hovered high in the blue windy sky. The grass verges glinted bronze and red beneath the sun.

With a jolt it occurred to Géricault that he and Alexandrine had never strolled the laneways, with their scent of hawthorn and elderflower, never lain like sweethearts among the buttercup gleam of the meadows. Always they'd been enclosed in darkened rooms, feverish and whispering behind locked doors.

Alexandrine's voice still rang in his ears, rained on him like pebbles against glass, breaking up his world.

Only one thought pounded in his mind, insistent as a metronome—she carried their child—she carried their child—the same maddening tempo as his horse at full gallop.

Géricault urged his horse faster.

The stallion raced along the wide rutted road. He was kicking up great clods of earth, enjoying the broad sweep at the curve of a river. At the next bend, a nesting swan rose from the reeds, beating the air with her wings. Rushing out, she darted her serpent neck before them and hissed with all her might. At the sight of the creature, the horse reared, flailing the air. The strength of his hooves was enough to kill a man. Instinctively Géricault held on. Supple as a jockey, he adjusted his balance, bearing all his weight on the reins against his mount's wild bucking leap.

Finally he brought the horse to a trembling standstill, every muscle twitching across its flanks. White-lipped, Géricault sat without moving in the saddle.

He ran one hand along the stallion's neck. The horse pricked up its ears and shifted from hoof to hoof as if finding a way to restore their equilibrium. Géricault lowered his heels in the stirrups. The horse walked on.

Alexandrine must hate me, he thought, and before she dies she will show me how much she hates me. Day after day, year after year, her silence behind those walls will shrill in my ears without end.

Again a deep sense of longing descended on him like a hunger—there had been a time when he had deluded himself into believing that he loved her, but he knew he had not. And this pained him more than having any lover wrenched from his heart.

Dusk was gathering and the dark shadows of the trees closed in on him, became menacing.

Towards midnight, Géricault stopped at a coaching inn. Numb with fatigue, he dismounted and handed his horse to a young boy who appeared with a lantern from the stables. The stallion gave a broken sigh when the youth led him away.

Gales of laughter greeted Géricault as he walked with a heavy tread towards the tavern. Like an outcast, he peered through the window. Groups of journeymen, merchants and pedlars crowded the long trestle tables strewn with pewter platters and jugs of ale. Everyone seemed to eat and drink and swap stories without a care in the world. As if there could be no end to their riotous gaiety, no presentiment of a vengeful Noah or of flood tides, no apocalypse in sight. Géricault felt he had trespassed and would soon cast a pall on this place of merriment and light.

At the far end of the room, a young gypsy girl held a fiddle tight to her chin and tapped one foot to the quickening rhythms of the refrain. Géricault noticed other women among the crowd, laughing with their mouths full and wiping grease from their lips, leaning towards their companions, bawdy and lascivious and showing off plump cleavages in anticipation of the night to come. The sight sickened him. Yet he also yearned for the comfort of soft rolls of flesh, the dimpled slabs of their buttocks and thighs. Knew he would find consolation in pendulous blue-veined breasts.

When he opened the door, the saloon rang with the stamping of feet and a ragged chorus tackling some rough tavern song.

Géricault made his way to a trestle table. The knot of people gathered there made room for him as he sat down.

He called to a boy darting up and down with trays to bring him a jug of wine. The gypsy swung and leaped at her fiddle and, arms linked, a ragged mob danced and jigged round and around in spinning circles. Géricault drank steadily without enjoyment. At the head of the table was one of the women he had seen through the window, a mass of red hair piled in coils on her head, her breasts heaving against her gown.

When she laughed, he noticed her teeth were white and sharp and even. He filled and refilled his glass, unable to take his eyes from the rise and fall of this woman's cleavage.

Again he called for the boy to fetch a round—this time for everyone—and when the jugs arrived, the entire table cheered and clapped. The woman darted him an appraising, insolent glance and lifted her tumbler.

Géricault relished the flush which the wine and the heat of the room brought to the woman's skin. For all her wide girth, she had a fine-featured face. He admired the dimple at the chin, the mole on her upper lip.

The dancing seemed to quicken in a roaring kaleido-scope of colour to the music's frenzied rhythms. The woman pushed back her chair and strolled his way. She put one arm around him and leaned forward, saying something, which he could not hear above the din. Géricault reached for her and buried his face against her gown. He nuzzled those breasts, revelling in their warmth, their fleshy scent. His hand searched beneath the rucked folds of her skirts and roamed the plump, supple thighs—she was dimpled at the knees and buttocks, just as he had imagined.

The woman brushed his mouth with her lips. 'You have a cheeky touch,' she whispered. Somehow Géricault managed to heave himself to his feet and follow the woman through the crowds. She led the way into the darkness, up the creaking stairs onto some dank landing, and finally ushered him into a room no larger than a linen closet, partitioned by a musty felt curtain.

She lit a candle, and Géricault watched her step out of her clothes, flinging her garments aside. The candlelight flickered over her breasts, the vast smooth dome of her belly. She was magnificent, standing there naked. He knelt before her, his hands reaching for the rough puckered nipples, while she splayed those colossal legs.

Again and again he took her with a ferocity that snatched away his breath, plying her limbs this way and that. There was no need for whispered endearments or words of passion and love, no need to teach her where his pleasure might be arrived at. Instead he surrendered himself to the rolling heave of such mountainous flesh, fierce and elemental as the ocean itself.

Géricault woke to a lurid dawn light and a stranger at his side. His skin itched with bedbug bites. He sat up, his head pounding. The woman turned over in her sleep, dragging away the sheets. Her lank red hair fell across the pillow and, with a shiver of disgust, Géricault noticed lice teeming her scalp.

Jumping to his feet, he hurriedly dressed, trying to quell the nauseous taste of stale wine in his throat. He threw several coins on the table and stealthily made his way down the stairs.

He stumbled outside and called for his horse. He could not face the long ride home, nor for his guests to see him dishevelled, the worse for drink like this.

Géricault imagined Alexandrine as she would be in a month—kneeling penitent, contrite, making her peace with God. A cold stone chapel, shafts of light slanting through stained glass. And his uncle, who would soon learn of his betrayal, pacing the cavernous rooms of some country estate, the sheets covering the furniture like shrouds. By Christ, he murmured, what have I done?

Wearily he mounted his horse, which whinnied, gently sidestepping beneath his weight.

He longed to march along a beach against a bracing wind and feel the salt tang on his skin. All at once it struck him, he would ride on to Le Havre. He needed ocean air to cleanse his soul.

Again Géricault urged his stallion into a gallop, and swiftly the ripened fields flashed by. The leaves of the poplars rustled and quivered and now a stand of oaks thick with dark green foliage and the slate rooves of a hamlet nestled in the valley below, until at last there were church spires and an oyster glimmer of open sea against light grey skies. Briskly his horse trotted through the narrow cobbled streets.

Géricault left him at the stables of a boarding house and strode along the esplanade. He barely glanced at the pretty women promenading back and forth beneath the shade of their parasols.

His boots crunched against flat level sands stretching in a wide curve as far as the eye could see. As he strolled towards the shoreline, gulls rose in a shrieking flock, sheered away in a sweep of the wind and settled several metres away once again. It was a high sea today. Green rollers crashed at his feet, rinsing a bubbling tide line of pebbles and shells.

Géricault picked up a worn flat stone and threw it past the thunderous swell. It skimmed once, twice, before disappearing beneath another swallowing wave. Such savagery in the ocean's spume-flecked flanks. No mercy there, should he choose to swim. He passed an abandoned sandcastle still bearing a tattered flag, water swirling through the sinking channels of a moat. A cormorant, wings outstretched, rested still as a statue on a knotted length of bleached-blond driftwood. He would love to live here at the fierce extremities of this salt-sprayed rim of earth, the only vegetation coarse sea grass and gorse stunted by gales, away from his uncle and the prying eyes of Montmartre.

Géricault wheeled round at a sudden sound of laughter. A woman was calling to her child, who raced towards him flying a kite, which looped in the breeze, its scarlet tail whipping in the wind. Seeing a figure standing so still at the shoreline, the boy stopped dead in his tracks. Géricault could not bear to look at the child's face, his bright bold eyes staring up at him as the kite soared from the string held tight in his hands. Nor did he allow himself to glance at the mother, who had caught up with her son and in a light teasing voice began to scold him for running too close when the tide was about to turn. Giving them a curt nod, Géricault walked on.

He had learned Savigny's and Corréard's lesson well. If there is anything certain on earth, he thought, it's our pain. Only suffering is real. As for the rest of the spectacle, it's a mere vignette.

He followed a track scored with the web-footed prints of terns, leading to a desolate shingled beach south from town.

All afternoon Géricault anatomised the ocean, the calm ribbed expanse welling the horizon. He studied the luminous sheen, tricks of light winking through the wrinkled ripples of its pelt. He listened to its song, deep rushing sounds, the sharp rattle of pebbles sluiced and tumbled by the waves and the sudden silence exhaled like a gasp after each stinging slap of spume. When a cloud drifted like a dark rag against the skies, he was graced with a rainbow forming for one shining moment a perfect arc above the sea. Such colours there, lapis lazuli, turquoise, magenta, a brief and exquisite flare of crimson and the purest of greens that he would have sold his soul to smear on his palette.

And then in a burst of radiance, it was gone. For hours he watched the day change to evening. The sky dark as bitumen streaked with granite clouds towards the horizon. A group of women waded among the shallows, gathering cockles and whelks.

Géricault drew his cloak against the evening chill. Dusk, the witching hour, nightfall, when the crazed dreams of survivors began to stir and stalk, with whispers and the glint of a sharpened knife. He mourned his *cantinière* lowered into a watery grave, the currents plucking her red flannel pinafore, weighing the hem of a blue cambric gown. Down she went, sinking into the shimmering shafts of the deep, her plaited hair flowing loose, spreading out in long pale strands like whip weed. He mourned La Touche who must in gratitude have grasped Savigny's hand when the good doctor leaned forward, to slit his throat with a scalpel.

A roaring wave smashed in a great white line of froth and soaked the tips of his boots. Géricault thought of the raft blown on buffeting tides. He marvelled at the endurance of these men.

When Géricault returned to his lodgings, he ordered a servant to bring a flagon of brandy to his room. Outside, a thin slanting rain began to pockmark the sands, sending the crowds scattering from the promenade. Beyond the headland, a frigate heeled in the wind, the sails beating against the spars.

All night Géricault's thoughts returned to Alexandrine and their unborn child. His hands trembled each time he filled the brandy glass. Sometimes, if he allowed it, the sense of isolation overwhelmed him, became frightful. He told himself not to give in to self-pity. The walls spun and whirled, like the raft rushing against another crest of a racing wave and with a sickening lurch sliding down again.

At dawn, Géricault knew what had to be done. Lighting a candle, he filled the washstand with water and gazed at his reflection in the mirror.

He now saw a hard cruel face he no longer recognised, with a sullen suspicious expression, as if he were a common thief, one hand pilfering the moneybox, the other blotting the ledger. Someone you could not trust. Shadows beneath heavy-lidded eyes that stared back defiant—a libertine in the full queasy glare of an early morning sun.

He shook out the thick tresses that Alexandrine had so admired and, seizing a pair of scissors, began to snip and cut until heavy curls fell softly around his feet. He dipped his razor in soap.

There, it is done, he said aloud, staring at his shaved head in the mirror, proof that he would renounce all society, friends, and pleasure of any sort, until he had completed his tableau.

He too would incarcerate himself behind thick stone walls. Never venture outside except for the purposes of work.

How the world would shrink, the vaulting skies no more than skeins of light sliding beneath a closed door, between shutters, a barred grate. Géricault shuddered at the thought.

Montmartre

———

September 1818

WHEN GÉRICAULT RODE through the driveway of his house in Montmartre, every sinew in his body aching from the long ride from Le Havre, he found Savigny and Corréard playing cards on the terrace. They hailed him with a cheery wave. His guests seemed full of vigour and health, sleek and contented as a couple of cats, whereas he—his complexion sallow, a brandy flask now his only source of strength—what had he become? He was wearing a tasselled Greek cap over his bald scalp, and Savigny and Corréard stared at him strangely as he passed.

'Welcome home,' Savigny called. 'We thought you had abandoned us for the delights of town.'

Wearily Géricault dismounted and told his guests he would like to see them in the studio within the hour.

Hurrying across the courtyard, the groom *tut-tutted* at the state of the horse, sweat-drenched, his head bowed, whinnying softly through his nostrils.

'Ridden him hard, sir,' the groom muttered, darting Géricault a disapproving glance.

'And he's not the only one,' Savigny declared. 'For you, my friend, look as if you've been carousing until the small hours.'

Géricault flinched from the intensity of that gaze. Now Savigny was contemplating his Greek cap.

'Good Lord!' he exclaimed. 'What on earth have you done?' He nudged his companion. But Corréard barely looked up from his game.

The thought flashed through Géricault's mind that he should seize this moment to confess the whole truth and lay his soul bare. Let Savigny and Corréard, these shipwreck survivors, be the judge of his sins. They, who presided over the mercy killings and tipped the corpses of the sick over the side. Ah, the relief in it—for how petty his crimes in comparison and how swift the redemption that would come.

And when he had completed his confession, Savigny would swirl wine round and around his glass and study Géricault with an amused expression. 'So you indulged in a dalliance with your aunt,' he would say. 'Why, I don't blame you, for she's a remarkably beautiful woman, although shame about the child. But mark my words, no harm will come of it. I'm sure your uncle is a solid sensible man and bound to take this in his stride.'

And just as he had done, his guests now would try to tease out the story from the first seduction to the inevitable end, and unlike them he would recount in every detail each lingering caress, the warmth of her flesh beneath his touch, the scent of her skin.

Thinking out this scenario, it occurred to Géricault that having reached the final act in this narrative of illicit love, the denouement of a doomed pastoral romance, he now required an audience. He imagined himself on stage, the women weeping into their handkerchiefs at Alexandrine's cruel fate, denouncing him as a monster, nothing but a cad; the men silent and sympathetic—what a fool, they would never have let matters get so out of hand—but with a grudging admiration always on his side.

Yes, Géricault was tempted to confide, but he did not want his guests to see him reduced, cleaved in half like this. Just one word, one enquiry about his aunt, and he'd be undone.

And with a pang, he realised they were all burdened with their own eyewitness accounts, burning to tell the truth yet shamed by the outcome. Heroes or villains, survivors or victims—in which category, he asked himself, did he belong?

How easily he could fabricate his own version of events and set his conscience at rest—Alexandrine the schemer, who had married Caruel for his money, the family wealth. And not content with that had seduced her young nephew and tempted him from his true calling with the wiles of a courtesan, some vile siren's song. No choice in the matter. There, it was done. Alexandrine, her lovely hair cropped close to her head, would lower her eyes as the nun fitted the wimple and fastened it tight beneath her chin.

With effort Géricault rolled up every sketch and painting of Alexandrine in the studio, including the last commission, their allegory of illicit love, which he stacked beneath the divan. There they would gather lint and dust. He knew he would never find the courage to gaze again on the mistress who had chosen to live behind convent walls.

Then he waited for his guests to arrive. When he saw by the timepiece they were fifteen minutes late, Géricault began to compile a list, as a means of focusing his mind.

He would *not* paint the following:

One—the abandonment of the raft, the towropes cast over the side. Politically charged, contemporary and ensnared in the moment of the times. Melodramatic too, perhaps something to do with the Captain's theatrical moustache.

Two—the first carnage, or the mutiny: incoherent, chaotic, men up to their waists in water, no visible structure of the raft. No real sense of who is defending whom, just an avalanche of men kicking, thrashing, biting. He had struggled with these themes too long. Perhaps they were best suited to another form.

Three—cannibalism. Taboo subject, sensational and obscene. Too hard to elucidate. Some subtler literary analogy might work.

Four—the mercy killings. Again, confusion in the scene. Is the good doctor Savigny giving orders for the dead to be thrown over the side? Or are those slumped figures still alive? This scene required an opinion, a stance, a particular side. He was an artist, not a judge or a journalist penning some outraged editorial for the *Journal des Débats*.

Five . . .

Still he waited for his guests to arrive. Géricault reached for the brandy flask. Only one month before his uncle would find out, yet Savigny and Corréard were wasting each precious hour. He took a bitter sip, followed by another. It was a matter of adhering to a strict routine, he told himself. Even if he had to keep his guests under lock and key, he would hear their story out.

Outside, the chestnut trees were turning yellow and russet in the wilting afternoon heat. Autumn—Géricault could smell it in the scent of withered lilac drifting through the window, the sharp tang of burnt stubble from the cornfields. It was only the beginning of September and soon the season of swallows would be gone.

He thought of the creature gradually unfurling in Alexandrine's womb, the steady drum of its heartbeat, blood pumping its veins. Their child, the boy she would call

Hippolyte, an avenging angel bringing destruction and scandal. Seeing Savigny and Corréard dawdle across the lawns, Géricault slammed his fist against the casement.

IT WAS A PROBLEM of scale, Géricault decided that evening, studying the canvas. One day—the men on the raft knew not which, for they had long lost count of time—a white butterfly had fluttered from the skies and flickered against the sun before alighting on a sail.

Seated in the rose garden, Savigny had insisted it was he who had first clapped eyes on the celestial creature.

'How the light gilded the thin, veined membrane of its wings,' he said. 'But of course, no longer trusting the faculties of my mind, I dismissed the vision as a fanciful dream.'

A cloud of common cabbage whites darted among the buddleia and gathered in a shimmering halo above Savigny's head.

'All at once, I heard a shout,' he continued. 'Corréard too pointed in the same direction. And there it was again, so pure and still, from another world, a universe splendid and divine, not this floating hell infested with dying men.'

Leaning forward, Corréard watched a butterfly hover about the scented blooms until it settled on a petal's crimson rim. When it rose in a dizzying flight, he trapped the insect between cupped hands. Géricault could hear the frenzied whir of wings against his palms.

'There was talk among the men,' Corréard whispered, 'that we should devour this delicate morsel, so desperate had they become.'

Géricault watched Corréard's lips graze the tips of his fingers. The image repelled him. He knew he would feel better if it was cooler, but the air was heavy with heat and the sweet pungent odour of roses. Still he could hear the frantic simmer of the insect held in Corréard's hands.

Registering his expression, Savigny laughed and told him they swore the butterfly could be none other than a sign bringing news of a speedy approach to land. They'd no more harm its sanctity than sailors would snare and pin the wings of an albatross skimming the waves across storm-tossed seas.

Corréard threw up his arms and released his captive, which skittered away in a crazed fluttering dance. Géricault felt a tight spasm of pain constrict his chest. He could scarcely breathe. He had not had a decent night's sleep since he left for Le Havre and he wondered if a dose of laudanum would cauterise Alexandrine from his mind. And that creature swelling like a tick in her belly.

The following day, Savigny continued, and the one after that, the men on the raft witnessed several more of these butterflies seeking respite on the slack sail.

Sometimes but not often a large seabird wheeled against the skies, effortlessly borne on swift air currents. Then the men on the raft mourned their becalmed listless state and envied that creature carrying a map of the world beneath its gaze.

It was a question of scale, Géricault thought once again, examining his canvas, the raft cumbersome, the butterfly too slight, a mere speck on a vast expanse of sail. Entranced, the men gazed skywards and pointed to the heavens, but at what exactly? It was impossible to tell. Unless he used a sea eagle racing towards them, a glimpse of desert sands reflected in golden eyes. No, it wouldn't do either. He might as well paint Noah's dove sanctimonious and sentimental, cooing smug songs of forgiveness and redemption.

Moths beat against the lamps. Outside, the night was still warm, with a glimmer of moonlight through the trees. Horace's house seemed strangely quiet. Géricault pictured his guests at the theatre, squinting through their opera glasses, enraptured with Thérèse.

That night he intended to sleep, and he unwrapped the parcel Biett, his physician, had delivered.

With care he set the laudanum phial on the table among his piles of sketches, empty wine bottles and bladders of paint.

He poured a draught and drained it in one, drowning the bitter taste with a deep swig of brandy. The effect was immediate. All his tension and fear of the future dissolved.

Géricault felt he could spread his wings and fly high into the starless sky where the clouds piled thick and still and silent, where he would soar on the back of the wind and escape from his uncle and the approaching scandal.

When he lay down on the raft, strange images began to flicker across his mind.

Thérèse appeared in a dazzling vision, diamonds flashing at her throat. She danced around the bed, clicking a pair of castanets until his head pounded and he had to beg her to stop. For a long time, Savigny sat at his side. Blood leaked from a wide, red-raw gash to his brow. 'Is there no apothecary to attend to you?' Géricault cried out. But he received no answer and when he opened his eyes Savigny had gone.

At dawn, Alexandrine glided towards him stealthy and silent as a cat.

Géricault stroked the swollen dome of her belly and listened to the vibrant pulse of his child. Alexandrine stared down at him and smiled. Remote as a Madonna, a painted figurine wreathed with incense and flowers. Someone he could worship but no longer touch.

'He kicked just now,' she whispered. 'Like a kitten beneath a rug.' And leaning close, she laughed.

THE FOLLOWING DAY, Géricault found himself sketching a rapid pen-and-ink study of an old man cradling the body of a youth.

He had woken with a dull throb behind his eyes and a stale taste on his tongue. Perhaps, he reflected, he would have to take more than the four drops Biett had prescribed.

He turned again to his study and tried to concentrate.

Again he sketched the man quickly at the bottom of the page, more of a scribble, the details vague and irresolute. The figure leaned forward, his elbow against one knee, a fist propped beneath his chin. The folds of a head cloth spilled over his shoulders. His right arm pulled the corpse against him. The boy lolled senseless in his lap, legs splayed, his feet dangling over the edge of the raft.

Even in this loose improvisation, Géricault could discern a wise and noble face, a brow crowned with grey leonine curls. Stern, something of the prophet in him, Moses on the Mount full of moralising rhetoric.

Except, Géricault found, he had drawn the eyes expressionless, past blame, reproach or suffering even, past life itself. Is that it? he thought. What it would be like for

Alexandrine, behind bolted doors in a convent cell? What it was like for the woman in the hospital, sheets tousled at her throat? No redemption there from God or triumphant cherubs soaring on angel wings. He focused on each detail and enlarged those hollow eyes. Could that be death? And the youth clutched in the man's arms, his son perhaps? The corpse which dawn delivered and they devoured?

When Géricault drew the boy, he amputated his limbs at the thighs.

Then fasting had more power than grief.

Where had that line come from? he asked himself. Slipped straight into his mind like a slogan, a newspaper headline. And then, of course, he remembered, *Divine Comedy*, Canto XXXIII, Count Ugolino starving among his dying children in the Pisan Tower.

Then fasting had more power than grief. Except for Ugolino, day after day gnawing his knuckles to the bone, surrounded by dead flesh.

There he died; and even as thou seest me, saw I the three fall one by one, between the fifth day and the sixth; Whence I betook me already blind, to groping over each, and for three days called them after they were dead; then fasting had more power than grief.

Then it struck him—the father and son would provide the corner stone to his composition. An allegory more powerful than the actual act itself, which when literally portrayed lost all impact and meaning, became instead a pantomime of men and the vile scraps of their repast, a foot, an arm, obscene doodles from a caricature.

Again Géricault studied the sketch of the boy. Delacroix, he would be perfect. Lean as a whippet, he would not have lasted long on that raft. And all at once Géricault saw the raft at the forefront, the planks nudging an ornate gilt frame as if the viewer were standing up to his waist in swell. And the father? Quick as a flash it occurred to him, his tutor, Carle Vernet, holding the viewer in his gaze.

'Very clever.'

Startled, Gericault turned to find Horace standing behind him.

'So we channel the sensational, the unmentionable, through one of our favourite stories in romantic poetry. No one can mistake the figures, the father a very emblem of paternal grief crouched over his child, poised to devour the flesh. Much better than your earlier efforts. Although I doubt your guests will be pleased.'

Taking off his hat, Horace bowed and cleared his throat. He adopted a theatrical stance.

'*Remember Ugolino condescends,*' he began to recite,
'*To eat the head of his arch-enemy,*
The moment after he politely ends his tale;
If foes be food in hell, at sea
Tis surely fair to dine upon our friends,
When Shipwreck's short allowance grows too scanty
Without being much more horrible than Dante.'

Horace clapped his hands and laughed.

'Where did you come across such verse?' Géricault was outraged at the intrusion. He would have to speak with Horace, tell him he could no longer tolerate these interruptions.

'An English poet,' Horace replied. 'His name is Byron, although I doubt you've heard of him. But I'm sure he has heard of the *Medusa* for he slipped this shipwreck stanza into his epic narrative, *Don Juan.* It's become very popular. You should stay in touch and read more, my friend.'

Now Horace was staring at the Greek cap pulled low on Géricault's head.

'If you don't mind me saying so,' he eyed Géricault up

and down, 'I'm not sure what you're trying to achieve, but you look rather ridiculous.'

Before Géricault could think of a reply, Horace strolled across the room and began to flick through one of Géricault's sketchbooks. 'Let me give you some suggestions, or points of reference, rather.' He snapped the book shut and riffled through another. 'I would study Guérin's *Marcus Sextus*. Examine the anguish etched in that noble face, our Roman hero who, returning from exile, finds his wife dead. Remember how vividly those sorrowful eyes, the furrowed brow, impressed themselves on our young imaginations. Nor is it impossible to overlook the resemblance of this father to the despairing soul flailing among the bodies in Gros's *Plague Hospital at Jaffa*, a hellish place that corresponds to the raft.'

He smiled. 'As for the son, quote liberally from paintings by Guérin, Girodet and Prud'hon and you will find an interesting convergence on the themes of suffering and death.'

'This group will be the only one turned directly towards the viewer,' Géricault declared despite himself. He must not encourage him. Next thing, Horace would be helping himself to the brandy. 'Unconventional, I admit,' he continued however. 'Offering a prelude to the drama unfolding on the raft, a first chorus to the narrative in which the spectator is about to become involved. It's a bold idea, but hopefully I can pull it off.'

When Horace finally took his leave, Géricault cursed him for wasting his time. Damn Prud'hon and Girodet, the Vernets' smug clique of friends. In order to execute a composition of this father and son, he must *study the dead*—touch and examine the very texture of their flesh, observe how they appeared and smelled.

If he could not lure Savigny and Corréard to pose for him, he would make do instead with dead companions. He decided to drive to the prison morgue.

~

As he began the steep descent of the hill, the still humid streets shimmered like a mirage. For September, the heat had become intolerable. When he reached the Palais-Royal, even the river seemed to have sunk lower on her mud flat haunches and leaves dropped with a languid flutter from the sycamore trees. Géricault pressed on through a labyrinth of cobbled lanes until at last he reached a sentry box, at forbidding iron gates. The soldier on guard dozed in the shade and only opened one eye when Géricault explained his business: he, gentleman artist and anatomist, required access to the morgue. The soldier darted him a sardonic look.

'Been a long time since one of your lot came through.' He yawned and flicked a fly from his brow. 'Times have changed, I suppose. Too busy on royalty instead of corpses. I tell you, in the Emperor's time, we were hard pressed to keep up.' He laughed.

Géricault smiled politely and waited for him to issue the pass. The gates clanked open and he led the horse into a wide courtyard. All around, granite walls rose sheer and wide, mere slits for windows. A face appeared behind one of the barred grates and darted away again. Géricault thought of Alexandrine soon in some cold sunless cell. He couldn't imagine the horror of being incarcerated in such a place. Even his horse sensed the atmosphere of despair and flattened his ears.

He left him with a groom at the stables and the creature whinnied watching him go.

Géricault walked through an arched passageway leading to a churchyard with a long low building at one end. When he knocked on the thick oak door, a pair of eyes blinked at him through the grille. Again he explained his business, and showed his pass. Slowly the door creaked open. He stepped inside. Dim flares lit the vaulted walls.

A putrid odour lingered in the musty air. Géricault clamped a handkerchief to his mouth.

His guide, the mortician of this charnel house, stomped ahead, boots echoing against the bare flagstones. In the half-shadows, Géricault could make out trestle tables ranged in rows along the walls.

The man marched up to one and ripped away a coarse linen sheet, stained and soiled in places.

Géricault forced himself to look at her. So this was death, he thought, cold and motionless as a waxwork.

Although the skin was puffed and bloated, the lips stretched tight in a rictal grimace, she would have been as beautiful and desirable as the models of Pigalle—far too young and slender for his *cantinière*.

'Died of the pox, that one,' his guide muttered. He covered her face once again. 'If no one comes for her by tonight, she'll be heaved into the paupers' graveyard and covered in lime.'

Géricault placed a coin in the man's hand. 'Take this,' he said, 'for a winding sheet.'

The man pocketed the money with a sly grin.

'Now, over here—' he declared, striding to the next table— 'I have the very thing, a brace of conspirators against the King, fresh from the perch. They were executed this morning at dawn.'

Like a merchant now showing off his wares, he snatched the sheets with a theatrical flourish.

Géricault stared at them. Young men, one dark like himself, the other fair as Delacroix with tangled curly hair. Republicans who died for the cause. A thick crust of liver-coloured blood congealed at their throats. Their expressions bewildered and startled, their torsos tinged shades of green-grey, the skin coarsening like elephant hide. Life snuffed out. Where were the mothers of these men? he asked himself.

Who would wash and anoint their wounds with tears?

It was a wonder that Savigny and Corréard did not die like this, that they were not hauled to the tribunals by the King's spies. Horace should be made to look down at these men before he accepted another commission from the Comte d'Artois. Perhaps then he would find time to reflect on his former allegiance to Napoleon.

'And over here,' the mortician called. An old man with limbs tapered and sculpted as any saint.

'A kleptomaniac, died in his sleep.'

Ah, a peaceful death. Yes, a smile hovered about these lips. But no, he would not do, Géricault decided, an end far too serene for this tale of his.

He continued his tour of this gallery of death: courtesans, pickpockets, strumpets and procurers, the opium sellers and debtors piled pell-mell.

Some no older than ten, a young boy snatched by the scarlet fever, once renowned for his nimble hands and imploring beggar's eyes; a virgin bought by some Madame, unable to withstand the rough loveless passions of libertines.

Such suffering gathered here. Who to choose, who best illustrated his theme, the dead and dying on the raft?

When he took out his purse, the mortician gave him an eager glance.

Géricault told him he required the boy, the two decapitated male corpses and, over there, that sack of amputated limbs.

'They shall fetch a pretty price, sir.'

'It's of no consequence,' he said.

Contract concluded, Géricault watched as a couple of guards loaded the cadavers wrapped in rough hessian into a covered cart.

By late afternoon, when the grisly cargo arrived, Géricault helped the men heave the sacks into the studio. Once the guards had gone, a generous payment rattling in their pockets, Géricault unpeeled the sackcloth. Then he struggled to haul his models into place. He lifted the youth onto the raft and positioned him at the stern, for this would be the corpse cradled in the father's arms. He needed a pulley for the conspirators. They weighed so.

Géricault wrapped their heads each in a towel and arranged them near the parapet. He felt pleased with himself. At last he had succeeded in furnishing the raft. He crouched by the boy, gently turned him supine then prone and tried to stretch the mottled limbs this way and that.

Géricault imagined taking a knife in his hand and slicing a triangular flap from knee to groin.

It would be grey bloodless flesh of a quality you would not buy in a butcher's shop, but meat just the same, a lump of steak seared in a skillet. Yet Savigny and Corréard would have eaten their share raw. At the thought, Géricault fought a retch of bile in his throat.

The late-afternoon sun streamed through the shutters and cast fantastical shadows over the corpses on the raft. A fly circled the room, buzzed above the body of the boy and alighted on his thigh. Géricault brushed it away. The raw meat stench had already become unbearable. He was tempted to open a window but more flies would come in.

Even so, he knew he would have to discover the decay of the dead. He must calibrate in the most precise detail how long it took for flesh to wither from the bone. He had heard that carcasses spoiled quickly, within the first twelve hours.

Géricault rose to his feet and surveyed the carnage on the raft. 'Savigny,' he whispered, 'which one shall we keep, who will we tip over the side? The two soldiers over here or the boy cradled in that man's arms?'

He strode towards the parapet. Did he imagine it?—the corpse twitched, let out a breath like a faint sigh.

'Tell me, Savigny,' Géricault said now, standing alone in the twilight stillness of the room, swaying back and forth to the tilt of the waves. 'Which one shall we devour?'

Lightly he jumped from the raft. Not a sound from Horace's house. Out once again. He imagined Savigny and Corréard clinking champagne glasses beneath the glitter of countless chandeliers, whereas he, Théodore Géricault, had work to begin. And not the work of an *amateur*, this.

Steeling himself, Géricault took hold of the last sack containing the amputated limbs, which the men had unceremoniously dumped by the door. He sweated with the strain of heaving the load to the raft's stern. His fingers trembled and fumbled with the tight-knotted rope. Taking a deep breath, he ripped open the hessian—and choked on the bitter, putrefying vapour. How long had they been lying in the morgue?

Géricault cleared his sketches from the model stand and swept away the discarded paints. Snatching up the Oriental rug, he laid it carefully on the raised platform. He set down two candlesticks from the side table and lit them with a taper. Their sudden flare bathed the crimson fabric in a rich golden light. Géricault paused to admire the effect.

How, he wondered, to arrange this still life of his.

Pouring himself a tumbler of brandy, he contemplated the sack. The rank odour of rotting flesh rising from its mouth seemed to settle on him like a thick clammy fog, on his clothes, his skin, his tongue.

He drank the brandy in long greedy gulps.

Then, before he lost heart and found himself fleeing the studio, puking like a coward, Géricault upended the sack, disgorging a soft lifeless mound of carrion.

Where to begin with this scrapheap of mutilated sinew and bone? The limbs had been spliced and sliced with surgical precision and spread out for all to see on the anatomist's slab. He thought of the students craning forward, taking notes with sharpened quills so that they too would know the end and come away with death branded on their souls.

Finally, Géricault picked up a severed arm and one leg and placed them on the model stand. Amputated at the thigh, the leg was taut, muscular—taken from a young man. The arm, bandaged at the shoulder, had the slender wrist and hand of a woman. He moved the arm into a half embrace around the man's foot. There they lay as lovers would. So tender the pose. Géricault thrilled at the detail in the woman's forearm, the freckled skin downed with blonde hair. Her hand clasped the heel of the foot, her fingers followed the line of his toes, such intimacy in the caress.

Géricault knew he should quake from the horror of this scene but he willed himself to be strong. He would soon learn to study the colour of death textured as the finest marble and revel in the beauty of flesh pressed against flesh, no less remarkable than the shining fur of a freshly killed hare or the brindled plumage of a pheasant set beside an arrangement of pomegranates and pears. In time, he would paint them as they were and not betray his feelings with a sense of revulsion of any sort.

All evening Géricault outlined the calm sensual repose of those limbs enfolded and entwined. With a steady heart and eye, he anatomised every pore, the broad-rimmed nails ingrained with dirt on the woman's fingers, the tough leathered ridges on the man's sole. A youth, who once trod this earth with an eager stride and hopeful heart, so quiet he now lay.

Géricault worked until first light. With reluctance he put down his brushes. Outside, the mist-wreathed lawns were held in a perfect stillness. Géricault contemplated the corpses, their skin congealed like a soft purple bruise. He was tempted to keep them another day.

He scrubbed himself at the washstand and took a deep swig of brandy, before meeting his guests in the breakfast room.

ON THE TENTH DAY, fifteen men lay adrift on the raft beneath a cloudless sky, their thoughts circling like vultures, turning inwards, each contemplating their own death. Kneeling, they prayed, and Savigny distributed the last of the wine. Strangely they found themselves no longer oppressed by hunger or thirst. Perhaps their organs were closing down? Despite the scorched-desert sun, they shivered with cold. Not even the last wine taken drop by drop could warm their blood. Waves slapped against their feet. The planks creaked. The sail drooped about the mast. The bow dipped once again beneath slippery seas.

One of the soldiers, a captain of infantry, cried out, but no one heeded him, his fevered dream. Then another shout, from Lavillette this time: 'Over there, topmasts above the horizon.'

Savigny closed his eyes against their crazed delusions: *I see it plain, the harbour master's house at the mouth of the river; pinpricks of firelight ringing the coast. Seabirds, butterflies, harbingers of salvation.* Savigny drew his cloak about him and marvelled at the shortness of his life, barely thirty-one years, younger than Christ. He returned to the beginning, to his birth—delivered without a bruise from an expert midwife's hands, his mother's caress, the milk scent of her breasts. Then he remembered, as a child, marvelling at the flash of the guillotine's blade, the severed heads piling in wicker baskets like melons, and being devoured by a strange curiosity to study such a profusion of flesh. *Down with Robespierre and countless petty tyrants*—and the boy knew his calling. He, Henri Savigny, born to generations of tilemakers in Vernon, would become the finest doctor the nation ever had.

In the breakfast room, Géricault sketched him fast and furiously now.

Savigny had ignored their cries—*the topmasts loom larger. Why, the brig approaches.* He ignored the crazed scuffle on deck. Hoops wrenched from the cask, coloured handkerchiefs tied to a makeshift staff. A man, Corréard perhaps, pushed to the top of the mast so that he could wave a wretched bundle of rags, having squandered the last of the gunpowder and flares. *She comes close, now she recedes. Signal again. Wave with all your might, man! Hail the ship again.*

Géricault's pen spattered ink from the well and scratched across each page, desperate not to be left behind. The brig a mere speck on the horizon. The flags fluttered pitifully in the wind, the men strained forward, gesturing at the vast shifting expanse that separated them from salvation.

With a great welling of excitement, Géricault knew he had found his subject, at last—the first sighting of the *Argus*.

'You were among the men at the bows,' he said. 'Pointing, shouting, waving, cursing the gunpowder that had been so recklessly wasted. You did not want to die like the others. At whatever cost, you were determined to survive.'

Savigny looked up from the table and smiled. 'Perhaps you are right, my friend.'

~

In the studio his pale still models began to bloat. But Géricault needed the rot-stench of them, the spittle of nausea on his tongue, to go on. All day he stood at his easel. He had to keep the windows open now and could do nothing about the flies that swarmed the room.

Géricault tried to hold in his mind an image of the *Argus* appearing like a mirage on the horizon. Savigny and Corréard gesturing madly and calling in vain from the bows. Each thrilling with the hope of returning to France alive where, once their story was heard, they'd be hailed as heroes, feted and dined. But first the bath, a cake of soap, a cold crisp flagon of southern wine, and later some maid anointing flayed flesh with fragrant oils, followed by a kiss perhaps.

The end to be desired was *rescue*, Géricault said to himself. Drink, food, sanity, rescue. For ten days Savigny, Corréard, and those other souls, had clung to the planks of the raft, busy surviving.

And there, heavy with sail, the *Argus* ploughed the mist sprays of the horizon. Géricault tried to imagine it. The Captain stood on the poop, one proud eye on the rigging, the other on the helmsman. 'One point to the south,' the boatswain called out.

The Captain nodded. 'Carry on.'

What would I have craved the most, Géricault thought, if I were waving tattered rags from the raft? Alexandrine, her arms outstretched, gliding across blue shifting waters, those pouting lips half parted and waiting? Would it be his mistress? —or the fat, diminutive King of France, waddling painfully towards him on gout-swollen feet, his entire entourage applauding and paying homage at last to Géricault's great masterpiece, *Shipwreck Scene, Au naufrage de la Méduse, The Sighting of the Argus* . . .

Still he had received not one word from Alexandrine, no news from his uncle visiting his country estates while his young wife escaped the heat of Paris with her cousin in Versailles. An image came to him of Alexandrine there: a green-shuttered house, wisteria twining the porch, and Alexandrine strolling the walled garden, past espaliered trees of apricot and peach, gauging with each day the weight in her belly, considering how long she had before her confinement became obvious to all. He cursed ever having encountered his uncle's wife. How different their lives might have been without those six senseless years using them up, robbing their youth like an infection, a fever.

Géricault banished Alexandrine from his mind. Went over to his still life arranged on the model stand. The flies rose in a great roaring cloud at his approach.

Some extraordinary metamorphosis seemed to be taking place, for the skin on the man's thigh and the woman's slender arm seemed to glimmer with a pale translucent sheen, or perhaps it was a trick of the light. He leaned forward to inspect them more closely. Was he imagining it—he could have sworn the woman's forefinger moved a fraction, a slight spasm. He nudged the woman's wrist with the back of his hand, then recoiled in disgust. The flesh crawled with maggots! When he'd touched her, a wriggling white mass dropped onto the crimson damask rug. Blindly they squirmed.

Géricault kneeled and watched with fascination now, as they tried to creep back to their rancid feed of flesh. The blowflies have made fast work, he thought, picking up one of his sketchbooks from the floor. Looking across to the stern of the raft, he noticed the flies alighting on the corners of the boy's eyes and lips, on the blackened stumps of the two severed necks.

The sound of footsteps outside made him jump. The door swung open—surely he had not forgotten to lock it—and in strolled Horace, who at once clamped a hand to his mouth. 'Christ!' he exclaimed, staring all around.

He reeled across the room and leaned out the window.

'Have you taken leave of your senses?' He inhaled deep breaths. 'Has *this* been your occupation these last days? The thought that I joined you at breakfast,' he shuddered.

Again he gazed around the room, all the colour drained from his face.

'They're decomposing, for Christ's sake. They'll bring disease. But no doubt it's now your intention to study the effects of *plague* and *pestilence* among your neighbours and friends!'

Géricault smiled at him. Oh, he would soon make Horace see, when he alchemised these figures and trans-figured all that was odious in nature through the power of his art.

'Touch them,' he said. 'Encircle that slender wrist with your hand and inhale the corpse scent of their skin. I defy you to even conceive of the work I'm beginning to achieve.'

A breeze carrying a fragrance of mown grass and clover wafted through the open window and mingled with the bitter stench of putrefaction in the room.

Géricault ran the tips of his fingers against the yellowed heel of the man's foot.

'Stroke the muscles at the calf,' he said in a low voice. 'Explore every knot and tendon, the arterial vein on the inside of his thigh, and perhaps then you will begin to understand.'

Horace put his hands to his mouth as if to stifle a scream.

'This is the work of a lunatic!' he cried. 'Depraved, obscene. You could be *arrested* for less than this.'

'Don't tell me *you've* never been to the morgue,' Géricault retorted. He was becoming impatient with Horace now.

'Yes, we all have, but it would never cross our minds to bring specimens home and watch them rot in this heat. It's an affront to the dead.'

'No. Touch these limbs,' Géricault said, 'tell me what you see and feel.'

Taking a deep breath, Horace advanced towards the model stand. Flames from the candles flickered at his approach.

Before Géricault could stop him, Horace snatched away the rug.

The arm toppled from its embrace and rolled onto the floor with a thud. The composition quite sullied and ruined, there it lay on the floor—a severed arm, which stank.

Horace leaned over and retched into his handkerchief.

Géricault went to the sideboard and poured his friend a glass of wine. For a man who had choreographed thousands of corpses for Napoleon's battlefields, Horace must be losing his nerve, his backbone.

Without taking his eyes from Géricault, Horace retreated across the room.

'You must promise to get rid of these monstrosities,' he cried. 'Otherwise I'll notify the authorities at once. It's not a question of art, it's public health.'

Géricault had to laugh—this from a man who allowed his pet monkey to sleep in his bed?

'You'll not stay and take a glass of wine then, my friend?' he asked.

Horace backed further away until he stood at the door.

'These themes you're determined to explore will bring you down. Mark my words, they will.'

Again he shuddered at the sight of the corpses

positioned on the raft. With effort, he tried to compose himself.

'I know how seriously you take your art,' he began in a tremulous voice, 'but here you risk ruining your reputation, for this is a dark story and I'm given to understand that your guests are most reluctant for it to be dramatised in the ways you imagine. They fear that perhaps you're becoming too influenced by their tale.'

Géricault remained silent. He picked up the rug and shook it out before rearranging it on the stand.

'Dear God,' Horace cried, turning away in disgust. 'Call me a chameleon, who can paint any subject at will—but my portrait of the duchess progresses well, without affecting my appetite, sleep or *joie de vivre*. When the tableau is displayed at the Salon, the King will be pleased, and no doubt he'll award me a gold medal—whereas you, my friend, struggle and torture the soul with images of mutiny, murder and everything most horrible.'

Again he gazed around the studio as if he could not believe the vision which met his eyes.

'Even Savigny and Corréard complain you go too far. They never imagined you would bully them into the most mournful recollections, or that you would have the audacity to exaggerate the basic facts of their story. Now, I ask you, Theo, is this a fair way to treat your guests?'

Géricault glanced up. Horace was staring at him with an imploring expression.

'Please, leave me,' Géricault murmured. 'For as you can see, I have work to begin.'

Although the glutinous texture of the flesh repelled him, Géricault forced himself to take hold of the arm again and rearrange it on the rug.

'I intend to pray on your behalf,' Horace exclaimed, 'and prayer is something I've not done in a long time.'

Once outside, Horace broke into a run. Géricault listened to the clatter of his boots across the courtyard.

At dawn Géricault put down his brushes and stepped onto the raft. He prodded the boy with his boot and he rolled over onto his side. Géricault examined the corpse and noted with satisfaction that the maggots had burrowed deep throughout the night, had picked the eyes quite clean from their sockets.

He was tempted to keep his cadavers just one more day, but the stench had become so bad, so thick on his clothes, that he feared the putrid air must now carry across the courtyard and attract the attention of his groom and La Motte. So he braced himself and wrapped each one of his models in the soiled winding, and sacks, before dragging them outside. Géricault glanced across at the house. There was no one about. With effort he hoisted the two cadavers into the groom's large wooden barrow. He wheeled his first and heaviest load to the paddocks behind the stables, pushing and heaving with all his might as the wheels sank into the ragged dewsoaked grasslands. Finally, sweating and panting with the strain, he reached a stand of beech and upended his cargo in a soft pile of bracken. Now he hurried back for the boy and the sack of amputated limbs.

When Géricault returned, struggling against the barrow's weight, the sun had begun its steady upwards march across the heavens; and from the woodlands, the first piercing call of a bird rose higher and higher, finding its echo in another, until the trees rang with their song. He took up his spade and drove it easily into the moist clods of earth. Before long he had excavated a wide trench. He considered leaving one body exposed to the elements, but could not bear the thought of Horace's dog snuffling it out and returning to his master with a hank of human flesh in his mouth

ALL DAY, STEADILY, Géricault straightened and stretched his great canvas—the one he had bought for the final tableau. In the afternoon, pausing to admire his work, he knew he had set his ambitions high on this vast sail.

Soaring from floor to ceiling, the fabric seemed to mock him with its cream-white blankness. Shadows from the trees outside rippled against its surface and created monstrous images in a play of light.

At dusk, he heard the sound of footsteps outside.

'Leave me be, Horace,' Géricault cried. 'If you must know, I've got rid of them. Even that glorious sack of limbs. Are you satisfied?' He wrenched open the door.

To his surprise, it was the hack Grassin who stood there. The youth seemed thinner, more pinched in the two months since he had last seen him.

'Did you ever discover what became of your cousin, sir?'

'My cousin?' Géricault stared at the boy in blank astonishment.

Grassin was eyeing him with a hungry look. 'The one presumed lost on the frigate *Medusa*, sir. Were you able to find out from Monsieur Savigny whether he was still alive?'

All at once Géricault remembered the tale he had spun in the offices of the *Journal des Débats*.

Géricault shook his head. 'No,' he said, 'I never did.'

Now the boy was peering into the studio. Carefully Géricault shut the door behind him. He did not want the youth to see his real purpose, in the fearful detritus inside, sheaves of paper in drifts on the floor, sketches of cadavers everywhere, the stained rug draped over the model stand. Nor did he want him to catch a whiff of the fetid odour that might still linger there.

'Well, perhaps I may be of some further assistance,' Grassin declared with a triumphant air. 'For I've tracked down another man among the fifteen counted alive on the raft.'

Géricault studied the boy's expectant face. The thing was to look interested but not too interested, not sound too eager.

'Another survivor from the frigate *Medusa*?' He tried to contain the tremor of excitement in his voice.

'You should hear the rumours, sir,' Grassin exclaimed. 'They say this man escaped from the hospital where he was confined in Senegal, and trekked three hundred miles across the desert of the Sahara, that he ventured deep into the interior, further than any white man had been before—and prospected for diamonds in the mountains! He has returned to France a rich man, not that you would know it to look at him, sir. He goes by the name of the Helmsman.'

'How can you believe hearsay and rumours?' Géricault asked. 'I would have thought better of you, Grassin.'

The hack smiled. 'Oh no, sir. After I'd heard this, I sniffed him out from tavern to brothel until I found him.'

Géricault remained silent.

'There's a wine shop he frequents,' Grassin continued,

'a miserable den off the rue Jacob at the back of the Saint Germain markets. I've seen him for myself. From morning to night he sits in a corner by the window with a flagon of wine at his side. He says not a single word to anyone. You can't even wrest a glance from him. He just stares through that window as if he were somewhere else. He's not liked. No one goes near him. The old woman who runs the place says he frightens her to death.'

Grassin paused and gave Géricault a knowing look. 'Sometimes when he is in his cups, he starts whispering to himself, and berates Captain Chaumareys and the false pilot who brought the *Medusa* to disaster. Of course, when I heard that, my ears pricked up. I said to myself, I'm sure Monsieur Géricault would no doubt be keen to meet this man and I should arrange an introduction at once.'

At this Géricault wanted to laugh out loud. My, this boy never missed a trick, and he wondered how many assignments Grassin had undertaken 'freelance' like this.

'If such a person exists,' he said, 'what makes you think *I* can draw him out?'

Grassin shrugged.

'I don't pry into another man's affairs, but I would say, sir, that there's more to this business than the fate of your cousin . . . By the way, sir, how did you manage with Savigny?'

Géricault examined the boy's sly, pasty face. He's known all about me from the start, he thought. He imagined Grassin looking up his name in a file—heir to the tobacco firm, a wealthy artist, said to be working this shipwreck disaster into a tableau.

Géricault shook his head in wonder. Keen for business, already knowing that a different truth could be bought and sold every day, Grassin had ransacked town in search of someone else, a 'more reliable' narrator to sell him.

'How much?' he asked.

The youth gazed at him with a thoughtful expression. 'The same fee as before, sir.'

Géricault took out his purse and duly counted out the coins. 'If you are wrong about this man,' he murmured, pressing the money into the boy's outstretched palm, 'I will call you to account. Let us go now.'

Gleefully Grassin trotted across the courtyard and Géricault followed. He entertained little hope, yet the notion of meeting this Helmsman thrilled him to the core and he told himself to remain calm. Perhaps he could get to the whole story at last.

When they passed his guests, who were drinking champagne on the terrace, Savigny looked up and gave the boy a puzzled glance.

'He knows he's seen me before,' Grassin confided, striding through the gate, 'but can't think where.'

Once down the hill, Grassin darted through the lanes, threading the narrow backstreets of Pigalle like a rabbit in a warren. Géricault hurried after him—surely, alone, he would never find his way out! He'd hated that lost hour in the Passage Saint-Guillaume.

Finally they reached a cobbled alley running alongside the grey mud flats of the Seine. To Géricault's relief, Grassin stopped outside a dilapidated tavern.

He opened the door and they stepped into the gloom. The place was deserted, except for—as Grassin had described —a man seated motionless at the window, an empty wine flagon at his side. Cheap tallow candles set in tin stands flickered from the table and cast the man in an unearthly yellow light.

A woman shuffled behind the bar and set out jugs and glasses.

Géricault wondered how to approach this stranger, whose entire posture declared he wished to be left alone.

He studied the Helmsman. It was hard to tell his age; certainly he was much younger than Géricault's guests, and perhaps not more than a couple of years older than himself. There was a stark pallor about him, as if all the blood had been drained from his flesh. Yet his mouth was full-lipped, sensual as a cherub's, and seemed strange in that mournful narrow face.

He told the woman at the bar to bring him the finest Burgundy her cellar had, and she disappeared behind a felt curtain, calling to her husband.

When the proprietor returned, Géricault left the boy to gossip with the couple and carried the decanter to the man's table.

His hands trembled when he set the tray down. He filled the man's glass to the brim. Without glancing his way, the man drained the wine in one and uttered not a word when Géricault refilled his tumbler.

Tentatively, Géricault pulled up a chair and sat opposite. The man remained motionless, absently staring out the window with dark restless eyes, as if the reeking tides of the Seine, the flotsam of weed and timber, the scale glint of dead fish washed along the shoreline where seagulls scavenged in the mud—as if all this would yield some answer.

Géricault drank with him for some time in silence. He noticed a thin white scar, the length of the man's brow. But he did not want to scrutinise him too closely or distract him in any way. He would wait.

When the decanter was emptied, Géricault clicked his fingers and the woman ambled over with another. Then the man looked up and stared at Géricault with such intensity that he had to avert his gaze.

'My name is Thomas,' he said in a low, toneless voice, 'and all I possess in the world is my story—which I have branded on my soul.'

Géricault stared at him in wonder. It did not matter how much it might cost or how much time it might take, he wanted this tale and he intended to have it, even if he had to sit in this wretched tavern for all the days to come.

'My name is Thomas, helmsman by trade,' the man started again. 'On land and sea, I have fought hard for Napoleon, and was last commissioned on the frigate *Medusa*.'

Scarcely daring to breathe, Géricault pushed his purse across the table.

'Name your price, sir,' he whispered.

Thomas gave him a sharp, searching look and shook his head.

'When you've heard my tale,' he replied, 'it's up to you to decide.'

The Helmsman leaned back and half closed his eyes, as if reaching into the past.

'Did you know,' he began, 'there was no storm, but instead a perfect calm, the waters transparent, still as a lake, and shoals of fish gliding through the weeds like carp. How the crew sang, hauling in their catch. The ocean was flat as a pond and of a pure translucent green I had never seen before.'

Thomas swirled the dregs of the wine in his glass. Géricault reached for the decanter.

'You see,' Thomas continued, 'the discord lay not with the elements outside, but within us. No raging seas claimed our ship, dashing us against sheer cliffs or a reef jutting from the waters like a jagged row of teeth, no one even drowned. We could have lasted for months, as the vessel was sound. Yet we watched the carpenter build the raft and strip the decks of their timbers to fashion its loathsome planks.

'When the boats were lowered, it was balmy as a summer's day. We could see the bleached dunes of the

African coast. Perhaps we could have waded there at low tide, balancing our possessions on our heads. What fools we had been. The conflict did not reside with the ocean but festered on board ship like a wound, a sore like this wretched country of ours riddled with peace treaties you could pick off like scabs.'

Thomas stared fiercely into the candlelight. Then he leaned his forehead on his hand in a gesture of hopeless resignation. Géricault willed himself to remain silent.

'From that first night, all I had to do was survive,' Thomas said softly.

THE BROKEN ROPES HAD been salvaged and, fastened bow-to-stern around the mast, gave the men a makeshift rail to grasp in the choking welter of the swell. I tied myself with my belt to one of the projecting timbers at the bows and clung to this decking with all my might. Only my body understood. My mouth opened for the cold slap of air against my face then shut before a rush of spray. When I could take no more, my stomach clenched into a tight knot and vile brine burst from my throat. All night puking and sobbing, I listened to the cries around me, the shrieking for help. The screams of those lost over the side became fainter and fainter, and finally faded away.

All night my thoughts came in gulps—the boats will return. I will not die. Keep watch for the boats. Don't let me die—on and on in an endless rhythm.

Dawn—when I opened my swollen eyes for a fraction, I fancied myself back in France. Great battlements and colonnaded palaces reared in the flaming skies.

I rejoiced. I was alive. The swells had subsided. I unclasped my belt. From the parapet, the surgeon Savigny was calling out names, and drawing up a list of the dead.

Twenty souls lost in the night. Looking back, I should have understood, should have foreseen . . .

La Touche, the one man on whom we had counted to navigate the raft to safe haven, leaned senseless against the men, in the crush, his leg ripped to shreds. He didn't stop shouting, *My sextant, my compass all lost, all gone.*

As the ship's surgeon, Savigny was superintendent of the rations, and at first fixed the wine at three-quarters of a pint a day.

When the engineer, Corréard, and his men succeeded in setting up a mast and ran a sail trimmed from one of the main topgallants, Savigny called a council and made a speech.

'Fear not,' he announced, 'we have every hope of reaching land—and when we arrive in Senegal, we will soon revenge ourselves upon those who have so basely abandoned us.'

Although his words were met with applause, I could see the sail was of little use and would only serve when the wind came behind us.

The day passed like a dream. I concentrated on the boats, the creak and strain of their timbers, the sudden *thwack* of canvas, and imagined the morning tides rushing them shorewards. All day I willed them to return.

Stupefaction, despair, revenge—even hatred against the cabin boy, Léon, a sweet, angelic child no more than twelve years old, who had lost Lavillette's compass—these were the thoughts that wheeled and circled our minds.

No compass, no chart, no anchor, nothing to guide us except the rise and set of the sun and the stars.

At dusk I was set to stand guard over the rations—on the parapet, three barrels of wine, one cask of flour. It was easier at the centre. There were even moments when the waters only sluiced my calves. The last of the sun warmed my back. It was a comfort, a balm.

The officers kept a keen watch on the men and the sea. At one point, I heard Savigny: 'The bastards have given us nothing in the way of provisions. If the boats don't come for us, they won't sustain all.'

At that, Corréard spat. 'We're already forsaken, for they'd not risk their lives on these treacherous seas in search of such a precarious vessel.'

Under the doctor's supervision, it was my duty to issue the flour, no more than a spoonful to the men as they were mustered to the parapet in groups of ten.

That first time, Savigny weakened: 'For Christ's sake, double the wine rations.'

The piteous tone in his voice took me by surprise, but I too longed for a deep draught of wine just to ease the bruised ache in my bones.

Eagerly the men pressed forward, each in turn draining the cups we had, and held them out again. They were allowed a third and fourth measure. Ah, the joy of it, guzzled down our greedy throats, drowning the fear, the anguish in our souls.

We should have slept that night swaying like somnambulists against the lines of the ropes. We should have drifted on a great tide of dreams. Instead the wine turned sour in our stomachs.

A shout among the men—*Smash the raft so we can all meet our deaths.*

A scrimmage, a sudden scuffle at the stern. All at once, without warning, the officers fired their muskets into the crowd. The shots seemed to ricochet in the darkness. It happened so fast, no sense to it at all. And every time the fighting died down, with no sound on the raft except a whispered prayer, it broke out again—

Then I too took up my gun, like an automaton responding to some half forgotten command, a crazed call to arms . . . I imagined myself in the mud trenches of the battlefield, those clover meadows blackened and mired. All night I stood at the ready. Another cannon stoked, filled and fired.

What to say of the next morning?—the obscene dawn rose to greet us and only sixty souls alive.

No one could exactly remember—no one understood—yet the evidence was clear in the blood on our hands, the filth of our soiled clothes. No one dared say a word. We watched the officers tip the corpses into the sea.

Night fevers, the surgeon said. And—*At least the raft has lightened.*

I held my musket tight. Refused to give it up. All day crouched at the swinging bows, I stared at that merciless expanse, mesmerised by its shimmer and triumphant dance, those cruel mocking seas indifferent to our plight.

All day I willed a white sail to appear on the horizon.

At the violet hour, at dusk, one of the officers approached and nudged me alert with his foot.

'When the call is given for the rations, I expect you to join us on the parapet.'

Then he clawed his way back through the cluster of men to the raft's centre.

A crescent moon winked and blinked briefly before disappearing behind a canopy of clouds.

Chilled by a buffeting gale whipping the waves, I issued the rations. Just one cup of wine, which eagerly the men gulped down. Despite the rising swell, the officers on the parapet called out the names to come forward. And the piteous souls took their cups in outstretched hands.

I could tell what those officers were thinking. They should have taken their places in the boats, not in this floating hell packed with the depraved dregs of Napoleon's demobbed troops.

And it struck me with an illuminating clarity: however many of *us* would die—those on the parapet would return to France alive.

I considered this possibility and turned it over like a bright smooth pebble in my mind. It would not go away.

I knew I'd been offered a choice. Either take my place among the officers, or suffer the same fate as the raw recruits, those foot soldiers sprawled on the raft's outer planks.

I cast a military eye over the rabble, bickering among themselves, attempting to thieve one another's rations, and I knew it was of no use. Even though the officers were absurdly outnumbered, the men did not stand a chance.

Put it this way—there was no madman among us. No crazed assassin craving bloodlust. It was quite the opposite, even I had seen this: a simple matter of arithmetic—the numbers did not add up. Divide the provisions among some one hundred and fifty men and you arrive at the following: three or four days, at the most. I believe all of us had weighed and considered the bare facts as we knew how to— within three days not one soul would be left alive.

And once one arrives at this, the next course of action is, of course, indisputable. Faced with the same set of circumstances, wouldn't anyone have done the same?

THOMAS PAUSED AND stared straight ahead at some distant point beyond Géricault, beyond the broad river and the glimmer of lights on its banks.

Géricault found himself sweating. His heart pounded and his mouth felt dry. His mind jumped from scene to scene with a confused and frenzied motion.

Hadn't Lavillette the carpenter warned him? For all our sakes, he had said, stick to the facts as Savigny knows them.

He waited for the Helmsman to continue, and did not dare startle him with a sudden sound of his voice.

Thomas took a deep breath. He raised the glass to his lips. His face was flushed with the wine yet he continued to speak in a measured almost impersonal tone.

All that night there were shouts for mercy. The officers lunged forward from the parapet, slashing the air with their bayonets and sabres, these gestures repeated again and again over the swell of the crowd. After each slaughter, they kissed one another and gave their thanks to God.

Gelatinous with fatigue, I too was reduced to nothing but nerves, bone and skin consumed with the terrible effort of keeping myself alive, even if it meant murdering the innocent who had nowhere to run, nowhere to hide.

It was indestructible, a savage machine moving with slow and deadly precision. There was no escape for any of us. The defenceless, those whose weapons were thrown over the side, writhed beneath blows like animals. The armed were invincible.

It was absurd.

This dawn we were reduced to thirty-nine—Savigny the surgeon; Corréard and the ten men under his command; La Touche, his leg now raw from the brine; the *cantinière* and her husband, the sergeant; Léon the young boy had somehow survived; the soldiers cowering in the shadows of the sail. The raft had lightened and, as I awoke, seemed magnified in size—stretched fore and aft like some mighty vessel. All that day the sea and sun scoured and bleached the rank timbers, cleansed and washed away our sins. At dusk we no longer cared, could barely remember the clash of sabres like the flare of some distant, sweat-soaked dream.

Although there was no reason to kill any more, I kept my musket close at my side. For so did Savigny and the others on the parapet.

By the fifth day, mere mortal, shrunken now, we writhed and whimpered on the sodden parapet. One of us, I think it was Savigny, declared he was even prepared to eat his own excrement. I had tried, but could not bring myself to do it.

Many of us prayed to the ocean, talked and cajoled the endless swell, and all the time Léon ran back and forth from one side of the raft to the other, calling out, 'Mama, mama!' He received no answer except the immense voice of the sea. Still he beat the air with his fists, thrashing his way through us, stumbling over our ulcerous legs, heedless to our agonised cries. When the boy came too close to a group hunched on the parapet they would curse him, reach for their sabres and then with faltering hands lay their weapons aside. Lavillette, who for days had remained, back turned, at the stern, eventually beckoned Léon to approach him and, with tears streaming his cheeks, held the child tight in his arms, soothing his terrors and delusions. He called that he should be given an extra tot of wine, and vowed to exchange his life for the boy's.

Léon took too long to die, sobbing in Lavillette's arms, too long for us to wait. Of course, there were rations aplenty, meat we had butchered in great slabs lay spread out to dry on the deck and hung from the mast. Even the *cantinière* gobbled her share, her lips and teeth stained crimson. And I too, retching and sobbing, crammed my mouth full, time and time again without pause and restraint. *The custom of the sea*, it is called. Not unusual among shipwreck survivors—yet the comrades *we* devoured were not victims of the ocean, but slaughtered by our own hands.

Breathing deeply, Thomas stared at the empty decanter. Outside the wind beat against the window with great rocking gusts.

'I wonder,' he said, 'if I could ask you for a glass of wine.'

Startled, Géricault roused himself from the shadows.

'Forgive me,' he murmured, 'not to have seen to it before.'

STIFFLY GÉRICAULT ROSE FROM his chair and stumbled across the room. Grassin and the woman had disappeared. They were alone in the tavern.

Géricault felt soiled, as if he'd been steeped in blood from an abattoir. He needed to soak in a hipbath or at the very least wash his hands. He found another decanter, set out for him on the counter. When he picked it up, the walls seemed to close in on him and the floor spun beneath his feet. He glanced at Thomas, staring, as always, straight ahead, as if held in a trance.

Géricault tried to organise his thoughts. But his mind remained shrouded in darkness, a blank.

If Thomas's story were to be believed, he should feel outraged, appalled. But instead, a terrible, feverish thrill of anticipation began to course through him. His heart quickened at the thought that finally he might apprehend those fatal days on the raft. Come at it now with certainty and understanding.

Until this moment, the makeshift vessel had been no more than a stage, a frame to the story. He had smelled its rank odour, inhaled the sweet putrefaction of the dead, even choreographed the horrors of each passing hour, but never had he fully understood. Never had he witnessed the squalor of men kneeling to feed on their own excrement and human flesh, nor felt their hatred and despair, their baseness and compassion.

Géricault knew he could savour the stench now. Far worse than the corpses he had buried deep in the ground, far worse than the Revolution's guillotine massacres of L'Abbaye and La Force, where drains had to be dug to direct the blood flow, far worse than the first whore he had hired at the tender and expectant age of sixteen, who had thrust his head between her greasy thighs. No, nothing had prepared him for this. And now he was ready.

At the still point of the raft stood the officers, princes of mercy and sacrifice, busy surviving. Beyond, the splendour of the sea brimming the horizon.

Géricault thought of Lavillette cradling the youth Léon in his arms, whispering words of comfort, waiting for him to die. And when the last convulsion had passed, perhaps he too had devoured the child. So the old man in his sketches was Lavillette and the boy Léon. Not the father or son he had imagined.

Géricault carried the decanter to the table and filled their glasses.

'Tell me about the mercy killings,' he said.

On the fifth day, after the last slaughter, Lavillette—with a sudden outburst of horror—cast his weapon into the waves. Then Corréard did the same as well as the ten men under his command.

Then it was my turn. But no. I crept away and kept a distance at a far corner at the bows.

To be fair, and this was the irony, Savigny was scrupulous in tending the wounds of the sick: La Touche's stinking leg, the *cantinière*'s smashed thigh and her husband delirious from a gash to his brow. The doctor went from one to the other, administering wine, holding tumblers to their lips, which drove the rest of us mad for the smell of liquor—that sweet grape balm would have soothed our parched tongues, and we wept with the thought. It was *then* we hated them: La Touche who had failed us, the *cantinière* still so slab-faced and porcine, huge as a piglet gobbling and sucking her share, her husband tormenting us with recipes for rillettes recited over and over again. Each time Savigny unstoppered the wine, we wanted them gone, except the *cantinière* who should be stored in a barrel.

Unable to endure it another moment, I rose and went to them and held the musket steady. The sergeant was easy, like an old rooster, barely struggling in the grip of my hands tightening around his throat. For why, I reasoned, waste my last precious shots?

He was light as a bundle of rags when I threw him over the side.

Then Lavillette advanced, towards the *cantinière*.

'Since your husband has gone,' he declared, 'you must join him there.'

How she kicked and thrashed and bit anyone who came near, screaming to Corréard: 'By Christ, don't you remember, it was a *good woman* you'd saved!'

But he turned away now and remained silent. Savigny stood off, alone at the stern, watching and waiting without saying a word.

In the end, I stove in her head with the end of my musket.

La Touche lay without moving. So close to death I could scarcely see a breath. Yet as I bent to him, he fixed his frightened eyes to mine. And he opened his mouth, to speak, but no words came out. I kicked him hard against the chest, and he died in the darkness cast by my shadow.

Then Savigny distributed the rations of wine reserved for the sick.

Thomas fixed his gaze on the flames guttering on the table. Géricault sat without moving. He could not bring himself to look at the Helmsman, at the hopeless defeat in his face.

'You must understand,' Thomas said softly, 'we had drifted off the edge of the known world of judges, laws and tribunals, courts and assizes, juries and prosecutors. Only the ocean bore witness and—

'How it testified against us with voices that roared in our ears, condemned us with the hammer of anvils struck against wood! We bowed our heads and stood on trial, waiting for the life sentence to be passed: That if a ship appeared and we stepped ashore alive, we would never point an accusing finger at our companions. I knew then that without retribution—without one soul brought to justice, not even myself—no one rising in protest and demanding vengeance, there could be no consolation, not one moment of solace. Even if I returned to my sweetheart in Rochefort, I would lie sleepless in the warmth of her embrace, forever fearful beneath the starched sheets of her bed.'

The candles dimmed. The tavern was now completely dark.

'*Inconsolable*,' Thomas murmured. 'Can there ever be a more desolate word? Not many men could endure such a fate, not even a murderer such as myself, and so I lay on the sodden planks of the raft and prepared to die. Prayed those rough timbers would be my gallows.'

He rocked in his chair as if the motion calmed him, helped him to think.

Géricault leaned forward. 'But then finally,' he whispered, 'a white sail appeared on the horizon.'

Thomas nodded.

The wind had died down and a great silence filled the room. Géricault could feel the immense weight of it pressing down. His bones ached. The candles had melted. The first glimmer of dawn light now slanted through the window. The woman had reappeared and began sweeping the floor.

Thomas glanced about him with a bewildered expression, as if he had woken from a deep sleep and could no longer recall where he was.

'I have fought on land and by sea,' he said. 'I can tell you of the horrors I have witnessed on the battlefields of Lutzen, Brautzen, Dresden, Leipzig, Montmirail and many others. I can describe the forced marches, the privations of all kinds—yet none of them bore any comparison . . .'

His voice was almost inaudible and Géricault had to crane forward to hear him.

'Before,' Thomas continued, 'I had only to be afraid during combat. On the raft—well, now I understand.'

He closed his eyes and sat there, lost in his memories, his face expressionless.

Géricault waited for him to continue, but Thomas remained silent.

'What do you understand?' he whispered.

Thomas blinked and contemplated Géricault as if he had just met him.

'Whoever survives by violence is a traitor,' he murmured. 'And there's no prettifying that.'

Géricault thought of his guests dressed in all their finery applauding from a gilded box at the theatre, and shameless Thérèse showered with flowers curtsying and blowing kisses their way. The good doctor and his friend the engineer had invented new versions of themselves, like moths bursting from chrysalis shells and spreading their wings for the first time.

To his surprise, Géricault found he did not care. Let them brush against their new life, those bright and burning candelabras. He was armed with the truth at last. He would survey his canvas through the eyes of Thomas, eyewitness and shipwreck survivor, the Helmsman who had saved himself and returned from the unknown alive.

Thomas pushed back his chair and slowly rose to his feet. With a heavy tread he walked across the room.

Géricault could see in his mind a red banner unfurling, Thomas heaving a man up the mast and crying out—'Step onto my shoulders, I've got you now'—someone with more strength than himself, who, with arms outstretched, would signal the ship—

He did not want this man to go.

'No, wait,' he cried, proffering his purse of coins.

Thomas paused, one hand on the door.

'You can have my story. I do not seek payment.'

'Shall I find you again?' Géricault asked. He could not bear the thought of losing the raft's truth-teller and touchstone.

'I have witnessed peace,' Thomas replied, 'I have seen war. I have seen the splendour of the empire and the squalor of human misery. I have seen my own cowardice and the arrogance of my ship's companions. I have seen combat and surrender, death and survival. I have told you all I know. In two days, I shall board a packet from Calais and return to these shores no more.'

With a nod, Thomas stepped out to a morning of autumn brilliance where even the dull muddied waters of the Seine seemed to sparkle beneath a cloudless sky.

GÉRICAULT MANAGED TO RETURN to Montmartre without losing his way. As he walked up the hill, he wondered whether he should confront his guests with this version of events—tell them he'd spent an entire night listening to the Helmsman. Of course, Savigny's reluctance, his deliberate evasiveness in revealing the essence of this tale, made sense now.

At last Géricault could see Savigny plain; a man in perpetual flight from himself, unable to confront the truth, the corpse stench and rotting flesh, the humiliation of men setting on one another like a pack of wild dogs, and the shame of knowing that had he been a true man of honour, he would have died with the others. He had saved himself and from the moment he had stepped onto the parapet, a life sentence had been passed.

He was strong, this doctor, Géricault told himself. He believed he could defy the stalking truth just as he had outwitted death on the raft. *Inconsolable*, Thomas had said. Thomas understood, Géricault thought, Thomas at least could surrender to an inconsolable life.

And it struck him that had these men not survived,

their story would have vanished without trace. Perhaps he too was implicated in the fate of those who had perished on the raft. Perhaps he had somehow been selected to stand witness to the living and the dead.

That afternoon, Géricault's guests appeared unexpectedly at his studio.

Géricault watched them with interest as they came in, glanced all around, and examined the sketches on the table.

It was hard, he had to admit, to reconcile Thomas's account with these elegant sophisticated men keen to see how their story would be told in the polished gilt and marble galleries of the King's Salon.

Savigny was riffling through the sketches. Perhaps, he thought, by some extraordinary effort of will, this surgeon had succeeded in outrunning his tale, and was now taking an interest in the theatricals of the grand finale.

'The problem, as I see it,' Savigny began, 'is that you've conceived the narrative as a spectacle perceived from a distance, placing the viewer in the passive position of watching the raft as it passes by, the men actors gesturing on a floating stage.'

'Thereby reducing both form and meaning,' Corréard added, 'detaching the viewer from the central action.'

'The spectator needs to participate in our suffering,' Savigny continued, warming to his theme. 'It seems to me that the narrative power hinges on a choice juxtaposition of near and far elements. The approaching rowboat at a middle distance, the raft embedded in the foreground. The emotional crux of this drama *relies* on the moment of rescue.'

'Rowboat?' Géricault looked at them. 'Rescue?'

'Why, yes,' Savigny replied, holding one of the studies to the light.

'The eye must be held by the frantic efforts of the oarsmen, the men crowding the raft's bow signalling the flimsy vessel as, precariously, it rides the crest of each wave. The entire energy of the composition caught—in a strong diagonal thrust from the raft to the boat.'

'Gentlemen!' Géricault cried, snatching the sketch from Savigny's hands. 'You quite misunderstand my purpose. It's the first sighting of the *Argus* that I wish to portray.'

'The *first*,' Corréard enquired— 'when the ship was seen only to disappear again?'

'Exactly,' he replied. 'An emblem of universal suffering, of longing. Isn't that what we call the human condition? Don't we all hail salvation in a lover or a beautiful woman glimpsed across the street? Yet in this there's no triumphant cry of recognition, just a fleck nudging the rim of the horizon, heedless and indifferent—imagine the Captain at the helm admiring the taut trim of the sails, the ocean splicing the bows. How hopeless our signals. How black the starless skies, all that pitching and straining and calling. To what end?'

Géricault thought of Alexandrine. No divine intervention there, no ship reuniting them at the eleventh hour. And here scant consolation for the frigate's Helmsman, the one called Thomas: rescue would not save him; nor Savigny and Corréard who at first burned to tell their tale yet found that at every turn they had to edit and sanitise their account, dress the monstrous truth in finer clothes.

His guests had yet to understand how he was a changed man and knew what it was to curse the empty heavens.

Corréard moved to the window. Behind him the chestnut trees sighed in the burnishing wind.

'So you offer no redemption,' he said. 'The viewer is

not allowed to rejoice in the fact that help is at hand. They too must vacillate between hope and despair. The *Argus* continues her journey. She wasn't even searching for the raft, she was only dispatched to salvage treasures from the *Medusa's* hold. So. Once again we're forsaken and alone on empty seas . . . Oh, Géricault, I implore you, this tableau of yours is altogether too Godless and bleak.'

Savigny looked up from the sketches, 'There's no drama or sense of apotheosis in your narrative. Nothing happens! The ship sails on and slips over the horizon. The raft plunges through another wave.'

Apotheosis, don't make me laugh, Géricault wanted to say. He would paint the truth, even if it condemned his guests to an eternal and inconsolable longing. No salvation.

'Listen,' Savigny said, his voice tight with rage at last, 'you've chosen the wrong moment and deliberately discarded the most compelling episodes. The critics will accuse you of generalisations. Who are these people, they will demand, what is their nationality? Under what skies do they navigate? To which era of ancient or modern history does this hideous catastrophe belong? They will not know that this is *our story.*' Savigny turned to his friend. 'A tale told by us, Savigny and Corréard, of abandonment and betrayal.'

'Let us explain further,' Corréard interjected. 'Describe word for word exactly what it was like. Hear us out, for then you will agree to paint the moment of our rescue.'

With a theatrical gesture, Savigny stepped into the bow of the replica. Corréard climbed onto the parapet. Exactly as Géricault had wanted them.

All afternoon, they said, the men on the raft swung between hope and despair. Some imagined the *Argus* became larger, others that the Captain's course carried her further out to sea. In vain they waved handkerchiefs and flags. Then at dusk when the skies dimmed with a thin misty light, the *Argus* vanished from sight. Silence fell among them. They took down the flimsy bunting, the ragged sail, and made a shelter in which to die. They wrote a brief account of their ordeal and nailed it to a stave on the parapet in the hope this narrative would reach the Government, family and friends. They prayed that their story would survive.

Lying under the shelter that night, Savigny had a vision, that some ship, even the *Argus* perhaps, would one day sight those lashed planks, the sharks still following their stinking wake. There would be a shout for a rowboat to be lowered—the men then fighting the currents, pulling the oars with all their might, and an officer, clambering among the cadavers and ripping the tattered note from its nail . . .

Savigny sat with his hands over his eyes, moaning to himself, so reduced in the flower of his life, more beast than man.

The wind tore at the makeshift shelter. Savigny lay down and prayed for sleep. The raft swung like a toy boat in a pond. He thought he should like to gaze at the stars for the last time. He had observed that death creeps over the sick at the pale green threshold of dawn. It could not be more than a few hours. Taking care not to disturb his companions, Savigny stumbled to his feet and stepped out onto the bows. Oh, to inhale the sharp brine scent of the night.

More out of habit than necessity, Savigny pissed, surprised at the amount produced, for his parched tongue had swollen to the roof of his mouth. No need now to hold out a tin cup and drink, a blessed relief in that. Not having to swallow that acrid tepid liquor. Sirius the Dog Star blinked and winked from the heavens. Clear indigo skies prophesied a cloudless day, which Savigny hoped never to witness.

Then all at once, a shadow loomed close through the waves. He watched it approach with a sense of detached amusement to see which delusion his mind would conjure next: a castle, a church spire on the crest of a hill, a vertiginous mountain path winding through the Alps. Please, not that one, the crunch of gravel beneath his boots marching upwards.

A brig this time, the bowsprits quite plain through the mist and a group of men gathered on the poop deck. An officer pointed and called out: 'Anyone alive?' Why bother to answer these crazed harpies of the night? Savigny admired the vessel swift as the *Medusa* bearing down with a full white sail. Stately and regal. Reynaud would have approved of the trim in her canvas. Poor fellow. He wondered what had become of him; the brave second in command who, left to his own devices, would have long since brought the frigate to Senegal. A longboat dipped through deep troughs in the swell with the cries: 'Anyone alive?'

Savigny raised one hand. Tears coursed his cheeks. Corréard leaned over and put an arm around his friend.

The problem lay in the sentiment of the scene, the shouts of joy from the exhausted survivors, rescued by this divine sleight of hand. With what raptures indeed the good ladies of Paris would receive such a tableau, reaching for smelling salts and dabbing their eyes behind fluttering fans. And the critics would applaud a narrative of this immensely satisfying kind. How good to feel that the Lord in his magnificent benevolence presided at the eleventh hour.

Lately, Géricault had learned to hate sentiment in all its

forms, including the commissioned tributes of modern art. Forget the thousands slain in some soon-forgotten war. A King or Emperor would always gallop through blood-soaked battlefields sanctifying those prepared to die for cause or country. Forget the severed head of the Princess of Lamballe when you could admire the ornate brocade, the damask gown of the Duchess of Angoulême attired in the very height of fashion, which no doubt many fine dowagers would imitate no expenses spared.

No, Géricault thought, it would not do, this chocolate-box confection of war and revolution. The languid grace of some Empress parading through a pilfered palace or the simpering smiles of royalty the mob would have butchered not that long ago. At the theatre or the opera house, he expected to be roused. There he was willing to shed tears and clap his hands, but not at the Salon, which he held sacred as any Sunday temple where he hoped to meet God's gaze and seek no redemption there.

No, leave the fine portraits and court commissions to the Vernets and their honoured friends.

Here was his space, scorched implacable skies, clouds raining dust. A ship glided against a grey glimmer of the horizon, sliding onwards like a bead threaded through an abacus.

All night, Géricault worked at his canvas, pleased with his efforts. He had found a way at last to fuse composition and narrative into one.

He admired the vigour and dynamism of these men in action, the powerful span of their shoulders, those muscular bodies straining and surging forward with the same pulsing energy as the ocean.

Some might ask, he reflected, why he had decided not to depict the survivors as they were, flesh-flayed and cadaverous, their skin blistered and scourged from the brine and sun? Even the corpses imbued with an unnatural strength. Yet tears of compassion he would not have.

Instead his viewer would be made to participate in the drama and experience the suffering of all castaways since the beginning of time.

GÉRICAULT WOKE MID-MORNING to a great pounding at the studio window. He leaped to his feet and hurried into his outer clothes. Hearing a clatter of hooves and La Motte's voice calling for the groom, he wondered at the commotion, hoped there had not been an accident.

Géricault flung open the door and was shocked to find his father standing before him, dark in black breeches and coat high at the collar. 'How can you have been such a fool?' Georges-Nicholas cried. 'Don't you have money enough for the most sought-after courtesan in town?' he roared, pushing past him into the studio. 'Instead you chase after your *uncle's* wife.'

So the scandal was out. Géricault looked around the courtyard, expecting his uncle to come rushing towards him.

The time must have come for Alexandrine to send word of her condition and inform Caruel of her decision to live behind convent walls. Yet, to his shame Géricault found himself thinking, There's not the time for this now, I must get back to the raft. But for weeks he had been waiting to be called to account and now the day had arrived.

Georges-Nicholas was gazing about him in disgust—
'And this is how you idle the precious hours, when most
men are employed in sensible, profitable work!'

At least, Géricault thought, he had managed to restore
the studio into some state of order, the scaffolding beginning
to climb the canvas, his sketches piled in their correct
sequence on the model stand, the paints arranged along the
trestle as he would have them on his palette. No corpses or
putrid odours now.

'What is *that* contraption?' Georges-Nicholas was
staring at the raft. But before Géricault could reply, his father
dismissed it with an abrupt wave of his hand. 'I refuse to talk
in this squalor. Escort me to the house at once.'

He turned on his heel and marched across the courtyard, his heels ringing against the flagstones, Géricault at his
side praying that Savigny and Corréard were absent.

Georges-Nicholas burst into the downstairs parlour
and La Motte appeared, flustered, wiping her hands on her
apron.

'Bring me a pot of strong coffee,' he said, giving the
decanters and bottles crowding the sideboard a disapproving
glance.

When La Motte scurried away, his father rounded on
Géricault. 'Why, you seem to be running a veritable tavern,'
he exclaimed. 'On every count you're a disgrace, my son.'

Géricault remained silent. Through the window he
could see Savigny and Corréard engaged in some animated
discussion in the rose garden. Don't come to the house, he
prayed.

'This morning,' Georges-Nicholas began, his voice
tense with rage, 'Caruel came storming into my office and
interrupted a particularly delicate business meeting, just at
the point when my client was preparing to sign the contract.'

He studied Géricault with a look of hatred. 'You have

no idea how many weeks I spent drawing up that transaction,' he cried. 'Caruel was in a terrible state and began
to declaim, for all to hear, that you—' Géricault flinched
at the accusing finger pointed his way—'have broken his
heart.'

Géricault felt himself burn with remorse and shame.
The scene was exactly how he had imagined.

'Never,' Georges-Nicholas said, 'will he recover from
such a deep sense of betrayal from his favourite nephew, and
other such nonsense. As for his wife, so deep runs his disgust
that he never wants to clap eyes on that deceitful, lying face.
Let Alexandrine rot behind convent walls, he said. She'll
never laugh in the sun again.'

At the mention of Alexandrine, Géricault felt himself
sicken. He thought of his mistress engaged in the profound-
est piety which called for the destruction of every human
memory. The notion terrified him. If only he had stayed in
Rome. He cast his mind back. And in a flash, it occurred to
him that the very first night after his return, that dinner with
Caruel, must have been the moment when they conceived
their child. In the six years they had shared, it had to be that
fatal night. Not more than ten minutes at the most together
outside the privy. He winced at the irony of it.

'I feared for his sanity,' his father was saying, 'and even
considered summoning a physician, anything to silence the
clamour that was ringing through the hall. Imagine—
crowds probably gathered in the street! I had to remind
Caruel to retain some sense of control and direct his efforts
to avoiding a scandal—which might ruin the family business, and our reputations.'

Had I any sense of decency, Géricault thought, I would
have resisted those early flirtations and honoured the name
of Caruel.

'Are you listening to me, boy?' Georges-Nicholas was

glaring at him with those cold grey eyes Géricault used to fear as a child. There was a rustle at the door and in flew La Motte, setting down a tray and pouring coffee from a pot.

'You should know,' Georges-Nicholas continued, 'that your uncle and I were to embark on a joint venture, and now of course that's quite out of the question.'

He paused and waited for La Motte to leave the room. Géricault watched him take a fastidious sip from his cup.

'I did tell Caruel,' Georges-Nicholas confided, now lowering his voice, 'that I always thought he'd made rather a fool of himself by taking on such a young wife, and a silly one at that. You should consider yourself fortunate, I told him, that she's gone of her own volition. Now you've disposed of the creature, you must pull yourself together and find another, one more suited to your age this time . . . But Caruel flew into a terrible rage and created an even more appalling scene.'

Géricault found his father observing him with distaste. 'It was then,' he said, 'that he told me about the child.'

He shook his head. 'Damn pity. That wife of his—well, perhaps you were young and impressionable at the time. But an illegitimate child is not to be countenanced.'

There was a silence, then Georges-Nicholas thumped his fist on the table, making the cup rattle in its saucer. 'It's a wretched business all round. You should be ashamed of yourself.'

Géricault listened, chilled as ever by the unfathomable distance between his father and himself. Yet in that hard, stern face, he recognised all too well the similarities they shared: a cold, loveless heart; ruthless self-righteousness; contempt for women, perhaps.

'Strong words were exchanged and, shortly after, Caruel marched out. I've learned he has left Paris, with no forwarding address, and before long documents will be piling on his desk, with no one in authority to sign them.'

Georges-Nicholas clicked his tongue with exasperation.

Géricault pictured his uncle, the cuckold that he had made him, fleeing the scandal, enraged beyond imagining—and yet it occurred to him that had Caruel truly loved Alexandrine and wished for her happiness then he should never have imprisoned her in the forlorn cell of their wedding vows. What right had he to expect that or any other sacrifice from someone so much younger than himself? And with that thought came the bitter realisation that they were both guilty, both stood accused of not giving Alexandrine what she most desired: freedom from one and devotion from the other. Deceit, adultery, incest, what did it matter in the end when of the three of them, Alexandrine was the most betrayed. And she had known it. This was what Alexandrine had meant when she'd left him.

'I must add,' his father was saying, 'you're forbidden to go out in society until all rumours have died down. I've arranged to pay a yearly stipend, and finance Alexandrine and the child for life, on condition they remain in the country and out of sight.'

It then struck Géricault with tremendous force that his child would not even be raised by Alexandrine's loving hands: the boy would be fostered to some farmhouse outside the convent walls.

'And if I hear that you've tried to communicate with your aunt in any fashion,' Georges-Nicholas declared, 'I shall annul her stipend and that of the bastard offspring, of course.'

The final blow. Géricault immediately saw that, however hard he tried, he would never discover what might become of his child. His father would pay a considerable bribe to conceal the child's true identity, in case one day he came knocking on the Géricault factory door.

Géricault felt a sudden rush of loathing for this father of his forever keeping a tight control over any hint of misrule with his stipends and provisions, bank accounts and payrolls, and now tidying the mess created by his son.

He watched him pacing up and down, well in his stride now, raising one hand to make another point.

He's *enjoying* this, Géricault thought—and then a memory came to him, of his mother worn down by her husband's constant lectures and scornful disapproval. Now Georges-Nicholas had found a way to triumph over his son at last, and with far more ammunition than the failure of his *Charging Chasseur*, despite the Gold Medal it had won.

'It goes without saying that Caruel will cut you off. Not that it should make any difference, as you choose to live with riff-raff in the filth of Montmartre instead of with the fine upright citizens of the Hôtel de Ville. You say you want to be an artist—you've certainly behaved well by your uncle who gave you every encouragement, haven't you? You're a sorry disappointment, my son. Look at you—dishevelled, unkempt, the clothes hanging off you as if you've not eaten for weeks. Now that I've paid off your whore, I want nothing more to do with you.'

And Georges-Nicholas turned away and marched out the door.

From the window, Géricault watched his father advance towards the carriage, stern and austere in his dark suit, pausing to tip the groom with a dismissive arrogant gesture. Géricault thought of his mother's legacy and wondered how long it would last.

There, the cords were cut and sinking beneath the swell.

GÉRICAULT TRIED TO FORCE himself to work, but his hands trembled each time he lifted a brush to the canvas. His heart pounded hard in his chest. He was astonished at the fast, quiet, ruthless efficiency with which his father had worked—Alexandrine and their child financed for the rest of their lives, and he knew the settlement would be generous, to keep her quiet. Although he knew his uncle and father would never again exchange words, they would reach a lucrative arrangement over the business, for both were merchants at heart. There, it was done—the scandal dealt with and contained within the hour. At noon his father would open the door to his clients as if nothing had occurred, except for a dispatch sent round announcing Caruel's resignation. Business resumed as normal. Géricault felt humiliated, shop-soiled, as if his life and the fate of Alexandrine and their child meant no more than a mercantile transaction, a cheap bill of exchange filed away in some drawer.

At dusk Géricault put down his palette. He needed a drink, and a strong one at that. He searched through the decanters and bottles strewn on the sideboard, and came across a curious cut-glass container, which one of Horace's friends had pressed on him, claiming that this liquor had the power to illuminate the senses.

You could breathe every sound, the eager young poet had said, and hear the very colours vibrate all around, each odour and scent evoked sensations of lightness and weight, a particular texture you could touch with the tips of your fingers. Extrait d'Absinthe, an aromatic liquor distilled from wine and wormwood.

Géricault contemplated the bottle and carried it over to the raft. Perhaps, he thought, this absinthe will help me at the canvas until first light.

He diluted a measure in water and admired the milky sage tint in his glass. He then downed it in one. The pungent aniseed aftertaste burnt the roof of his mouth. Géricault lay down and waited for the dose to take effect. Apart from a slight drowsiness and a flush to his cheeks, he felt nothing. This time he prepared another measure and took sip after sip, grimly and without pleasure, but anticipating some delicate, shimmering evanescence to come. Just when Géricault was beginning to doubt the efficacy of this potion, the walls began to hammer and shudder, the ceiling spun, and he flung himself retching to the edge of the raft. A terrible whirling sensation hollowed the pit of his stomach.

'What's this?'

Géricault woke to Horace standing in the doorway, the monkey perched on his shoulder, framed by a dazzling pool of light.

His head pounded fit to bursting. He wished Horace would leave him alone, return to his straw-stuffed mannequins or the bare breasts of some maid.

Horace kicked something and cursed. Stooping, he picked up the empty bottle and gave it a sniff. He put it down on the table.

'So you think this will summon the muse? You fool.'

Géricault wished he could unburden his heart. Tell Horace about the nunnery and the child. But he was too shamed.

Horace strode towards him.

'Look at you. I suggest you get dressed and join your guests.'

Géricault found himself hauled to his feet. The sudden motion made him retch. The monkey jumped from Horace's shoulder took a leap for the table, sending plates, the bottle, the dregs in the glass crashing to the floor.

'Get out, get out,' Géricault cried, leaning over the washstand and splashing cold water on his brow.

Crouched beneath a chair, the monkey dipped his fingers in the shards of glass, gave his thumb an experimental lick and, with a shocked expression, let out a high-pitched shriek.

Horace laughed. 'See, this sensible Singe would never dream of going down your wretched path.'

GÉRICAULT'S TUTOR, CARLE VERNET, had agreed to pose as the father, and Delacroix as the son. Vernet had confided in a missive that a sojourn in Montmartre would suit him well. Back in vogue with his dandified equestrian canvases, he was finding himself quite exhausted with card games, balls and soirees at the Royal court.

Don't you welcome these times, he'd written in his neat fastidious hand. *How I loathed the cold Corinthian splendour of the Empire, those hideous military uniforms. Now if the Duchesse d'Angoulême could only be persuaded to powder her peasant skin, why, she'd be quite a pretty thing. Sad no lady in waiting survived the guillotine to advise her on such matters.*

In due course, Vernet's carriage had arrived, drawn by four prancing grey stallions, *un petit cadeau* from the King. He had jumped from the equipage dressed in all the latest satin and lace finery, pointed boots sharp at the heel.

'How pleasant it is to spend some days away from the demands of the King and court,' Vernet declared.

~

In the studio Géricault opened the champagne with an expert hand. He knew he would have to ply this impeccable courtier with chilled Veuve Clicquot before he could begin to inhabit the mind of an unaccommodated man stripped bare, crazed by shame and grief.

'You spoil me, dear fellow,' Vernet exclaimed, watching the bubbles rise in his glass. He took a sip and shuddered with delight. 'Perfect, quite perfect.'

Vernet glanced at the vast canvas and the expensive paints. 'I always thought you were ambitious, but never to this extent. It must have come at a pretty price.' He turned to him. 'Am I to be the first figure you paint? How flattering.'

Nodding, Géricault brought Vernet his studies, the abandonment of the raft, the mutiny. He had hidden the cannibalism scenes, not wishing to put his tutor off the task.

'So dark,' Vernet exclaimed. 'The figures seem to rear from pitch blackness. What an effect . . .' Examining the study of the rescue, he narrowed his eyes. 'Don't tell me,' he announced, 'bitumen—why, quite clearly I recognise the texture.'

He graced his pupil with an admiring gaze. 'I'm astonished, for this shading must have taken considerable time.'

Géricault felt himself flush with pride. At last someone who understood what he was trying to achieve.

'I have to begin at dawn,' he replied. 'Using such a slippery oil makes it impossible to continue on the morrow what I began the previous day.'

'Still sculpting with paint! Do you remember, I once dubbed you Rubens' pastry cook?'

Vernet ran a gloved finger over a thunderous sky towering above the figures crouched on the raft.

'This bitumen you use,' he enquired. 'How do you manage to apply it? It sticks to my hand like tar.'

'A careful process of dilution, sir.' How he relished this exchange of techniques in their craft. 'A risk, I know.'

Vernet set down his glass. 'You have work to do, so we must begin. Where shall I take my place on this raft of yours?'

Géricault motioned him to the stern and asked him to sit cross-legged, staring straight ahead, resting his head on one hand.

'Tell me who I am,' Vernet said.

'You cradle your dead son in your other arm. You desire only to die. Your entire attitude is weighted with remorse and shame.'

Vernet grasped a satin bolster against him as the boy, and adopted the pose. With a sigh he slackened his features in an attitude of despair. Elbow propped against one knee, he leaned forward, his gaze fixed at a distant point on the wall. Quite perfect, Géricault thought, exactly the right expression. But there was the starched cravat and the heavy brocade of his sleeves, which gave him the air of a dandy pleased with his immaculate toilette.

'Monsieur Vernet,' Géricault ventured, 'your attire, magnificent as it is, distracts the eye . . . that intricate gold stitching, the embroidered lapels of your coat.' He braced himself. 'Could I ask you, sir, to remove your clothes? I've an outfit here that might suit.'

He held up a frayed pair of pantaloons.

Glancing his way, Vernet shuddered. 'Very well,' he muttered, and unbuttoned his collar. Géricault handed him the garment.

After a time, the model was in place again, and Géricault draped a crimson cloth over Vernet's head. There, finally he had it.

'Imagine the scene,' he began. 'You're moments from death. You've no strength or interest in a ship outlined against the horizon. You pay no heed to the shouts of your companions. The wind whispers in your ears like a lament or prayer. There's tumult on board, ragged flags flown, handkerchiefs raised. But you're resigned to die and wonder that you've already survived this length of time.'

At this, Vernet coughed to stifle a giggle. The cloth slipped over his brow. With irritation, Géricault reached out and secured it with a pin.

'You've witnessed horror and torment. You need death to creep over your soul like the deepest sleep.'

Again Vernet focused his gaze on the wall. But a twitch began at the corner of his lips. Trying to conceal his impatience, Géricault waited for the laughter to subside.

'Forgive me,' Vernet managed to say at last, 'most unprofessional. Please pass me the wine. I'll start again.'

Géricault waited as Vernet settled on the raft. It was a matter of creating an illusion of flesh and fabric, air and light. He knew his tutor would be shocked when he saw he intended to execute this figure completely without preparing the canvas—for if he did, he would see it whole and not have the desire to go on.

When Delacroix appeared as arranged, Géricault motioned him to take his position in Vernet's arms. Quickly the boy stripped and tied a loincloth around his waist. Géricault watched him clamber unsteadily onto the raft, set the bolster to ease their joint pose. Yes, he will do, Géricault thought, down to the goosebumps prickling his pale pelt.

As Géricault worked, he noticed Vernet glancing his way with a perplexed expression. Delacroix contemplated a fly circling the ceiling: clearly he'd resigned himself to hours of boredom.

By late afternoon Delacroix dozed and, when he began to snore, Géricault had to leave his canvas and wake him with a sharp nudge, for the sound of a mouse was enough to interrupt his concentration.

~

When the light faded at last, he put down his palette with a sigh. How swiftly, he thought, the sun ran its course over the earth.

Stiffly Vernet rose to his feet and began to dress, Delacroix helping with buttonholes and stays. Not until he was once again attired in all his finery did Vernet stand back to inspect his pupil's work.

Géricault watched him, hardly daring to breathe. Vernet must understand; surely *he* would find some words of encouragement for the work.

'So, you believe you've reached a level of maturity and experience to break all the rules,' Vernet said at last. 'You've not even bothered to block out each section, simply daubed the figure of the father straight onto the empty canvas, without a rough sketch or preparation of any sort.'

Delacroix examined these first stabs at the composition. 'But sir,' he exclaimed, turning to Vernet, 'there's a bravura in these firmly traced contours. The solidity of the work appears none the worse for it.'

Géricault flinched at this praise from a mere boy, when he yearned for Vernet's response, for him to say—I have every confidence in you and I suggest you rent a studio in town where you can work day and night without one single interruption, not even from my son.

'Perhaps,' his tutor instead conceded, 'but I would advise *you* not to ape our friend by flying in the face of convention. Has no one shown respect for anything I've taught?'

What could Géricault say? Explain that blocking the canvas into known measurable squares with every figure held in a perfect symmetrical shape would destroy all he held true? No mystery or journey there. He could not do it. He might as well colour a grid.

Delacroix continued to stand before the canvas, his face strained and pale.

'Don't tell me. I know. Quite hideous, isn't it.' Horace was leaning against the doorway. 'Believe me, Father, against my advice our friend is determined to create a most monstrous spectacle and refuses to listen to my counsel or abide by any rules. There's nothing you can do to stop him, so you may as well go along with it.'

Seeing Géricault's stricken expression, Vernet indulged him with a smile.

'Come now,' he announced, 'perhaps this bold experiment will work.'

Horace went over and linked an arm through his friend's. 'Forgive me,' he whispered, 'I'm only concerned for your reputation, that's all.'

'Why?' Géricault replied, irritated beyond measure. 'Unlike you, I've nothing to lose.'

When they took their leave for Horace's house, Géricault stood before his canvas.

He had begun the base of a pyramid, the figure of the father staring at the viewer. Beside him, a man rose like Lazarus from the dead and gazed towards the group hailing the distant ship. A face loomed out of the shadows of the shelter, his features in a hopeless expression of resignation. At the apex of the pyramid, still half imagined and glimpsed in the mind's eye, Corréard and Savigny pointing and hailing and a Negro climbing the mast and a crimson flag unfurling. How, he pondered, should he fill the immeasurable distance between? Géricault saw Lavillette plain, his chin resting on one hand, the boy in his embrace. A companion crouched behind them, unwilling even to venture from a makeshift tent. Another struggled forwards on his hands and knees, the effort enough to kill him.

Was it necessary, Géricault wondered, to characterise these last fifteen souls, give them faces and names, pay tribute and immortalise every survivor in the final tableau? There lay the danger of overcrowding and diffusing the action with narrative complexity, which would bring him back to the original problem he had faced in the mutiny scenes. No, it was impossible, he reflected, to give these figures each a separate role.

Contemplating the sketches, Géricault decided that somehow he would gather the figures into four distinct groups and fuse several bodies into the one motion, repeating the same gesture over and over in endless variations on the themes of suffering and survival. The group dominated by the father and son, Vernet and Delacroix—or Lavillette and the cabin boy Léon—occupied the space of the raft's lower half, first engaging the viewer in attitudes of lassitude and despair, heedless of the excited clamour at the prow. By way of contrast, grouped on the other side of the mast, four men would watch the horizon with intent searching eyes, Corréard and Savigny among them. To give strength and depth to the ascending line, a struggling mass would rise towards them, arms upstretched in frantic pleading. They would prove the most pantomimic and therefore the most problematical. And the last group, the central focus of his composition? Géricault had yet to decide.

Later Horace joined him for a glass a wine.

'Why, only now Delacroix has returned,' Horace declared, darting his friend a reproachful glance. 'He told me he ran like a fool all the way to his lodgings on rue de la

Planche at the far end of Saint-Germain, to recover from the impression your composition made on him.'

Horace sighed.

'He can't stop babbling about your sketches being the best argument for beauty, a sublimation of all that is most monstrous in nature, and other such nonsense.'

At his words, Géricault smiled. At last someone who understood. If he applied himself, Delacroix would do well.

THE NEXT DAY, Géricault assembled his cast. So began the choreography he had devised: Vernet resumed his position at the stern, cradling Delacroix in his arms; Horace knelt, his entire weight balanced on the thrust of one leg, a fist raised above his head raging at the Gods.

When he posed Savigny and Corréard in the bow, they astounded him by averting their eyes from the muscular flesh all around. He would have thought they had become accustomed to the sight of naked men by now. Then he had Joseph, the boxer from Horace's studio, lean against two empty barrels crowding the centre of the raft.

Before picking up his brushes, Géricault paused to admire the corporeal strength of the forward motion, straining towards the distant ship like trees bent before a gale, except—there was a problem. He looked at Vernet's assistant, Montfort, signalling from the mast. The central focus seemed wrong somehow. He glanced at the boxer lighting a cheroot.

'Hey, Joseph,' he cried. 'Help me move the barrels to the forward end of the raft.' With a sigh, the boxer stubbed the cheroot beneath the sole of his foot and hoisted both barrels. Corréard and Savigny scurried out of his way.

Géricault had him set them down at the apex of the prow. 'Stand on that barrel.' Dutifully the boxer jumped onto the lid, his athletic back turned and every muscle in his torso stretched taut and lean.

Now Géricault knew what needed to be done. He summoned Delacroix and Montfort to join Joseph. 'Delacroix, lift your right arm and wave the flag. Montfort, clasp Joseph around the thigh so that he can signal the ship with all his might.'

He asked the boxer to stand so only his dark body jutted against an imagined skyline high above the horizon. He handed Joseph a bolt of crimson satin and instructed him to roll it out when he gave the sign.

'Savigny,' he called, 'point towards the ship and turn to your companion who—Corréard!—eagerly scans the seas beneath the canvas shadows. Tell him the *Argus* has been seen. Shout it out, man, at the top of your voice. I want to hear you rejoice.'

Savigny adopted a stiff theatrical stance like an actor auditioning some spear-wielding part. 'No, not like that,' Géricault exclaimed in frustration. 'I want to see every tendon stretched in the upward reach of your arm, the wrench of your shoulders as you twist back to your companion.'

How limp, the gesture. He hadn't got it at all. Géricault gave the boxer a nod. 'Demonstrate how it is done.'

Joseph jumped down and grasped Corréard who reeled back in surprise. '*Over there*,' he prompted, showing the pose, '*topmasts above the horizon*. Come on, you must know the words by now.'

Once again Géricault told his actors to resume their positions. Horace hid a glass of wine behind the mast and knelt on the stern. Vernet stared ahead with a mournful gaze.

Finally Géricault strode across the room and swung open the door. 'Don't move,' he said. A fierce autumn wind whipped through the room. At Géricault's sign, crimson folds of cloth snatched away from the boxer's uplifted hand—this was the climax Géricault wanted.

He must sink the horizon to emphasise the towering rise of the men culminating in the crowning figure of the boxer supplicating the heavens. He must crop and adjust and alter the focus. If he narrowed the margins of sea and sky, the raft would overwhelm the viewer with a sense of oppression as if they too were trapped on this hopeless vessel. The massive foregrounded figures in Vernet and Horace would haul back the horizon, heightening and dramatising the isolation of the men grouped around the mast, its sail the hue of tanned leather.

Colour would defeat colour in scatterings of vermilion in the head cloth of the father, the drapery of the man crouched beside him, the sash of the man raising himself on the right, the cloth unwinding from the boxer's hand—all serving to intensify the ashen monochrome of the shadows tinged from dark brown to the sleek black of pure bitumen.

At the left of the canvas, the brightest light would fall from a luminous blue patch of sky shot through with pale yellow, heralding dawn perhaps, the rising sun sending a fierce orange glow through banked clouds. Not so the sharp cold crepuscular shafts, slanting across the raft and casting a pallor over the figures, hinting at yet another night to come.

As for the ship, the *Argus*, a mere speck against wind-ploughed clouds, which the viewer would have to crane forward and search the canvas to behold. Then all those who clapped eyes on his tableau would be made to share the experience of shipwrecked men. Not only the despair of these men, but of every soul ever abandoned on heaving fathomless seas—his composition would smash the barriers of time.

And when once again the viewers strolled onto the street, the cafés so warm and gay and brightly lit, the pretty girls promenading at their side, perhaps they would glance up at the stars wheeling the darkening skies and with a shiver listen to the great roaring emptiness there. For they were so alone, drawing their cloaks against the chill of the night, creeping homeward on this whirling clod of earth, the cold planets shining from above.

Montmartre

———

August 1819

AFTER EIGHT MONTHS, Géricault had resurrected five more men from the waves to ballast the foreground of the tableau. Now, he had twenty figures on the raft instead of the fifteen of Savigny's account. But the accuracy of their version mattered not to him now. He was too tired, bone tired.

He had felt nothing except a senseless passion for this work, which made him rise at dawn despite sleepless nights and allowed him to prepare his palette with a steady hand, which guided the way up the scaffolding and planted his brush in a pool of darkness blacker than the devil himself, which held him in thrall day after day, month after month.

Often he had visited the Louvre to see David's *Sabines and the Léonides* again, and would ride back to Montmartre discouraged and disheartened. How to describe those tremendous figures full of breadth and depth and life? Once he told Delacroix, whom he had hired as his own assistant, that his efforts seemed clumsy in comparison. But the youth had said nothing.

Most nights during this time he had hardly slept, thinking of those bitumen black gargoyles creeping across the canvas, like the monstrous patterns he used to see as a child flickering and leering against the wooden panels of his nursery room.

One spring morning, Géricault had received word from the mother superior at last, written in an old-fashioned spidery hand: *Alexandrine Modeste Caruel at four in the morning the nineteenth of April delivered a healthy boy.* Reading the note, Géricault had felt as if his sides would crack.

Most days he found it helped to give in to despair. The dusks had lengthened and the chestnut trees shook out their white blooms once again. And for a long time, Géricault's guests, Horace, and his retinue of friends had been mere shadows to him. Their entrances and exits, the musical intervals, the picnics and dances and strolls through the meadows were cued by some unravelling plot, which he no longer followed.

But now it was summer again. Géricault had finished in time. Savigny had returned to his book and intended to open a publishing business specialising in political pamphlets. He had confided that he would call his shop, *Au naufrage de la Méduse.*

Horace had long since finished his portrait of the Duchess, and while awaiting his triumph at the Salon he amused himself with lucrative commissions from the court. Barely three weeks remained until the King opened the exhibition at the Louvre.

Géricault thought of the King's Salon. He imagined his tableau hung in the great gallery of the Louvre, and when the spectators sashayed from exhibit to exhibit, a flute of champagne held in one hand, they would be spared no redemption from his canvas. It would cram their eyes with the raft's wide spread, place them in a terrifying perspective and make them reel from the vast plunging distance between raft and rescue. This vision they would never forget.

For his tableau had been accepted by the King. The committee had sent a missive. His shipwreck scene had so impressed the judges that he had been given the greatest honour—of choosing for himself where on the vast walls of the galleried room the composition should be hung.

So now the day had arrived.

Tired as he still was from the work, Géricault made sure he was dressed for the occasion. This was the very cusp of fame. But he was alone and afraid.

With great care, La Motte had laid out cream breeches, a broad satin sash, his best linen waistcoat trimmed with silver braid. Worn out with anxiety and lack of sleep, Géricault adjusted the gold buckles on his belt, slipped a single white rose through the buttonhole of his lapel, and rearranged the starched lace folds of his cravat. He pomaded his hair with eau de cologne. It had grown back thicker than before and curls now twined the nape of his neck. Having worn that paint-stained smock and his old riding habit for so long, he cursed the stiff tight buttons at his wrists and throat. He felt entombed in all this finery.

Géricault knew he should ask Horace or Vernet to come, to help him reach this important decision, to advise him on where to hang his tableau on the packed walls of the Salon Carré. But pride held him back.

~

When Géricault finally climbed from the carriage, the crowds milling across the grand paved square swam queasily before his eyes. He pressed through and climbed the steps of the Louvre. With effort he swung open the heavy double doors and strode along the gilt and glittering corridors.

Somehow he managed to dodge the horde swarming at the entrance of the Salon Carré. People gathered, separated and reformed, forever squinting upwards to where hundreds of paintings already lined the immense walls and long gallery beyond.

By the window, he saw Ingres surveying the scene. The great master paced beneath his vast offering, *La Grande Odalisque*, a terrifying nude of riotous concubine flesh, which had been hung to perfection, neither high nor low in the middle section. A clever choice, Géricault thought. He needed to find a similar position.

With a patrician smile, Ingres greeted colleagues and acquaintances—an imperceptible nod of the head, his gestures refined and studied, adopting the nonchalant stance of the famous who feigned not to notice they were on show. Briefly his pale blue eyes rested on Géricault then darted away in recognition of some important figure entering the room.

To Géricault, it seemed that beneath the shining carapace of that fame, Ingres appeared smaller and frailer, more mortal than you would imagine.

Behind him was Gros, wearing his trademark shabby blue smock; he held court before a group of journalists who scribbled down every word. Gros glanced at the folds and rumpled swathes in the ultramarine cloth of his exhibit, *The Assumption of the Virgin*, with a look of irritation.

'It's a meat market and I couldn't care less.' He pushed a sweep of dark hair from his brow. 'Believe me, I'm not

lying awake at night worrying about it or any other prize.'
The journalists leaned forward. 'I hope artists aren't only
thinking about their aspirations for medals—but many are,
I'm sure.'

Anonymous and invisible, Géricault began to revel in
the spectacle, this parade of artists and their work—he
marvelled at their confidence, the sense of power they
exuded. Invincible as gods, their presence intoxicated
everyone in the room. Wildly gesticulating, Gros now
warmed to his theme, still denouncing all those who set
store on prizes and medals. 'These men are only kept going
by the thought of fame,' he declared. 'Fame is their most
pressing need.'

Géricault set off for the Theatre Italien, where many of
the entries were still assembled. There, breathless and half
suffocated, he paused by a window to regain his bearings.
Ladders and scaffolding everywhere. Men shimmied across
the planks shouting instructions, hoisting the vast canvases,
which swung back and forth, straining at the ropes like
leviathans hauled from the deep. Géricault looked around
the packed gallery walls. It was like being in a battle. Every
conceivable space was filling fast.

For a long time he stood miniaturised before his own
canvas. He was amazed by its sheer length and height. He
wanted to stopper his ears against the roar of that molten
broiling sky, the rough ragged seas, the pitiless stretch of
horizon welded by shadows and blankets of darkness.

'Monsieur Géricault.' A young official hovered at his
side. Turning round, Géricault tried to focus his tired gaze
on the young man who was unfolding a complicated plan
of the room etched with arrows and names. Géricault
thought he might faint in this heat.

'Would you be so kind as to show me exactly where
your tableau should be hung?'

Suddenly frantic, Géricault looked around the room. There was Guérin ordering his canvas to be lifted between two arched windows overlooking the main courtyard. He envied this commanding position. He knew he should go and ask Guérin's advice, but again pride held him back. Besides, the official was gazing at him with such a polite, expectant smile on his face.

'Monsieur Géricault.' Now the youth spread out the plan before him as if it were a newspaper. 'Show me the place you have chosen.'

Géricault decided to tell him he was unwell, overcome perhaps by the heat, and he would return tomorrow. After all, he explained, it was an important decision and not one to be made lightly.

The official shook his head.

'I'm sorry, but this is the last day, sir.' He eyed him sadly. 'All the canvases in this section have to be hung by six o'clock tonight.'

The boy surveyed the room, and all at once his expression brightened. 'Why, look, sir,' he exclaimed, pointing to a space above one of the massive panelled doorways leading to the east wing.

'I'm surprised that's not been taken. His Majesty will be able to see your tableau all the way through the galleries.'

He snapped his fingers at two workmen who hurried towards him. 'Exhibit number 143 above the doors there,' he instructed. 'Be quick about it or someone else will request that spot.'

To Géricault's horror, they slid his canvas onto a trolley and began to wheel his life's work, his masterpiece, across the polished oak floors.

'Make way, make way,' they called to the crowds. Breaking into a trot, the official followed.

'No, wait,' Géricault cried, pushing through the throng.

People turned to stare. Guérin nudged his companion and they exchanged mocking smiles.

Géricault could feel damp patches of sweat seep through his waistcoat. Once again he mopped his brow, aware that he was making a spectacle of himself.

But the pulleys were already in place. Two extra men had appeared to take the weight. Leaning back, grimacing with the strain, they heaved on the ropes, lifting the canvas higher and higher.

Géricault watched his painting rise and sway above him, bumping against the walls. He had to step back to view the composition and when he did, he wanted to rail against the heavens. The power of the piece had entirely lost its impact and become flattened and diminished. So high up, the canvas would never draw the viewer into the scene, into the suffering and despair of the men on the raft.

'Stop!' he cried. But no one heard, or they ignored him. With a triumphant smile, the boy proffered a pen so that he could sign his name on the plan.

Géricault hated him then, the lank blond hair that fell across his sallow face, the look of quiet satisfaction as if he actually took pride in this job. Snatching the quill, he noticed a tremor in the boy's ink-stained fingers.

Bah, he thought, he should not be so hard. Perhaps by dangling his tableau before him like the trinket it was, this official had shown him the truth that he, gentleman artist, amateur dilettante, had once again failed.

Géricault returned to Montmartre drained and exhausted.

His guests made the point that, since he had deliberately avoided the most dramatic episodes in their narrative, such a Godless, pitiless tableau *was* best placed out of sight. Indeed, the higher the better for the hapless viewer.

'At the very least, you could have called it "The Raft of the Medusa",' Savigny declared at supper that evening. 'Scene of a Shipwreck is far too vague.'

How they wearied him with their endless carping and complaints. He was tired of arguing. Besides, he had not laboured day and night for eight months with the sole purpose of causing embarrassment to the Ministry of Marine. His tableau had broken free from the anchors of time.

'Nevertheless, people will recognise your portraits,' he replied, in what he hoped was a soothing tone. 'They will say the man reaching out towards the horizon is in fact Corréard the engineer, and the other signalling by his side, Savigny, the brave surgeon of the frigate Medusa. You mark my words, they will.'

'Perhaps in our lifetime,' Savigny declared in a peevish voice. 'But should your work last the centuries, no one will know who we are in this shipwreck scene of yours.'

Again and again, right up until the last moment, they had tried to persuade him to have the ship's name emblazoned on the crimson cloth unfurling from the Negro's hands. But he had refused to be bullied further. This was his composition, his narrative—it no longer belonged to them or anyone else. Not even to Thomas, the Helmsman, that harbinger of the truth at last.

Leaving them now to their games of cards, Géricault withdrew early. How drab and empty the studio seemed without his tableau, how bare the walls without the scaffolding and ladders.

Géricault kneeled beside the abandoned raft and, despite himself, dragged out his sketches of Alexandrine once again.

All night he riffled through the canvases, unable to sleep, sifting over the past and mourning that which might have been.

ON THE DAY OF THE Salon, Géricault woke in a sweat of dread. This was the time he had strained every effort towards, just like his figures on the raft. Today the house opposite seemed unnaturally quiet. He imagined Horace at his toilette, pomading his hair and making sure he was exquisitely turned out for his patrons, the King and the Comte d'Artois.

Although he had little appetite for breakfast, Géricault hurried down and, to his surprise, found himself alone in the dining room. Surely Savigny and Corréard would not refuse to accompany their host to the Salon, despite their profound misgivings about his tableau.

La Motte bustled in with a tray.

'That will do, I'm not hungry,' Géricault said, trying to hide the impatience in his voice.

'Well, I'm sure your guests will be,' La Motte replied before flouncing from the room.

All at once the doors swung open and in walked Savigny and Corréard. When Géricault turned round to face them, what an apparition met his eye.

Savigny attired in a lilac suit, white satin breeches and an emerald green coat, which by the expensive fit were the work of the best tailor in town. Corréard similarly clad, accessorised by a damask cloak and scarlet plumed hat. They gleamed with vigour and health, made him feel like an old man in comparison.

'Well, what do you think?' Savigny enquired, sashaying up and down. 'Much as your final analysis of our narrative is bound to disappoint, we felt we should come out in style for this momentous occasion and show the King that we, publishers of political pamphlets, *Au naufrage de la Méduse*, are not to be trifled with by the Bourbon court.'

Géricault rang the bell for La Motte.

'Bring us champagne . . . today we must celebrate.'

And then he found himself clinking glasses with his guests, these two dandies unrecognisable as the souls he had rescued from a garret not even one year ago—perverse that it should be he who had diminished and lost weight. La Motte had had to take in his waistcoat . . .

His hands trembled when he raised the champagne to his lips. He drank to Hippolyte his son, and to Alexandrine.

AT LEAST ONE THOUSAND paintings lined the Salon Carré and the long gallery beyond. Géricault was dazzled by the glitter of gilt and shining canvases stretched frame-to-frame, row upon row—vast religious compositions, Madonnas and Virgins, scenes from the Old Testament, the lives of saints reeling from the walls.

And royalty, dynastic narratives in every variation: Henry IV, Marie-Antoinette, Jeanne d'Arc, Clovis and Clothilde, the Duchess of Angoulême. The ceiling fairly spun with them. Strange to think these glorifications of the Bourbon restoration were conceived in studios which not so long before had sublimated the victories of Marengo, Austerlitz and Eylau.

Géricault saw Horace surrounded by his retinue of city friends, strolling towards a canvas before which an admiring crowd had gathered. It was positioned exactly opposite Géricault's tableau. A sensational scene, entitled *Massacre of the Marmelukes*, a panorama of soldiers advancing and regrouping, dying in the old Empire style. Horace took his place among the entranced viewers and bowed to their fervent applause. So this had been his secret all this time,

Géricault thought. Trying to fob him off with Marie-Antoinette's plain daughter! Oh, he was a sly one, Horace. Instead, Géricault noticed that it was Carle Vernet who stood beneath a magnificent portrait of the Duchess.

Corréard and Savigny meanwhile were escorting Thérèse, resplendent in a gold and silver brocaded gown, in a turn around the room. How at home his guests seemed in this milieu of artists, peering at each exhibit. It was hard to imagine them sprawled against bare planks adrift on the ocean . . . Géricault studied his canvas. Were those the same men?

There was a fanfare of trumpets. A silence fell upon the crowd. Then, a corpulent figure, smaller than Napoleon, hobbled along the corridor—the King of France had arrived. How old and frail he appeared, crippled by gout and leaning heavily on a cane.

Taking small deliberate steps so as not to overtake the monarch, the Duchess and the Comte d'Artois came behind. Géricault saw now that Vernet had enlivened her, pared down the slack folds of flesh and added lustre to her pockmarked skin. Géricault wondered at her years in the tower, watching her family ascend to the guillotine one by one. That she should be alive, nodding at the crowd who once bayed for her blood!

Suffering and survival. In all this splendour, it occurred to him that only he seemed to have given expression to the themes of their times.

Slowly, the entourage moved from exhibit to exhibit, addressing and complimenting the artists, who scraped and bowed, waited on the King's every word.

Géricault found himself swaying on his feet with

exhaustion. He had not eaten in a long while. The glass of champagne he took at breakfast now thumped at his brow.

The King had reached Vernet. Géricault noticed Savigny and Corréard had sidled into the crowd, not quite game to brazen it out.

The King raised his arms in admiration.

Expressionless, his niece peered upwards at this fictional creation of herself.

Then, painfully, the King moved towards Horace, who kissed the monarch's extended hand. The Comte d'Artois glanced at the composition with a puzzled expression. Surely this was not the work he had commissioned. Even so, he made a great show of praising the exhibit, announcing in a loud voice for all to hear that these Vernets, father and son included, were most certain to receive gold medals. An excited frisson rippled through the room.

Géricault stared at his own canvas, so diminished and miniaturised above the vast doorway.

He tried to examine it as a stranger would, dispassion-ate and detached. Was it good, what he had done? Perhaps it was a brilliant achievement, one that would stand the test of time—

A loud cough at his side made him jump. A liveried footman loomed imperiously before him. And then he was face to face with the King of France.

Blushing, Géricault bowed.

For a long time the King looked up at the canvas, then he clicked his fingers with exasperation. Two assistants darted towards him.

'I can hardly see this work,' the King declared. 'Bring it down.'

All at once there was a bustle of activity, ladders appeared from nowhere and were propped against the wall, a pulley wheeled its way across the floor. Ceremoniously, Géricault's great canvas was lowered, until the King's line of vision met that of the father cradling his son.

Géricault saw the monach step onto the raft flailing to keep equilibrium, his slippered feet sliding and skidding across soaked planks. The King of France clambered over the father, recoiling from the corpses all around until he entered a makeshift shelter and reeled from the cadaverous shadows huddled there, reaching out for him, clawing, fighting, biting. He stumbled and found himself engulfed in a tumult of men desperately crawling towards the Negro who waved a crimson cloth, which streamed against the skies.

A grip on that shoulder warm as sunlight. Someone hauled the monarch to his feet. One arm outstretched to the horizon, Savigny turned to him and said—but his words were swallowed by the wind whipping cruel waves against the raft's bows, swelling the sail so it tacked in the opposite direction of salvation and rescue, just as Géricault had intended.

For a long time the King stood motionless on the raft. Silence in the room and the galleries beyond. No one stirred. Finally he espied the *Argus*, already disappearing over the peaked troughs of the horizon.

The King shuddered and drew his cape close about his throat. He tapped the floor with the tip of his cane and signalled one of the footmen to bring him a chair.

With difficulty, aided by his niece, the King sank into red velvet cushions.

Géricault imagined him being lowered over the ship's side, the ropes creaking with the strain and the crew waiting below on a golden barge laden only with valises, grabbing at the mahogany chair legs carved in an Etruscan style.

The King continued to contemplate the composition. 'Monsieur Géricault,' he said at last.

'You have made a shipwreck which isn't for you. This catastrophe is not ours. And you have compelled me to participate in an experience which is not to my liking.'

He seemed cheered by the notion.

So, Géricault thought, this monarch was the first to understand.

'I know, Your Majesty,' he replied with a bow.

Still the King sat and studied his tableau, the footmen standing beside him, the expectant crowds waiting in silence.

Géricault stood alone at the top of the steps and gazed down into the foyer, at the waiters weaving through the throng of the King's Ball. A wooden stage had been erected, on which a group of musicians was seated busy tuning their instruments. He could see Horace leading Savigny and Corréard, their arms around Thérèse, towards a raucous group of friends. He knew he should go and join them, get drunk on champagne and celebrate with the rest. There, the greatest artists of his day were gathered. The King had choreographed a truly historic occasion.

Instead Géricault made his way back through the Salon Carré, until he reached the room where he had first kissed Alexandrine. He glanced up at the gold-leaf haloes of the smiling Madonnas. Through the doorway came a fanfare of trumpets, signalling that the ball had officially begun, and his future. Yet the very notion of descending into the bray and the chatter, the Vernets and their clique of cronies, overwhelmed him with a sense of exhaustion.

Surely this moment was the pinnacle. From an early age, this was what he had always desired.

Standing alone and uncertain in the shadows, Géricault

thought of his son, and wondered whether the child had already been wrenched from his mother's arms for some wetnurse from a neighbouring farm. Now he heard a roar of applause. The King must have made a fine, rousing speech. Géricault imagined Horace raising his glass and cheering with his friends. Why could he not be more like him?

Downstairs, Géricault threaded his way unnoticed through the packed foyer. He crossed the vestibule and paused on the threshold. He looked back at the gaiety and light. Vernet was holding court before a huddle of journalists, among whom Géricault recognised Grassin. Everyone was dressed in all their finery, the musicians hard at their violins and cellos, and Géricault slipped away into the night.

GÉRICAULT RIFFLED THROUGH the newspapers and journals strewn on the table. Ah, here, he had it. *La Gazette de France*:

All is hideous and passive—not a trait of heroism or grandeur upon which the soul and eye can for one moment repose— nothing to indicate life and sensibility—nothing honourable to humanity. This picture is truly said to be a work to rejoice and glut the sight of vultures.

Shafts of light streamed through the windows. The newspapers were beginning to crinkle and yellow. He knew he should throw them away. The most asinine and foolish of all—Géricault growled beneath his breath when he came to it—had to be the *Revue Encyclopédique*:

He could have made it horrible, and he has made it merely disgusting; this picture is a heap of cadavers from which one turns away. If he had rendered the subject in all its energy, all its truth, if he had dared show the unfortunates of the Medusa, *driven by the pitiless motives of self-preservation, fighting over the corpse of one of their comrades in order to prolong their existence by a few hours, then, to be sure, he would have inspired horror, but he would have been sure to attract attention.*

Géricault threw that review against the wall. He almost laughed, though, when he read the next in the pile:

Courage, M. Géricault. Try to moderate an enthusiasm, which might carry you too far. Being a colourist by instinct, try to become one in practice; being still an imperfect draughtsman, study the art of David and Girodet.

And even praise came only in breathless, exclamatory tones—*My heart trembled on seeing the Shipwreck of the Medusa, I shudder while I admire; what movement, what verve—*

Verve? he said to himself. Well, that was not the effect I intended at all.

The only man in this country who came close to apprehending the driving force of his tableau had been none other than the King of France. And who could fail to see the irony in that. All Corréard's and Savigny's hopes at discrediting him had backfired. There was even a rumour that the King might buy the painting for his own private collection. This last possibility made Géricault smile. Perhaps the King also tired of pallid sycophantic fictions and craved reality from time to time.

Surrounded by all this print, Géricault's head pounded.

A long day stretched ahead. Not even noon, not even out of his dressing gown. Géricault was too tired yet to contemplate beginning another work.

Horace was touring the Languedoc region with the Comte d'Artois, his house closed and shuttered until the end of autumn. How quiet everything seemed. He needed to get away too—travel to some distant land, say, and find meaning in flowered silks and temples leafed with gold . . . the Orient, perhaps.

Even Savigny and Corréard had gone—to set up shop at the Palais Royal. And their printing press was proving a success, riding on the back of the notoriety surrounding the raft.

Géricault picked up the *Gazette de France* again, then the *Revue Encyclopédique*, scanned their creased pages once more.

Bah! he declared. Artists must turn a deaf ear to the noise made by these merchants of hot air.

From outside, a sound of skylarks, long rapturous notes. Lately he had noticed it pained him to listen to such keening joy for long.

WHEN GÉRICAULT WROTE TO Horace telling him of his plans for a voyage to the Orient, he received an angry reply penned in a hurried scrawling hand. *What is it you think you lack here? You have wealth and talent, your first efforts in a difficult art have been crowned by success. Why take on the risk of travel in unexplored countries? Don't you have an almost inexhaustible source of inspiration here at home? What more do you want?*

Géricault sharpened his quill and dipped its nib in the well. A single sentence to Horace should suffice. *What I want is the trial of misfortune.*

Still no word from the King and soon, he knew, he would have to ride into town to collect his canvas. But perhaps he would ask his groom to do it.

That evening Géricault watched a transparent sickle moon hover above the chestnut trees, sending out a yellow sliver of light.

A sharp rap on the door from La Motte made him jump. Géricault took the tray from her, a bowl of barley soup.

~

The following morning, Géricault was cheered by a note enthusiastically penned by a Mister William Bullock from London, proprietor of the Egyptian Hall—an imposing edifice in Piccadilly, auction house and occasional gallery, featuring artefacts and scientific oddities. Géricault wondered in which category *his* work belonged.

Eagerly he read the letter, silently thanking his mother for teaching him English in his youth.

With the utmost success, Bullock wrote, *I have shown a sensational canvas of* Brutus Condemning his Sons *by the painter Guillaume Léthière, at an admission charge of one shilling a head, which proved most profitable. I am most keen to try out your Raft on the English public.*

Without a moment's hesitation, Géricault dispatched a reply—he would sail on the packet *Iris* from Calais at once. At last, he thought, the adventure he had been looking for.

HIS IMPRESARIO, BULLOCK, a genial corpulent man with an indefatigable enthusiasm for life, had found Géricault lodgings in the Strand. But despite the theatres and bars, how grey London seemed! The women staid and buttoned to the neck. The men, equally encased in drab woollens and tweed, went about their business with looks of dull resignation. And such refuse everywhere—all manner of detritus, discarded papers, orange peel, oyster shells piling the gutters—which was shocking to behold. And stray dogs roaming the streets, odd mongrel breeds with flea-bitten, manged coats.

Géricault knew Bullock intended to do well out of the Raft. From every journal, an advertisement framed in ink proclaimed:

MONSIEUR JERICAULT'S GREAT PICTURE, 24 feet long by 18 feet high, representing the Surviving Crew of the Medusa French Frigate on the Raft, just descrying the Vessel that rescued them from their dreadful situation; this magnificent picture excited universal interest and admiration at the last exhibition of the Louvre and is now open for public inspection in the Roman Gallery at the Egyptian Hall, Piccadilly: the public attention is

respectfully invited to this chef-d'oeuvre of foreign art. Admission
one shilling.

All prefaced by a couplet from the poet Southey:

Tis pleasant by the cheerful hearth to hear
Of tempests and the dangers of the deep.

No matter, Géricault supposed, that they'd misspelt his
name.

Although Bullock had assured him he would return to
Paris covered with gold, the man's constant good cheer and
gaiety only wearied Géricault to the soul. On the first day,
Bullock had taken it upon himself to provide a tour of the
sights and had hired a barge on the Thames for the very
purpose. They set off from the Embankment at dawn and did
not return until night. All day Géricault's head thumped and
Bullock's voice boomed in his ear, reeling off dates, facts and
figures relating to every building they passed: St Paul's Cathedral, its vast gold dome glinting in the light; the Monument;
the white pinnacles of the Tower; the grand observatory at
Greenwich, the elegant facades of the Marine Offices, overlooking immaculately clipped lawns. Then back again in the
opposite direction to the magnificent Botanic Gardens of
Kew, the palaces of Hampton Court and Richmond's ancient
parklands. And all the while the thick brown waters of the
river slapped queasily against the tarred timbers of their vessel.

Géricault struggled through Bullock's meals of beef,
suet puddings and claret. Yet Bullock's generosity knew no
bounds, and he took a childish delight in his vast sprawling
city bound by leaden skies.

On the few occasions when Bullock was unable to
chaperone his guest, Géricault wandered the streets unable
to shake off a sense of unease, an unaccountable malaise that

had oppressed his spirits ever since he left France.

He found there was something about the town that weighed so, the narrow cobbled lanes grimed with soot and dust. From every conceivable direction a grandiose ugliness met his eye, coal wagons toiling up muddy slopes round the docks, distant views of rooftops, chimneys, ship masts and that dome of St Paul's half hidden beneath a shroud of yellow smoke.

One morning he passed a paralysed woman propped like a corpse in a clumsy wooden wheelchair, against which a drunken attendant rested. On the other side of the road, a hearse rolled through the fog. He tried to sketch an old vagrant with an emaciated dog at his side, a piper playing some tavern tune. He wanted to catch every detail of street life—the hats of the beggars, the harnesses of drayhorses— but to no avail. His efforts seemed slight and trivial.

Once Géricault became lost in a labyrinth of alleyways and when finally he emerged, he found himself in front of Newgate Prison, where a multiple public hanging was taking place. Three men ranged on the gallows were being readied for the drop—already two of the condemned had hoods covering their heads.

The man on the left resisted the reverend's last counsel and stared out with a defiant expression. Briefly, his brooding eyes rested on Géricault as if singling him out as the one responsible for his fate.

What struck Géricault most in this scene was the mundane everyday sense of routine. The two hangmen went about the tasks in a bored listless manner, one tying the hoods, the other climbing the ladder to swing on the ropes. And all the while the crowds milled back and forth, many not even pausing to watch the spectacle.

Géricault did not stay. Before the men were tipped from the planks, he hailed a cab to take him back to his quarters.

Each night, Géricault was invited to soirées hosted by members of the Royal Academy and other patrons of the fine arts. He was disappointed in the English school, which he found distinguished itself only by such subjects as landscape, seascape and genres of the lowest kind.

Still, he must attend these stultifying evenings of affectation and snobbery, the interminable dinners, course after course ferried and served by footmen and butlers with an excruciating adherence to protocol, which made him want to dash his plate to the floor; and the talk thin as vapour, each word so carefully chosen, so vacuous and polite that the general conversation carried no meaning at all—so different from the verve, dash and wit of Paris. And afterwards, when the good ladies retired in a shimmer of taffeta and pearls, Géricault had to endure the rounds of port and cigars and pretend to be amused by obscene jokes about Parisian whores. And each morning when he woke from a fitful sleep, his head pounded fit to bursting.

But the massing crowds did converge on Mister Bullock's Egyptian Hall, paying their silver coins, twenty thousand at the last count.

The impresario rubbed his hands with satisfaction. He told Géricault he expected at least five thousand visitors more and hoped to send *The Raft*, as he called it, to a similar exhibition in Dublin.

Ireland. Géricault shivered at the thought of visiting yet another dull drab land.

For a week it had been raining desultorily, splashing down, turning the streets to rivulets and swamps. In five more days he would board the packet to Dublin.

Migraines and lassitude afflicted his mind.

However, the critics at least showed a keener appreciation of this 'new Melo-drama, the Shipwreck of the Medusa or the Fatal Raft,' as it was termed, than their colleagues in France. In every newspaper, Géricault found himself described as a French artist of great eminence and promise. Of course Bullock, a tireless advertiser, might have had a hand in this, knowing as he did every scribe and hack in town.

But a review from the *Literary Gazette* managed to lift Géricault's spirits for a while.

In this tremendous picture of human suffering, the bold hand of the artist has laid bare the details of the horrid facts with the severity of Michel Angelo and the gloom of Caravaggio.

Yes, he confessed to being mighty pleased with that.

The light brought into the piece and thrown upon the upturned faces of a centre group powerfully assists in arresting the attention. This seems to break on them from the illumination of a cloud above their heads, and is contrasted by much surrounding gloom, and this again by the bright rays of the morning. The powerful element of the mighty waters is very happily depicted by the hand of the artist; and taken altogether his work is, as we before observed, one of the finest specimens of the French school ever brought to this country.

After reading that particular tribute, Géricault treated himself to a bottle of champagne at the Gaiety Theatre.

The show was tawdry, the chorus girls lumpen and their gestures clumsy. But one caught his eye, narrow-hipped as any model in France, with a mass of curls piled on her head.

It had been a long time since Géricault had felt a

woman's caress and as he watched her he became consumed with desire. These were good upright girls, protected by their proprietor, but Géricault knew it would not take him long to find another. By the interval, he had left, and was prowling the streets hungry as a wolf.

Soon enough, a woman crossed his path. He inhaled a cheap rose scent from her gown. Light from a lamp shone against her face and she gazed his way, her features sharp and lean, not altogether pretty, but he liked the predatory, professional way in which she assessed him.

'How much?' he whispered.

'One shilling,' she replied, not taking her eyes from his.

The same price as to see his Raft. At that, Géricault laughed. Had twenty thousand souls or so passed through her doors in the last month? Like him, this whore did well from her art.

She led him through a maze of alleys thronged with drunks and thieves and women like herself. Géricault found himself shrinking from their insolent stares and made sure he kept one hand on his purse as they passed.

Finally they reached a dilapidated shop three storeys high, which in its wretchedness could have been the very garret where he first discovered Savigny and Corréard. He followed the woman upstairs, to a dark fetid room furnished only with a table and cot bed. She lit a candle and threw a lump of peat on the fire. The embers blazed briefly. Then, when Géricault went over to her, she looked far older than the glimpse he had caught of her in the street. She began to fumble with buttons and stays. He thought of Alexandrine and the pleasure he'd had in stripping her of all her expensive finery.

Now the woman was stepping out of her gown, which was worn and patched with age and none too clean, the hem ringed with mud. She wriggled out of her petticoats and chemise and stood shivering and naked before him.

All desire left him at the sight of those slack breasts and thighs, the goose bumps mottling her grey skin.

'Come on,' she said, treating him to the same insolent stare as the women crowding the alleyways outside. 'What are you waiting for?'

Géricault unfastened his cloak and flung it at his feet. If it was going to be done, he thought, it was best done quickly. He took her brutally, against the wall. And there finished, he was quite undone. Not more than a minute for the price of one shilling. No longer than a single glance at the Raft.

'Line up, line up,' the touts cried already at the door. 'Come and see Monsieur Jericault's great picture, twenty-four feet long by eighteen feet high.'

But Dublin was far prettier than Géricault had imagined, the river flashing and snaking beneath bridges, past grand warehouses and spired cathedrals.

How good it felt to be free from the constraints of London, the mud flats of the Thames reeking at low tide. Here he could breathe at last.

The Raft had been dispatched to this Rotunda, a theatre in the Georgian style. Already Géricault had made seventeen thousand francs from Bullock and was assured to receive much more by the journey's end. Indeed it was true, he would return to Paris a rich man.

And in Dublin he had rather missed his impresario Bullock's entrepreneurial and promotional skills. He reflected that Bullock must have found him a dull companion, oppressed as he was with migraines and fevers and London's granite skies. Géricault would have liked to sit with him now in a gay Irish tavern, scarlet geraniums spilling from windowsills, and toast him with a fine beaker of the barley wine that was said to be good for the blood.

Since his congress with that woman whose name he had never asked, Géricault found himself assailed with a strange contamination of the lungs, and an ache in his throat as if he had spent the night with Horace smoking innumerable cigars, sometimes accompanied by palsy, a dry, retching cough and sudden shooting pains in his groin.

But he was convinced that here, in this verdant land, he would fully recover.

Inside the Rotunda, Géricault met Bullock's colleague, a pale plump fellow called Bloom who proffered a sweating palm. The theatre was damp and old, the cracked walls mildewed with neglect.

Unrolled and stretched in its frame once again, his canvas seemed darker, more mottled than when he had last seen it in the glitter of the Egyptian Hall. Géricault examined it more closely. Had he really painted the tableau in such strong shades of black, which threatened to eclipse the crowded figures on the raft? He touched the cruel ebony ridge of a wave washing the stern. The bitumen stuck like glue to his hand. Would it never dry?

Bloom shuffled through the dank cavernous room, the floor littered with leaves.

Géricault looked around at the windows splattered with bird droppings, plaster peeling in scrolls from the ceilings, his tableau half hidden in shadows. The place was a mess. He must tell Bloom to clean it—

But seeing Bloom sneeze against the sleeve of his coat, he took pity on him, and described instead the magnificent frescoed interiors of the Egyptian Hall—the cornices outlined in gold leaf, the enamelled sarcophagus that dominated the foyer, a central courtyard planted with palms—hoping this man would take the hint and make an effort to at least sweep the hall before the expectant crowds lined the streets for the official opening tomorrow. 'You can count on me,' Géricault said, 'to make a speech and discuss my work in every detail.'

Without gracing him with a reply, Bloom gazed up at a flock of pigeons nesting in the rafters. A feather spiralled through a dusty shaft of light.

'I fear we may have a spot of competition, sir,' he said at last, 'from the Palace Theatre across the way.'

Géricault went to the door and stared across the square. How could he not have noticed the announcement inscribed in black letters against a scarlet drape? *Novel Marine Peristrephic Panorama of the Shipwreck of the Medusa.*

'A most unfortunate coincidence,' Bloom said when Géricault went back inside. 'Opened yesterday and fairly drew in the crowds.'

Bloom peered at the tableau and tapped its frame. 'Still,' he declared with a weak smile, 'I'm sure this picture of yours will hold up well.'

For an hour Géricault stood in a snaking queue, shuffling slowly forward until at last he reached a uniformed man at the door.

'How much?' he asked.

'Two shillings,' the official replied, holding out his hand.

He could not believe anyone would pay such a sum but the foyer swarmed.

When Géricault gave the man the coins, he received a ticket with the words *Marine Panorama* embossed in silver curlicue letters across one side.

Pushing through the throng, he made his way up the steps to the auditorium. He was astonished to see there was hardly a seat to be found. So many people already inside, fanning the air with their programmes and calling out to friends in excited tones. He managed find a cane chair at the back. Soon there seemed to be standing room only yet the crowds continued to spill through.

Géricault noticed a full orchestra in the pit tuning their instruments. Surely this cheap panorama was not being set to a musical score!

'Jemima saw the show yesterday,' a girl next to him confided in her companion. 'Just like moving pictures, she said.'

All at once there was a roll of drums. The room darkened and the audience fell silent.

The red curtains swung open with a fanfare of trumpets and a clash of cymbals. A huge sheet of canvas slowly unwound to a dramatic serenade of cellos and violins. Of course, Géricault recognised the life-size figures, Savigny and Corréard among them, farewelling France. The *Medusa* surged through clear blue waters—crude lithographs made vivid by primary colours. To tremendous applause, this first scene disappeared from view and was followed by another, depicting the abandonment of the raft. The cowardly Captain lifted his sword to cut the towropes, and the audience hissed and booed as the leering, moustachioed villain glided past.

The heat in the auditorium was becoming unbearable. Sweat trickled down his neck. He loosened his cravat. The orchestra played with all its might, mimicking the rhythms of storm-tossed seas, and now a clap of thunder from the wings.

The girl seated beside him screamed and clung to her friend. Géricault could barely watch the tumble of men and sabres next to slide past, or listen to another clash of cymbals. Who could be responsible for presenting this spectacle, this travesty to be viewed without one single intelligent thought? Such melodrama, the pull and tweak of tawdry emotions demanding a response from them all.

They should be called to account for denigrating these men! Except—the thought struck him—that Savigny and Corréard would no doubt applaud with the rest.

Géricault wondered how long this gaudy pantomime would go on. His head throbbed with the constant clapping and stamping of feet. Everyone was howling now and peering through their hands at the cannibal scene, the sight of those survivors chomping the raw flesh of their companions. There were cries of delight at the carnage and blood, the special effects daubed with the cheapest of paints.

Then the soaring note of a harp, echoed by a lute's gentle strum, milked their tears. Oh, death was nigh, judging from the limp figures sprawled on the raft beneath a yellow glare of sun.

Géricault fought an impulse to jump onto the stage and declare that these spectators had been cheated of two shillings a head. He wanted to herd them into the Rotunda, explain his motives, the months of effort to transform catastrophe into art. He wanted to make them understand the true nature of what had taken place on the raft.

The trumpets and drums reached a thumping crescendo. The winding canvas ushered the climax into view. And at first Géricault did not believe he was seeing the apparition which slid from the wings. A painted toile wheeled round and around on a set of pulleys—the first sighting of the *Argus,* aping his creation in a smudge of muddy browns.

He looked around—the crowd was cheering, some were standing with tears streaming down their cheeks.

Perhaps it had something to do with the flickering shadows cast by the torch flames at the foot of the stage, but everyone seemed tinged with a garish green light, which exaggerated their features and gestures and transformed them into caricatures of the most ghoulish kind.

In what monstrous portion of Hades had he found himself?

Rising to his feet, Géricault stumbled up the aisle. By way of finale, the orchestra played a frenzied waltz. He hurried down the stairs and out onto the street, where he was confronted with another queue inching towards the theatre doors.

'Roll up, roll up,' the ticket touts were shouting. 'The show will start again in an hour.'

SEVERAL DAYS AFTER THAT monstrous display of moving pictures, Géricault woke still drunk from the night before, and remembered as he dressed—hands trembling, his face ashen at the washstand—that he had agreed to participate in that most British of pursuits, a fox hunt. Bloom had arranged the excursion, thinking it might lift his spirits to mix with the English gentry, although he despised them, Géricault could tell.

As he dressed, he considered cancelling the engagement, but decided a fast gallop in the clean bright air might clear his mind. Besides, he had hired an expensive riding habit for the occasion.

Bloom stood in the square and watched the meet gather— the uniformed lackeys with their trays of punch and sherry, the braying laughs of the riders, the clipped accents so harsh and different from his own.

The beaters' whistles, the baying of the beagles, the huntsman's horn shrilled in Géricault's head as he mounted his horse, a bay stallion with a mean look, shying at every sound. Reining him in tight, Géricault reached for a glass of sherry, and another, until the pounding at his temples receded to a dull throb.

'I hope you have a good ride, sir,' Bloom said, taking his glass with a deferential nod.

At the blow of the bugle, they were off, clattering through the streets to the outskirts of town. They cleared the wide ditch of the church grounds and galloped by the river along a towpath flanked with fields of barley and rye. A beech coppice on a hill lay before them and the bugle gave the signal. A fox had been seen.

At last Géricault revelled in the exhilaration of vaulting a high hedge of hawthorn. He exulted in the huntsman's rallying cries as they veered towards the thicket and the fox's lair, the hounds loping ahead, snouts down to catch the scent. Then they all crashed through the woods fragrant with a sharp sap scent of ferns. But their wily prey had eluded them, and was making for a stand of willows by the river.

Géricault brought his horse to a canter as they came to a fallen beech still sprouting a high hedge of pale leaves. The beast arched his neck and fought for his head. But Géricault urged him on, kicking his flanks with the spurs. And as they reached the jump, something stirred and rustled in the undergrowth.

Whinnying with all its might, the stallion reared. Caught off guard, Géricault flew from the saddle, and his boot caught in the stirrup.

He was dragged—through bushes and thorns—his body flayed by sharp roots and stones. Then, standing stock still, the horse gave one last buck. Desperate to free himself from the weight, the sack of flesh and bones impeding his flight.

Géricault lay on the sodden earth with his left leg at a strange angle. Blood seeped against his thigh. He felt grit in his mouth and a thick salt taste he could not define. He gazed up at a shimmer of beech trees, a streak of blue sky, the play of shadows and light filtered by the morning sun. He felt no pain. Instead he saw the world around him in the finest detail as if he had clapped eyes on it for the first time. Probing the air with its horns, searching for dangers, a dung beetle crawled from a log spongy with moss and lichen. Ants scurried on their swarming mission. A crow circled overhead and alighted on a hollow stump, raking the rotten timber for earwigs and wood lice. And then Géricault spied the fox, trotting lightly through the bracken, his tail outstretched in a tawny plume, his eyes narrowed and thoughtful, calculating the next move.

Montmartre

_____

January 1824

DELACROIX VISITED FROM TIME to time, but Géricault could tell it disgusted him to have to sit by the bedside of a dying man—his malady in the vile spittoon, the broken opium phials, the leeches squirming against a glass jar waiting for Biett's tweezers, when once again he would be cupped and bled. He envied Delacroix's youth, those long years stretching ahead. At his age, when he was twenty years old, Géricault too had longed to shine, to illuminate and astonish the world.

Sweating, exhausted, he lay back on the pillows.

A door slammed. Someone in a hurry, he thought. Biett, of course. His physician, brisk and solicitous, with an impeccable bedside manner—soon he would be with him, kneading his dead limbs like dough.

Géricault strained to listen. He heard La Motte's voice, followed by the doctor's.

Never had he felt so alone. Even Horace was gone. He'd won the richest of honours—the Rome Prize and a three-year residency at the Villa Medici, to which aspiring artists flocked to pay court to the grand master. The house opposite was now deserted, the windows boarded up, the only sound a loose shutter banging in the wind.

Géricault had long lost track of the number of months he had lain in the room where his mother had died. From floor to ceiling the walls were crammed with all his sketches, endless copies of the great masters, horses in every pose and stance, studies for his *Charging Chasseur*, the *Wounded Soldier*, portraits of his mother, of Alexandrine.

Mere vignettes all. Except one, gathering lint and dust beneath his bed. The composition he refused to discuss any more, or even look at. Savigny and Corréard had made such a name for themselves with their publishing venture, *Au naufrage de la Méduse*, that they'd forgotten their former host. They were always too busy, or working on their book, the *Narrative of a Voyage to Senegal*.

There were times when Géricault would cast his mind back and try to remember, but the days made no sense to him any more. They slipped by swift and greedy. It had been five years, he knew, since Biett had found the tumour fastened to the base of his spine—from that wretched riding accident in Dublin. Géricault could remember the bay stallion he had hired, its mean look, and then the vile abscess swelling to the size of a cantaloupe, which he had attempted to lance with a needle.

He should never have gone to England in the hope of seeking some trial of misfortune.

Now there was only Biett, who had made it his personal mission that this patient would not die under his charge.

Biett had proposed an operation but Géricault would rather submit to the rack. So at regular intervals, the good doctor sat at his bedside and outlined the various methods he had devised to straighten three vertebrae compressed in the small of Géricault's back, using all manner of braces, steel tubing, and other nameless contraptions. Whenever

Géricault dismissed him, Biett would bow like a courtier then turn to him and say: 'Monsieur, I would advise, nay, implore you, sir, to agree to these procedures, for otherwise you've not much time.'

But Géricault refused to play the corpse on a dissecting table. After all, he reasoned, he was not dead yet. Alone once again, he would stare at his sketches and canvases. There was still so much to achieve, and he'd done nothing. Absolutely nothing. The prospect terrified him.

Not even so much as five good paintings justified his life.

Through the bedroom window, he saw it had begun to rain again, a soft fine drizzle misting the pane, blurring the chilled green meadows beyond. Winter grew. Winter in everything.

I shall never walk in the sun again, Géricault murmured. How hard it was to die. He wished he was ready. He could not bear the thought of another day waiting for the night to return with its dark waves of pain and insomnia and a morning even more dismal than the one before.

Géricault dreamed of working on enormous surfaces with buckets of paints and brooms for brushes, painting horses the size of life and women, such women.

On these inspired canvases, he would pour blood, light and darkness in turn. He would give himself up to drunken orgies and create a series of pictures superimposed on one another, each new layer translating the language of dreams and raising it towards perfection. He would compose a terrible hymn in honour of destiny and anguish at leaving this world with so little done.

Acknowledgements

First I would like to thank my publisher Nikki Christer and my editor Judith Lukin-Amundsen for their intuition and invaluable critical judgement which made the book possible. I also thank my agent Lyn Tranter for her support and patience; Glenda Adams, Joyce Kornblatt and Clare Moss, who generously gave their time to comment upon various drafts; and Alex Snellgrove for an inspired cover design. I am grateful to Tasmanian artist Terry O'Malley, and Robert Aldrich at Sydney University, for their meticulous efforts in putting me right on historical matters; the staff at the Mitchell and NSW State Libraries, and Jillian Maddison at Bicheno Library for helping me source research material.

I would also like to thank the Literature Board of the Australia Council for the grant which allowed me to finish the book.

I could not have written this novel without the following historical sources on which I relied heavily: *Narrative of a Voyage to Senegal* by J.B. Henri Savigny & Alexander Corréard, The Marlboro Press, Vermont 1986; *Géricault, his life and work* by Lorenz A.E. Eitner, Orbis Publishing, London 1982; and *Death Raft* by Alexander McKee, Charles Scribner's Sons, New York 1975.

Although inspired by and based on the life of the French artist Théodore Géricault, this is a work of fiction, and certain dates and names have been altered to suit the purposes of the novel's narrative.